G000065449

# BENEATH 5TH CITY

## Book 1 of 5th City Chronicles

### Jesse Sprague

Copyright © 2020 Jesse Sprague

All rights reserved

The characters and events portrayed in this book are fictitious. Any similarity
to real persons, living or dead, is coincidental and not intended by the author.

No part of this book may be reproduced, or stored in a retrieval system,
or transmitted in any form or by any means, electronic, mechanical,
photocopying, recording, or otherwise, without express written permission
of the publisher.

Cover design by: ebook launch
Edited by: Amy McNulty
Printed in the United States of America

# PROLOGUE

Bodies lined the floor, leaving no room between the revealed flesh of men and women. Their chests rose and fell, but beyond this, they were as still as death. A door opened in the seamless sides of the black room they occupied.

A being entered, followed by three others of its kind. They were formed in a shape and size akin to human, but there the similarity ended. Their flesh was as black as pitch and flowed in slithering tendrils like the beings were composed of thousands of tiny snakes. Sometimes, a gleam of white bone appeared from beneath the fluid flesh.

They called themselves gods, and here, with humanity piled at their feet, no one would challenge them.

Each god's face rippled in a featureless mass around its single, red, jewel-like eye.

As they strode, a current on the air lifted the humans crumpled around the room to clear a pathway, laying body over body. Each man and woman was naked and shaved.

The gods approached a human female.

Breaking away from the others, a god placed a fingertip on the woman's flesh. When touched, she rose and hung in the air as if lifted onto an invisible examination table.

"This one need not have come to us," the closest god said. Its face reformed while it spoke, mimicking her features except for the eye that remained in the forehead. An imitation of the woman's eyes showed disgust from the liquid-black face as they stared at her unconscious form. "She's nothing special."

The others' red eyes glittered in assent.

The woman disintegrated when the god's snakelike finger drew away. Ashes fell to the floor.

Then they moved on to the next, no different from the others to the gods' eye. Her sleeping face bespoke innocence and strength. She did not possess a look that would have graced fashion magazines, which were a significant source of how the gods defined human attractiveness. Her nose was too large, and she carried too much weight at the hips and belly.

"She is not acceptable," one said, but it continued looking. They had delved into many human theories of aesthetics when they studied humanity. Never in their travels had the gods found a race so enamored with its own face and form. The process of choosing a group of survivors based on physical appeal was new, the rules underdefined.

"No."

"She *is* beautiful," the first said, altering its initial decision. The front of its head rippled as the black tendrils shifted until the woman's smiling features formed on its inky face. It motioned to its newly formed mouth. "See how she smiles."

The god wore her smile, though the human woman's true mouth was slack.

"Yes. Beautiful," the fourth god said.

"I consent," said the first. "She can join the other Companion candidates."

"I consent," said the second.

The woman floated to the wall, and it engulfed her. Once their accepted specimen disappeared, the gods moved on to the floating form of an ebony-skinned man.

# CHAPTER 1

"**S**he is beautiful." The words echoed in Val's head. Her blood seemed to have turned to ice, though her groggy brain couldn't process why the words terrified her.

"*Help! No!*" Ethan's young voice rang. She knew the sound was only in her brain, and this awareness caused two things. The first was a stabbing sorrow, and the second was that she awoke instantly.

Val blinked at the blurry room, her hands bunching in the sheets. At first, her mind tried to make this her home. To make sense of where the shapes lurked. Breathing fluttered around the room and her mind tried to make it Rick's breath. But it was too distant and too plentiful.

*Where am I? Shit.*

Memories raced through her brain. She'd been at her sister's house, holding her nephew in her arms. Her sister, Evie, cowered, not moving, not protecting; Ethan had no one but Val. She'd tried to stand between Ethan and the door... Oh, god. The door had folded in on itself, crumpling with a squeal of metal. And a large humanoid figure stood there, composed of gleaming, black metal, with long, spindly fingers that stroked the wall like feelers. It had no face, only a single red glass dot marking where a forehead should have been. The metal of his flesh rippled. She'd leapt at it, trying to do something, anything and then...

She squeezed her eyes shut and held them that way, blocking out both the memories and the new horror around her. Val's brief glimpse of the world was hazy with sleep and disorientation. All she'd noticed was that it was not home. And if she reached beside her, she wouldn't find her husband, Rick—wouldn't escape the nightmare. And if she didn't look any further, maybe she didn't have to know more.

Someone sobbed off to her right.

Beneath Val's eyelids loomed the face of the dark "god." Like streams of dirty oil, its flesh flowed, never settling into a form that made sense. She couldn't hold off a memory of it standing over an ocean of people and proclaiming itself a god. Proclaiming that it had come to reclaim humanity. If she looked at the surrounding room, would that face lurk there? She didn't want to know.

Then she saw the face of her little nephew, Ethan, frozen in fear. Evie had been so young when she'd given birth to Ethan that Val had spent most of her own youth taking care of them. But in that one moment, the moment that had mattered most, she'd failed them. Her mind recoiled. She could almost feel him gripping her leg as she held a knife and faced the apartment door, waiting. The knife had proved useless. Ethan's scream rang in her mind. Her eyes opened.

A white bed lay under her, covered in nothing but a white sheet. Her legs peeped out of a gown that was equally bleached.

She let go of the sheets. Her ring finger felt empty. Barren.

Hands trembling, she touched her head as the cool air stroked her skin. On top of her head was only smooth skin, and when she lowered her arm, she gasped. A scar had crossed her upper wrist since she'd fallen from a tree at age ten. It was gone.

She glanced at her ankle and the tattoo she'd gotten the day she'd graduated as an RN was also missing. Her thumb ran over the place where her wedding ring should have been. It was as if they'd erased her life.

Val's jaw tightened at the sound of a woman weeping on the bed to her right. Tears were a waste of energy in any emergency. An alien takeover didn't strike her as an exception. Neither the aliens who'd pronounced themselves gods nor the metal drones like the one that had burst into her sister's apartment would be thwarted by tears. Despite a desire to hush the woman, Val remained silent.

*If Evie were alive somewhere, she would be crying. It wouldn't change a thing if someone ranted and railed at her to be useful. Some people don't have it in them. I'd want someone to protect Evie. People like that need someone to look out for them.* Val pressed her trembling hands together. *But who will protect me?*

No matter how she tried, she couldn't imagine Rick into existence in front of her. She couldn't create the firm muscles of his back as he stood in front of her, a wall of human strength. Nor could she feel his thick arms as they pressed her against him. Without him, there was no measure of safety, no ability to relax. *I must protect myself.*

Forcing her mind away from her own growing fear, Val tried to get her bearings. She lifted her gaze to a sea of pearly white.

Moments elongated around her before her mind made any sense of the surroundings. A large chamber, uncluttered by decoration of any sort, stretched off on both sides of her. Along the walls were beds, and on each bed was a person clothed in thin, white garments. She estimated there must have been at least fifty beds in the chamber. Other than a door at one end of the room, there was nothing else to see. Blank walls and a high arched ceiling. No windows.

*Well, this is grand.* Val wanted to yell out curses, but some of the other people in the room were still sleeping. *Let them have peace as long as they can.*

A few of the other occupants were sitting, but most lay still. Like Val, they were clean-shaven, showing the bare traces of stubble over their scalps. Despite the strange garments and hairless heads, everyone in the room radiated beauty. The faces that surrounded her belonged on movie screens and magazine covers. This was hardly a group Val had expected to find herself amid.

*Like a room filled with dolls. We're not even human. They took that away from us.* Anger tightened in her stomach, and she welcomed the flush because it drowned the fear.

In the space of ten minutes, no one remained asleep.

When the last of them woke, metal-skinned beings filed into the room. The metal covering their human forms moved constantly, like water rippling. They were as black as the gods they served, each with a red glowing eye in their forehead.

Val recoiled. *I hit one of those with a knife, and it did nothing. If the news reports were accurate... we hit their damn ships with everything we had. Whatever these "gods" and their helpers want, how could I possibly stop them?*

They came two at a time and split to either side of the room. Once spread out, they halted and turned to face the humans.

The man-shaped entities moved in unison, and once facing the shaved people, stood still as only machines could. They were not living beings—couldn't be. They were robots. Drones.

A shiver ran up her spine as she recalled the chill of a drone's finger on her. The touch had rendered her unconscious, and she remembered nothing more until waking to hear the god proclaiming its dominion over humanity. Her chest still ached from the drone's touch. She wasn't anxious to repeat the experience. After a darting examination of the room's occupants, Val estimated a headcount. The people outnumbered the drones by five to one. Which, considering, meant nothing.

*Fear won't do me any good. Cowering won't do anyone any good.*

Fingers itching for a weapon, she rose to her feet.

*Them. They did this. What did they do with Ethan?*

The others remained on their beds, in their cocoons of fear. Many turned to her, and a few tentatively lowered their feet to the floor.

Nails biting into her palms, Val stood tall and took two long strides up to the nearest drone. She felt the eyes of the others follow her movements.

*These monsters won't bring me to my knees. I won't cower.*

As the first to rise, she had the drone's attention. Reflected in its liquid metal skin were her wide, frightened eyes. She stepped forward, with the fingers of one hand curled around a nonexistent blade and her other hand in a tight fist.

*They did this to me.*

Her arm drew back, preparing to strike.

"You." The drone's blank visage formed itself into her own.

She stared into the night-black face, and her own glaring eyes stared back with a third glowing eye on the forehead. For the first time, she understood her features as something not her own. She forgot to speak and to move. Her fingers loosened. Thoughts of defending herself fled.

Her mouth smiled on the drone's face, and it was a cruel, taunting smile from the superior height. Unreasoning fear swept over her, leaving her breathless.

She stumbled back and averted her gaze.

Movement caught her eye from down the room. Everyone else's attention remained fastened on her and the metal thing wearing her features. Only she saw the man leap up, the whites of his eyes visible. The man rushed upon the closest drone. He struck out. His fist fell against the shimmering metal at the side of the drone's head.

His blow had no effect on the machine. Val gasped and then the drone lifted its twitching fingers and touched the man.

He crumpled to the ground. The thud of his corpse reverberated through her. Vacant, lifeless eyes stared across the room at Val. For a moment, it was Rick lying there.

Val's knees buckled and slammed into the ground.

*They killed him. Jesus. They just killed him.*

The noise of the dead man hitting the floor caught the other people's attention.

"This is how dissent will be met," the drones said together. "You will be as the gods wish you to be, or you will not be at all."

*That was almost me.* Val's body trembled. There was a silence that lasted the space of an unintentionally held breath.

"The old world is gone. The past is gone. There is only now. Over the next months, you will be instructed on what the future holds for you. This is as the gods have dictated. For now, you are to be given names. They will be your sole monikers going forth," the drones said. Then each drone motioned to several of the humans closest to them. "Come, now."

Involuntarily, Val thought of Rick. He'd tried that command on her once when he'd been drunk. He'd received a vodka tonic in the face. No urge to resist this time.

*Why was I so horrid to him? So difficult?*

Her heart beat in her chest, and she did not want the pounding rhythm to cease. Her life was all she had. So she stood with five others around the thing who wore her face. And to each, in turn, it gave names. None of them were names of the world she knew. It gave Val a name.

Jaisa.

# CHAPTER 2

Val didn't recognize the woman who stared back at her in the mirror. But then, she supposed, that woman wasn't Val—she was Jaisa.

*I'm Jaisa.* With diamonds glittering on her eyelashes and a sheen of bluish glitter making a gradient from the pale skin of her forehead to the now blue crown of her head, she certainly wasn't Val.

A halfmoon of white metal curved in front of Jaisa, blocking her from seeing the other men and women she'd entered the space with. And without their companionship, she was left alone with the creature the drones were shaping her into. At the center of the metal barrier, a mounted mirror reflected her every movement. Two more mirrors positioned to her left and right ensured she couldn't turn away without facing the drones who patrolled the back of the room. There was no way in hell she intended to do that.

A drone spoke from behind her. It spoke in the gods' language.

Of course, Jaisa didn't understand a word of it yet. She didn't understand until a second later when the silver headpiece sitting against her ear translated. It had said, "Dress yourself."

"In what?" Jaisa snapped. She spoke in English.

The drone's finger jabbed into her stomach. Then a jolt. A web of agony spread outward, making her limbs jerk. The taste of copper filled her mouth. The lapping waves of her punishment faded slowly.

"The languages of the world before are no more," the drone said.

Curled over, Jaisa couldn't see its hateful face. She gasped, fingernails biting into her palms.

"Stand." The command echoed in her earpiece translator.

*I'll kill that damn thing. They will not break me.*

Jaisa righted herself, her right hand flat over the still aching spot on her abdomen.

"Dress yourself," the drone repeated.

This time, Jaisa took the time to jab her command into the computer interface beside her. Luckily, this meant not looking at the drone. She spoke only when she had the translation for her words. "Dress myself in what?"

She knew the expectations already and what to expect of the drone. They had already gone through this process a few minutes earlier when it had approached and demanded she adorn herself. And she'd tried then to do as the metal-man wanted. She'd figured out the boxlike contraption attached to the barrier just below the mirror, but she'd found no clothes within.

The drone stepped forward into her space. It took all of Jaisa's will not to flinch away as its finger traveled past her shoulder.

*That touch killed a man. It electrocuted him... stopped his heart.*

Her fingernails pressed into her thighs.

*No, they did more than just kill a man. A damn monster just like that one stole my family. They probably killed Rick.*

*I should have been home with him. What kind of wife am I...? I wasn't even home for the end of the world. If Rick were here, I'd certainly never live that one down.*

Her thoughts took a swift turn as the drone's finger pressed into the side of the box and a second rectangular contraption popped out, this one with an opaque screen.

"This interface will aid you," the drone said.

Jaisa remained perfectly still until it strode away, its heavy footfalls vibrating the floor beneath her feet.

Once the drone was gone, she ran her finger over the screen and it jumped to life, displaying a perfect 3D image of her body. Next to this rendering of her, ten boxes showed different categories she could choose from with simple symbols.

Jaisa selected what looked to be pants. And then ran through an infinite variety of options. Some she recognized as reminiscent of different cultures, while others bore little resemblance to familiar garments. Putting those on would prove an unnecessary complication. Yet no matter how hard she looked, none of her choices looked comfortable, warm or even slightly practical.

*Why bother wearing anything at all if those are my only options?*

But a drone's thudding footsteps behind her answered that question. She'd wear the clothes because she didn't want to die. The drones had been very clear on what her fate would be if she didn't obey.

After searching through a number of categories, Jaisa settled on a "dress," which sadly lacked many features Val had found vital in a dress. Like full frontal coverage and a skirt that went past her upper thighs.

As soon as her finger clicked the *accept* icon, an impossibly thin metal arm emerged from the white partition. When it spread its three-fingered hand, a garment rested at the center of the mechanical palm.

Jaisa reached out to take the heap of cloth.

Before her fingers touched the fabric, several more arms zipped out of the partition and lifted the dress up. When the dress, and the arms, came flying at her, she leaped back. Not fast enough. One grabbed her waist from behind. Another lifted her right arm and yet another her left. Then more appendages tugged the dress over her head and began arranging it around her body.

*They're taking care of me?* Jaisa allowed herself to relax and through her tired desperation came a calming wave.

*Maybe... Maybe all this isn't as bad as it seems. Despite that man's death, if Ethan, Evie, and Rick are being taken care of like this, then...* Her mind fizzled out, unable to complete the excuses. The tenuous peace evaporated as easily as it had come. Her gut knew what these drones were and by extension the gods they served.

At least she wouldn't need to worry about a learning curve involved with getting dressed.

At least...

Jaisa didn't know if the sound that emerged from her lips was a sob or a laugh.

A week passed, filled with sobs and cementing on a brave face. These seven days were filled with drones and beautiful humans Jaisa had no way of speaking with. The time managed to be lonelier when in the company of others. After five days, Jaisa and the others had been moved from the large dormitories in which they'd first woken up into more intimate sleeping spaces. At least when quasi-alone in her room, Jaisa could pretend that the world outside the white walls was something recognizable.

She still didn't know why she was alive or what her life would be like from there on out.

In need of a break from her thoughts, she almost rejoiced when two drones entered her new dormitory room and ushered her and the others out. Without a word, all seventeen people left the room for a purpose that had yet to be revealed.

The hallway from the Jaisa's freshly assigned sleeping chamber showed no distinguishing features. Like everything within the compound, it was sterile and bland. What struck Jaisa as new was the color. Every other room she'd encountered in this place had been the same dull white, but the hallway she and the others were being led down contained darker pigments.

She clumped along down this dreary hall with the other men and women who'd been stationed in the same sleeping chamber as her. They all seemed completely faceless to her. No one spoke to anyone, and she sometimes idly wondered if she went into one of the other of the fifty sleeping chambers whether or not they would all be the same.

The farther they traveled, the deeper the walls faded into gray tones. And the more the color disturbed her.

A Barbie-doll woman beside her gave a choked sob as a black doorway came into view over the shoulders of their prison mates. She babbled something in a language Jaisa didn't know.

Jaisa shook her head and grabbed the woman's soft pink hand. If she'd known the right words to say to calm the woman, she would have said them. The drones had forbidden the human dolls from speaking the old languages. But the woman beside her was beyond subtle cues, and the aliens' language, of which Jaisa had learned only a select few phrases, seemed to have escaped her tongue.

If the woman continued to babble, the drones would come.

Since the first man had died, the drones had killed no one, but the atmosphere was heady with fear. Knowledge lurked behind every eye that the next death was just around the corner. And other than obedience, they still had no idea what the gods wanted from them.

When the woman did not calm, Jaisa pulled in a hissing breath. She couldn't say anything to fix the situation. The feeling of helplessness that Jaisa was slowly becoming accustomed to weighed around her shoulders and neck like a steel collar. *I won't watch her die. I won't.*

Jaisa gave her a solid slap across the cheek.

The woman stood stunned for a moment before holding her cheek and stumbling forward with the others.

A drone near the doorway had Jaisa fixed in its red eye. Her hand stung with the force of the blow, and her heart slammed against her ribs as if they were walls keeping it caged. The red eye blinked rapidly.

*Is it communicating? Recording?* Jaisa forged on ahead, tensed for retaliation from the drones.

"Thank you," the woman beside her said in a trembling voice.

The words of the god's language were accented, but still, Jaisa understood the phrase—one of the few she had learned. There was no response to give. At least, none she knew.

*I'm not helpless. Not really. Even here, I have choices. I simply need to find out what those are and use them.*

They passed through the black doorway and past the drones that stood guard. The interior of the room shone a crisp, bright white and in the vivid color, the prisoners tried to hide. They slunk into corners, against the walls, pressed against each other with barely room to breathe.

At the center of the room, upon a platform of kneeling drones, stood one of the tendril-faced gods.

The drones linked their arms together and knelt. Three layers of them, on the floor and on each other, their heads turned at odd angles so that each drones' blinking eye stared out at the room's shivering occupants. But they were not the part that chilled Jaisa.

No, the chill that spread down her appendages, only to be cast away in an angry fire from her heart, had been caused by the god who stood on the backs of the drones. Its red eye found her across the room and as she met its stare, the inky black flesh around the eye drew back, leaving white bone. With its two arms folded, the long, wormy fingers wriggled against the squirming black of its stomach, causing ripples. The drone's fingers, long and twig-like, were bad enough, but these moved like wicked entities in and of themselves.

Jaisa clenched her jaw and took another step.

A few brave souls stood close to the god's platform, though the majority of the people huddled against the gray walls. Jaisa marched toward this smattering of human strength.

None of them were familiar yet. They all kept to themselves.

Two small women, probably of Chinese descent, stood together, faces suffused with hope. They stood closest to the god, in a way that made Jaisa think them crazy rather than brave. A man lurked near them, fixing the god with a stare of adoration.

*I'll wind up strangling that crazy bastard if I let myself near him.* She kept her distance.

Farther back stood a pale-skinned man with strikingly pale blue eyes—stunning as all the others were, but without the muscle and bulk that had attracted Val to a man. The men in general seemed to fall into two types, pretty men like this one who were clean-shaven and slender, and "manly" men who all wore five o'clock shadows or beards and had thicker, more muscular figures. Val would have gone for the manly ones. This was not the world before, and she could no longer be Val. This new man stared at the god as if daring it to meet his eyes, and his finger traced a pattern on his bicep over and over, absently sometimes and with purpose others.

Another man stood a few feet from him, a muscular Middle Eastern man. His scowl had no patience in it, and his shoulders were tense, his hands balled into fists.

Jaisa ended her walk next to a dark-skinned man whose anger was clearly ready to boil over, but it was the slender man her gaze gravitated to again and again.

He resembled an artist more than a warrior. Maybe that was just the pretty boy look, or maybe it was his graceful hands, which moved with an elegant dexterity. Perhaps he had been a musician crooning with his guitar, a sculptor, or a painter at an easel. So how was he there, facing the god, when so many stronger men cowered?

*What was he before this? Who was he?* His long, elegant fingers moved constantly, and mesmerized, Jaisa's eyes traveled over him. Curiosity made him a true individual to her as none of the others had been so far. They were just a haze of lovely faces, but he challenged her.

As the room filled, more joined them at the front—some by choice and others because there was no room at the back.

Jaisa took her cue from artist boy and stared down the god. Someone needed to show strength. Someone needed to be the backbone for these people, and if an artist was able, then so was she.

When the last of the prisoners shuffled into the room, the lights dimmed, leaving a spotlight on the god. It appeared more octopus-like to her up close. The arms were no longer twigs, but more akin to ink swirls branching from tentacles.

The muscular man at her side tensed, and Jaisa placed her palm on his fist. It was a motion she'd used on Rick over the years. He'd never made a fist at her, but that restraint hadn't applied to others. Sometimes a brawl was more trouble than it was worth. She tightened her fingers around his fist until he relaxed.

Words emitted like a filthy residue from the god's face. She could not understand what it said, but the voice's slime covered her, and it was all she could do to continue looking on, to stand tall.

*This thing killed Rick, and I'm just standing here.*

Then, one by one, the drones translated in a cacophony of conflicting languages what the god had said. Even in the jumble of mixed up words, Jaisa understood most of the English translation.

"This is the last visit you will receive from the gods. You have been chosen as material, but only a select portion of you will be deemed worthy in the end. I have come today for two reasons."

The words fell as leaden weights. At the least, she'd thought she had earned the right to live. Wasn't she obeying these atrocious entities? But she knew what being deemed unworthy meant to the drones and assumed the gods shared this view. It meant death.

"First, to inform you that thus far we have been lenient, giving you room to grieve and adjust. That ends today. Each of you has been injected with nanites, microscopic machines that live in your blood. These nanites will monitor you for appropriate behavior. If anything you do conflicts with their programming, they will send a pulse to warn you. This will feel to you like a numbness that will grow to pain if you do not comply. If you continue to misbehave, a drone will be summoned to judge what punishment your behavior deserves."

*Why would they put all this effort into us?* The idea of tiny mechanical monsters inside her made her feel overripe in her skin, as if her body could no longer hold her blood and every ounce was about to rush forth. But worse was the lingering question of why... Why would they bother tracking them?

Then the drones went on in their translating. "The second is to give you each a chance to ask the questions inside you. This one time, I am here to set any lingering doubts aside."

The drones' voices petered out.

For the first time since the god had spoken, Jaisa glanced around. Would no one speak? No. They were afraid.

Then her eyes met with the artist's pale blue ones. He nodded at her.

"You," she started, expecting punishment for her use of English.

Instead, the god turned its many-faceted eye to her. "Use of the old languages is permitted for this meeting."

"You took our entire planet with no trouble... What could you hope to gain from ruling us? What do we have that you want?"

The drones translated before the god began its answer.

"You have nothing we want, yet someday you might. This is why your world was brought into the fold. Humanity showed signs of intelligence and violence. We could not allow you to continue to develop along those lines. Often before, as now, we have been called to save a race that verged on threatening us, themselves, and the galaxy. Now that your planet is ours, we will guide the best of humanity's minds into becoming the race they were meant to be. That they can do this under our guidance is a blessing."

"Why kill so many? Wouldn't we have been more useful in our full numbers?" the artist asked from across the room. His voice was a deep tenor, almost baritone, and it carried across the space as if he were used to public speaking.

"That is not the case. For our Chosen leaders, geniuses unappreciated by your former governments, to work at peak capacity, they must not be reminded of things they lost. This is true for you as well, though you were chosen not for your minds but your bodies' appeal. Reminders of the world you lost and reminders of self-governance undermine your productivity. Unfortunate as it seems to you, the culling of your numbers was needed."

"Why our beauty?" Jaisa asked.

"Incentive for those of humanity worth preserving. Of the treasures this planet offers, your people value their own faces the most. So you are payment to our Chosen in the form they will most appreciate. You are to be trained to be Companions and your purpose is to please, serve, and entertain our Chosen. At the end of your training here, each Chosen is given an opportunity to purchase one of you. Those selected will have earned a place in the world we are building."

The man next to her tensed again; his shoulder coiled readying to strike. Jaisa slapped his fist, the sound of the contact ringing through the silence.

She met his angry stare. He jerked his arm away.

*Live—that's all we can do for now.* If only she could force her thoughts into his mind. *I want to destroy them as much as you do.*

The god descended from the back of the crouching drones and took two steps toward Jaisa. One of the god's tentacle-like arms slithered out, and the tendrils at the end stroked Jaisa's cheek.

Her legs shoved back, and she stumbled away, her gaze cemented to those awful twitching appendages.

"This one shows prudence." The god met her eyes, and there was a smile in its words. "We are not done dealing death to those who do not deserve survival."

The god disappeared in a flicker of lights, which like a thousand fireflies, consumed its darkness. After its disappearance, the room fell into the drone's control. Jaisa sank into the back of her mind, where she could be Val, and allowed the drones to herd her back to the white room.

Now she knew what the gods wanted of her and the others. Now she knew, and she wasn't sure it made anything better. Staying alive meant buckling under... and all for what? A life as a sex slave? They hadn't said that directly, but why else would a "Chosen" wish to purchase a "Companion"?

Jaisa didn't know if that life was worth living or even if she could make herself buckle under. Even if she could and she did... it certainly sounded like many of them would die anyhow if not picked. If that were to happen, she would have buckled under for nothing.

# CHAPTER 3

The chime announcing first meal brought Tavar to his feet. The white blanket that had rested over him puddled in a mess at the foot of his bed. As the other future Companions filed out, Tavar paused. At first, he didn't know why he needed to wait, but he trusted to his gut and paused.

Something subtle looked off—a shift in the dynamic he had grown accustomed to. He'd learned to trust his instincts in crowds after years of performing with his band everywhere, from seedy clubs to fancy weddings. Then he noticed a stillness in the flutter of bejeweled movement, a pocket of sound that didn't fit the general mood.

His finger moved to his bicep to trace *her* name. The simple action helped him focus.

Behind the line of slumped, hopeless figures, one Companion remained on her bed. She was not asleep but sitting up against her headboard with vague eyes focused outward. She wasn't seeing the room or its occupants, of that he was certain. She was lost in the past and unwilling to return to this moment.

*They'll kill her.* He navigated his way through the others filing out the room and knelt by the woman's bedside. Her cloudy brown eyes looked through him. Her fragile hands alternated between slack and rigor mortis.

"Come," he said, hoping a human voice would stir her from her despondency.

She blinked and shook her head. Her dainty body shrank

back, hands folded against her chest, as if anticipating the drone's touch.

"Please come," he said. He wanted to tell her that food would make her feel better, but that would be a pure lie.

She stared down at her fingers and tears dropped from her eyes. When she looked up at him again, a panicked smile had formed on her lips. A smile that spelled both madness and determination, the smile of someone poised to jump off a ledge.

In the nearly empty room, the thud of drone footfalls made him shudder. A shrill laugh emitted from her throat.

*It's coming.* The hairs on his arms rose in anticipation of the metal man.

The woman spoke in a language he didn't know—some Asiatic tongue.

*I can't save her, not after that.* Tavar met her eyes. Then he took one of her hands, despite knowing the touch was forbidden. *She made her choice; all I can do is see she doesn't die alone.*

The metal-fleshed monster moved into the doorway.

Tavar sighed, and as the drone reached out, Tavar brushed his thumb over the woman's hand. Then he held it as she died, ignoring the tingle of nanites warning against human contact as long as he safely could. The drone stepped back after she drew her last shuddering breath and turned to him.

"You must attend first meal," it said.

*Drone-assisted suicide, that's what her death was.* Tavar stood and headed to the dining hall, his eyes downcast as he thought through all the death. His mouth was dry, and an old ache started up in his chest.

He passed a man lying across the ground. His forehead was bloody and red smeared the wall above him from where Tavar guessed he'd struck his head until he'd blacked out. Drones were already approaching from behind. Whether they'd come to kill the unconscious man for self-harm, or someone else for harming him, it didn't matter. Someone would die.

Tavar hurried into the dining hall to avoid witnessing the second death of the morning.

*I'd give anything for a drink about now. Just a bit. Just enough to drown this out for a while. If the morning is already this bad, then it'll only get worse by nighttime. Just one drink. Only enough to curb the edge.*

His hand lifted to his arm. *Wendy. Think of Wendy.*

Tavar let his finger glide in the familiar pattern, reminding himself why he had to go on. Why he couldn't attempt to numb the pain, to get lost in addiction. So many had died. People who, like Wendy, hadn't deserved it, hadn't earned their fate. He might not deserve to survive, but these others did.

*For them. Because they survived and deserve to live. If only I had a drink.*

He sat at a table along the wall and closed his eyes, imagining an ice-cold glass. That first sip—like the promise of peace. The descending fuzziness...

The gods provided nothing like that in the training facility, and even if they did, he couldn't have let himself get lost in a bottle. *Not again. I won't go down that road again.*

When he opened his eyes, a woman stood in the doorway next to his table. Her green eyes burned into him. She moved toward him. He recognized her from the day when the god had come to announce what the Companions were being held for. She was the one who'd dared to ask questions. *That walk—I'd know it anywhere. She moves like a warrior. There is so much fight in her.*

That was someone who would never give up and let the drones kill her.

Her hips swayed as she walked over. Her long, black hair, grown by the alien machines, danced with every step. Silk bands wound around her body in an intricate web from one wrist to the other ankle, serving to accentuate her form. Beauty was everywhere, but something in the almost arrogant set of her shoulders, and the forceful power of her movements, captured him every time she was near.

Tavar shook his head, forcing his gaze away. Touching was forbidden. Even for a woman like that, it wouldn't be worth dying. He was being saved, they all were, for the Chosen of the gods.

She sat in the seat opposite him and leaned forward, her small breasts barely restrained by the joke of a garment.

*I need a fucking drink. Anything to get my mind off this.*

"I'm Jaisa." Her voice was smooth and confident, but not sultry, as the women in the Companion compound were being taught to speak. Her lips had been painted in an exotic shade of purple and tiny crystals dotted the ends of her eyelashes.

"Tavar," he said.

"You're alone," she said. She paused before going on, clearly struggling with the new language and finding words. "You're never alone."

Tavar took a moment to find his own words from the still unfamiliar dialect. "A woman died. I needed a minute." That, at least, was true.

"How can they give up? I don't understand." She shook her head.

*You wouldn't, but the rest of the world isn't like you.* "Everyone they loved is dead. They don't want to be strong."

"Did... Did children survive? Any?" Jaisa tossed back the fake black hair that toppled down her back and glanced around the room. "I've only seen adults."

"There are none in Chosen, either." The computers didn't list too many details of the Chosen but enough to get an idea of who'd been put in the ranks. Only those who'd proved themselves scientifically. But there were more people in the gods' new world than Companions and Chosen. "Maybe Half-ranks and Rankless?"

"Who?"

"In computers," he said. The words to describe it wouldn't come, but like everywhere in the training center, there was a computer here. He pressed the buttons along the side of the table and pulled up a screen for her.

He watched her face contort with anger as she read. *Someday, she'll explode. If we're lucky, by then, she'll be able to tear these alien bastards down.*

The Rankless were the people the gods had saved to keep the cities of the Chosen running. They lived without names or rights, working to keep the gods' fourteen cities afloat. The Half-ranks were interesting genetic specimens that the gods thought might be some use to the Chosen in their work —"saved" to be experimented on. Her anger was understandable.

Jaisa closed the screen, fire in her eyes. "How are you so strong?"

*Me?* Tavar smiled and shrugged. "I've been broken before."

Her eyes traveled to his hand. He realized he was tracing Wendy's name again.

Tavar stood. Talking about the past would get them killed, but even if it wouldn't, his past was his to bear. He wouldn't share that burden with anyone.

A summons from the gods was not to be ignored—especially with the drones there to enforce it. Jaisa hurried to the designated room. A cloud of perfume drifted out into the hallway, telling her exactly where the other Companions had congregated. She didn't think she'd seen the room before, but it was hard to tell. With no windows and locations that seemed to shift overnight, Jaisa had no idea where she was.

Honestly, she wasn't even sure they were still on Earth. For all she knew, she was in one of the aliens' spaceships in orbit around the planet. Or, heaven forbid, on a spaceship headed somewhere else entirely.

What if that announcement was why they had summoned the Companions?

With that in mind, Jaisa stepped through the door.

The other prisoners, painted with cosmetics and dyes the gods' machines provided, parted as Jaisa moved into the room. Her presence rippled through them, and the eyes of so many weighed on her shoulders. After only a few weeks in the compound, a divide had formed between Jaisa and the others. They looked at her with a mix of fear and expectation.

*What do they think I'll do?*

She forced her stride to remain even and stopped the trembling in her hands by folding her arms across her chest. Her jeweled eyelashes were heavy, and it took effort to look alert.

Just as Jaisa thought the hope and fear from the hundreds of gazes focusing on her would break her, the artist fell in beside her. Even knowing his name, *the artist* label stuck in her head. He smiled crookedly, and with his presence coupled with hers, the others relaxed slightly.

His smile was charming, if halfhearted. The glimmer of joy didn't reach his pale-blue eyes. As soon as the expression faded from his face, he traced his finger across his bicep. Up closer, the skin there was raw and irritated. The hand movement must be almost constant.

Jaisa focused to make sense of the swirls his finger made.

*W.E.N.D.Y. Wendy. He's tracing a name?*

The longer she watched, the more certain she was that he was scrawling a woman's name, again and again on his arm as if he could tattoo it there.

Jaisa slid her finger over her arm, but the letters that made Rick's name were useless and brought her no comfort.

She gave the artist a small wave, barely lifting her hand to shoulder height. "Morning."

"Or afternoon. Who can tell?" His arm moved as if to give a comforting hug but then stopped. The nanites discouraged them from physical contact.

Jaisa tried to think of a way to show she was impressed with his command of the language but couldn't think of a comprehensible way to say anything. She wished she learned that fast.

Besides that, she had nothing more to offer him, or to ask of him, so she simply stood, taking comfort in being next to someone she trusted not to dissolve into hysterics. Dreams of

Rick rotting on their doorstep had kept her up the night before. She didn't have it in her to deal with someone else's sorrow—not when she was drowning in her own.

A dozen drones moved through the room, organizing the Companions into lines. Jaisa lined up behind Tavar, taking the spot on her own to avoid the indignity of being herded.

At the front of each line, a screen descended from the ceiling. Jaisa had no way of seeing the images it displayed at first, but she heard the screams and wailing that erupted from the front of the line. Whatever the screens were showing was designed to break them.

Jaisa clenched her jaw. She wouldn't give them the satisfaction.

When she got closer, the images she saw appeared to be of the gods' takeover. There were pictures of the alien ships in the sky, huge, black, metal things with spider-like legs reaching out across the sky and joining to other ships in a giant web. And there were pictures of those same ships descending through the clouds above cities, firing a red beam of destruction. Other than these universal images of the takeover, the pictures, although brutal, had little meaning for her. Images of accidents, corpses, burnt buildings, sometimes entire fields of corpses flashed by. These images differed with each person, so they seemed to be targeted to the individual at the head of the line. After each set, the line moved, a distraught person fleeing from the front.

*They're showing us the things we loved. The people we loved... and what became of them. They have to make sure they've killed our pasts. It makes sense to them, but I can't do it. What if they put Rick up there? Ethan? Evie?*

When Tavar stepped up to the front, her gut clenched into a painful mess. His pain was all that stood between her and the images they'd chosen to bring her to her knees.

Jaisa steadied herself as she stared at the images flickering on the screen. All four screens lined up across the rooms showed the same terrifying, gut-wrenching pictures of death and decay. For now, the corpses strung up, laid out, and torn apart were not of people she knew. Staring at the images that flashed for Tavar, she managed to remain in control, even though her eyes stung with unspent tears. If she just maintained that level of emotional distance when it was her turn, maybe she could get through this.

For Tavar, a series of images passed of a wrecked city, demolished bar, and lines of crashed cars.

Her focus on these pictures brought another realization.

Unlike the ones shown on other screens, Tavar's images seemed impersonal. Aside from an elderly man and a doorman, no individuals appeared. No one to match the name he traced on his skin; his hand moved even as she watched. Wendy had to be important, so why wasn't she up there?

Tavar's images puzzled her. What sort of man was he? The distraction disappeared the moment he walked away, blank-faced, and she stood before the black screen.

The first image eased her in—a demolished bar, the place where she'd met Rick. A blackened karaoke machine and broken glass covered the floor. Their table lay broken and discarded. They'd spent countless nights there together, always seated on the same side of the booth, with his fingers rubbing the small of her back.

Then her sister's glazed eyes stared out from underneath a pile of corpses. Evie's hand reached out, frozen in death. Jaisa's arm twitched, wanting to answer the plea of Evie's outstretched arm. Jaisa forced down her emotions while she concentrated on keeping her breathing even, and her shoulders straight.

*I'll be strong. They will not break me.*

Her mother's car was a smoking hull with one blackened arm sticking out. Her father hung among a line of others. She hadn't seen her parents in years, but their deaths still hurt. That was only the warmup. Next came Ethan, sweet little Ethan, lying on a white floor, dried blood ringing his lips, and his eyes rolled back in his head.

Jaisa clamped a hand over her mouth to keep the cry inside. A whimper wormed its way between her fingers.

*I can't. I can't watch this. I'm sorry, Ethan. I should have tried harder, protected you. No... please...*

Her best friend, lying in the aisle of a shopping center amid stacks of rotting apples.

The instant her eyes closed in protest, the tingle began in her fingers. The sensation spread to her toes. Nanites revolted inside her. She considered keeping her eyes closed and letting the drones come take her life.

Free her from what was coming.

*I'm sorry, Rick. I'm so fucking sorry.*

She opened her eyes and met the destruction on the screen. A parking lot with Rick's car, bodies piled just across the way at the door of a building and dotting the black cement. She supposed she should be thankful that, like her mother, they hadn't captured his face in death. But they showed enough.

Tears streamed down her cheeks.

# CHAPTER 4

J aisa watched, seated on her bed as a drone focused its blinking eye at a screeching woman. Since seeing the images of their dead loved ones a few weeks before, this was the first outburst. But Hisha continued to shriek words they weren't allowed to say in a high, panicked voice—just asking for death. The red light on the drone's forehead fluctuated rapidly, carrying data. Then the blinking stopped, and it took its first stride toward them.

Hisha continued shouting. Her sunflower yellow clothes looked painted on her. But there was nothing bright about her prospects.

*I didn't even know her.*

If Jaisa's mind had been less numb, her own detachment from the coming murder would have upset her. As it was, she watched motionless from the edge of her bed with her legs curled under her. As the other woman shouted forbidden words, Jaisa gripped the ends of her emerald curls with equally green nails—longer than she'd ever managed in the world before.

Woman and men cluttered the room like so many brightly colored jewels. Though the men did tend toward slightly more muted colors.

Hisha looked no different. Just one of many priceless gems.

"No, Lily! Lily! My name is Lily!" The woman's face glistened with tears. Toe to heel, she stepped back from the drone that approached her, even as she continued to insist on the name.

Lily wasn't her name. It might once have been, but her right to that name was gone, just as Jaisa could no longer be Val. Val and Lily were dead. And claiming the old name would only gain Hisha the same honor. Jaisa held no hope for the outcome of this trespass.

Her fingertips pressed into the side of the bed. The drone's form blurred as Jaisa squinted her eyes until she could imagine it was just a man. Her fingers tightened on the bed as she pictured strangling the dark, blurry form.

She half-expected the nanites they'd implanted in her to activate, but they didn't. The nanites didn't care what the Companions thought. Probably that was wise because if the self-styled gods had insisted on humanity thinking well of them, they would have had no humanity left.

"Lily! I'm Lily." Hisha's voice was quieter now, her eyes focused on the drone.

Jaisa heard her words very plainly as, "Just kill me. I'm done." Her own lips parted as if imagining the taste of such words.

The long, white room fell into complete silence as Hisha's screams halted. All of the Companions, scattered on the floor or on their beds, stared as the drone approached.

Jaisa's emerald nails dug into the bed, and numbness tingled in her fingertips. Instantly, Jaisa relaxed her hands. If she let the nanites fully engage, she might end up with a drone striding toward her as well. Thinking about strangling was fine. Mussing the sheet while you thought it apparently crossed a line.

The drone reached the woman's bed. Its black finger rose, the elongated shape hovering in the air, then the tip brushed down Hisha's body. She screamed.

This wasn't right. This was not a sudden, mostly painless demise, as the killings before had been. The difference shocked Jaisa from the stupor she'd fallen into watching the exchange.

"What are you doing to her?" Jaisa exclaimed.

Not even glancing up, the drone stood over Hisha as she writhed on the floor. Apparently, whoever commanded the drones didn't care about the outburst, since Jaisa had spoken in the new language. Blood trickled from Hisha's nose, mouth, and eyes.

Jaisa let go of her bed and lifted her hands to her face.

Many people were too brittle to bend to the will of the gods. Minds cracked, folding under the terror and change, and the drones forever silenced them with a touch. But before this, the offending party had died instantly and without obvious agony. Jaisa's body poised to run to the dying woman, but her mind could not fight past the drone's presence.

"You have no pasts," the drone said when Hisha quieted.

Her vacant eyes were red, and Jaisa's compulsive fixation was unbreakable.

Hisha's head gave a little bounce, colliding with the floor in a final spasm, and then she was still.

The drone's voice was flat, "You began the day you were named. There are consequences for forgetting."

A hush fell that seemed like a vacuum after Hisha's screams. The drone returned to its usual place next to the dormitory door. The Companions in training were silent. Jaisa seethed, unable to move. The drones had left Hisha's body there to remind them of their lesson—she was sure of it.

Jaisa's legs were still frozen beneath her when Tavar got up from his bed. He crossed the room, looking at none of the others. Scooping up Hisha's yellow clad body, he turned and laid it on her bed. After covering her body discreetly with a sheet, he bowed his head. No more. His little observance done, Tavar crossed back to his bed and sat.

Jaisa stood and drifted over to Hisha's bed and looked down. No emotion broke free in her heart. Still, she needed to see Hisha's face—to remember it. Someone needed to remember her. Jaisa studied the features of the fresh corpse and wondered what her life had been like before.

At least in death, the woman was able to be Lily. Maybe

the sacrifice was worth it in order to not be a toy of the new gods.

When Jaisa looked up, the others averted their gazes from her. This reaction was typical. The other Companions made bonds with each other, but none of them befriended her. She was dangerous, their eyes said, and Jaisa didn't care. What did it matter what they thought of her? They weren't wrong, either.

There wasn't a day Jaisa didn't twitch to do something that would get her killed. The nanites couldn't account for almost-actions, but the people saw.

Alone in this inhospitable world, Jaisa performed like a perfect doll. The images of her loved ones had done as intended. Somewhere deep inside her, Val fought and railed, but Jaisa was silent and obedient.

Jaisa pulled the sheet over Lily's face.

She returned to her bed and knelt on the mattress. The gods had instructions for almost everything, and as long as she had instructions, Jaisa knew she'd be all right. She could follow instructions. It was moments like this, when they were free to sit, that Jaisa feared she would crack.

Eventually, Jaisa lay down. When she closed her eyes, her face was hers again; they hadn't stolen it. And in the dark behind her eyelids, the old world still existed. She saw the faces she'd forbidden herself to picture in the daytime. Today was a relief because it was Hisha's face that loomed. Lily's face.

Sleep came slowly, and as Jaisa's mind skirted the edge, Lily's face became Evelyn's and morphed again into little Ethan's. His dead eyes burned her, and Jaisa sat up, managing not to scream by biting her tongue. Next would have been Rick, and she was not in a hurry to see his face rotting away in her mind.

To keep her mind from the pictures trying to surface, Jaisa read the inscription on her headboard. The same thing was written on all the Companions' beds.

*The wicked and useless have been consigned to death, unfit to walk the world of the gods. So shall the winnowing of mankind continue.*

She touched the word *wicked* and then the world *useless*. Those words were irreconcilable with the faces of those she had lost.

Sitting on a stiff chair in front of a learning terminal, Jaisa said her language lessons aloud. Her voice was smooth and child-like, no matter how much she tried to be sultry. But in the few months since arriving in the compound, her pronunciation had improved, and despite everything, she took pride in that. There was little enough to take pride in when she got daily reminders from the mirrors that populated the halls that she wasn't attractive enough to be picked by a Chosen.

Each day she was dressed by a machine in fanciful garments and saw her face and form reflected back at her. Then she saw the others, perfect in ways she would never be.

Her words scrolled across the screen, marked where she had mispronounced or mis-conjugated. The words themselves were some tripe about the rules of disciplining the Half-ranks and Rankless they would be buying as slaves. She tried not to think about it.

After all, she might not survive that long. And it might not even be worth surviving for what was in store.

A woman down the room stood abruptly. Wearing little more than metal specks over her body and purple-black hair, she exemplified the perfection that the gods sought. Her chair bounced back, hitting the seat of the man behind her. Her agitation and the confused looks of the surrounding Companions drew Jaisa's eye. *What the hell is this about? She's looking at them like they're worms...*

The woman who went by the god-given name Drima yelled in a mix of an old language that Jaisa knew and the new one they were all learning. "They are gods!"

The two men Drima had been sitting next to drew back.

One forced his gaze back to his terminal, pretending not to hear.

"I don't see how we could not believe them, not love them!" Drima turned her eyes to survey the entire room. "They are what humanity needs, and we should all be grateful. They saved us!"

*That's English. She's speaking English.*

Only death came from using a language of the world before. Before Jaisa moved, a drone's voice stopped her. It addressed Drima. Jaisa stood and backed up to the wall to watch the exchange.

*But the things she's saying... she can't mean them.* As Jaisa's mind processed the meaning of the other woman's ravings, she did not want to be any closer than she had to be. *Saved.* That was the word Drima had used. *They saved us.*

"Drima," the drone said, "your desire to serve the gods is admirable. Know that there is another option for all of you, other than being Companions. You, Drima, have chosen the gods, and they will offer you and those who follow you in the next few months a place serving them. If you wish it, you need not be auctioned off with the others."

"How?" Drima asked.

Jaisa pressed herself against the wall. How could someone choose to serve them? How could this woman stand there and offer even more than they demanded? She was offering her devotion to the destroyers of the human race.

"You will be their priestess. When the new world is set in place, you will preach their word. Choose the gods and the gods will protect you."

"I choose the gods. How could I do anything else?" Drima smiled a radiant smile.

"Others will join you soon in this service, but you are the first, and the gods will honor you," the drone said. It led Drima from the room.

"Traitor," Jaisa whispered. It was the first word she had uttered in the old tongue. As she spoke, her fingers and toes went numb. The feeling spread up to her elbows and her knees.

Jaisa said no more, but the woman in the chair next to her looked her way. She was a dusky-skinned woman, and the blush of hair on her head was jet-black. Jaisa thought she'd heard the woman's name: Ladair. With a crafty twinkle in her amber eyes to show she knew and approved of Jaisa's misbehavior, Ladair smiled.

Across the room, Tavar looked up, and Jaisa met his eyes for comfort, not knowing what to expect from this other woman. Realizing she'd turned to this stranger set her heart pumping. *I trust him. Oh, don't let him be one of the ones to die. I don't know how I could lose anything else.*

"We are all traitors or dead," Ladair said, slowly and painfully in the new words. "Still, it is better tame than broken."

"Yes. I speak, did not think."

"Good. Enough are dead," Ladair said.

Jaisa kept that thought with her. Enough had already died. How many was that? Had millions died? Billions? It seemed a safe bet that over a billion were dead. But how many? She looked up the words she needed at the terminals she'd recently vacated and practiced saying it as she walked up to a drone standing guard at the doorway. It was the first time she had approached one of her own accord. Her stomach lurched in protest as she stopped in front of it.

The sight of one of them taking on her face never failed to horrify her. But her face reflected in the black metal did not show that horror, which meant that she was containing her emotions. In the weeks that had passed, she had learned to hide the feelings that welled up inside her. The drone waited for her to speak.

"How many humans have been killed?"

Those behind her in their seats tensed at Jaisa's words. An understanding of what the answer meant entered Jaisa as their reluctant eyes met hers. She did not really want to know. It would be too horrible. Now, she was stuck hearing it, as were those who had known better than to ask.

"Five billion, eight hundred and thirty-seven million,

four hundred and seventy-eight thousand, nine hundred and twenty-seven people, since the day of the gods' arrival until the moment you finished your sentence."

Jaisa wished it were not her face that gave that answer. How many people had there been prior to the gods' reign? Seven billion? Eight?

How many people lived?

Before anyone else could ask that question, Jaisa hurried back toward her seat. Almost six billion were dead. Ladair was right: Enough had died. It took all her effort not to run, but she passed her seat, her momentum carrying her to the far wall. There had to be some way to stop these invaders who called themselves gods. Even in her mind, Jaisa could no longer call them "gods" herself. The word refused to come. They were aliens. They were invaders, and somehow, they could be stopped.

Jaisa turned her head to one of the many mirrors that hung on the walls. The Companions were never deprived of their own images. Her expression was anything but blank. Carefully, Jaisa arranged her features, and as she did, she calmed.

*No, the invaders cannot be destroyed. They may not be gods, but they are out of my reach. They have killed so many already. I will not give up my life for the past.*

*But I will not serve them—never that.*

Was that possible? The options were clear: obey or die.

*How long do I have to live anyhow?* She stared at her imperfect features. *However I was chosen, it was a mistake. I look nothing like the others, and when the Chosen bid on us, I will not be selected. Then I will die, or I will serve them. And I will never serve them.*

Jaisa touched the brown shadow of hair on her head. The dark green eyes that looked at her out of the mirror softened.

*Is it wrong to want to survive?*

She left the mirror and walked back to her seat to continue studying.

Her walk was beautiful. She moved purposefully, and the sway of her hips accented by long legs was devastatingly attractive. All her life, she had walked this way and had never been aware of it. It was powerful. It was sensual. She was aware of it now.

# INTERLUDE

Three gods floated in the prismed chamber, watching the woman at the center. She lay strapped to a table, though her hair floated around her, dancing in the gravity-free environment. Tubes filled with her blood poured out into a vat, leaving channels under her skin. The black liquid that powered the drones was funneled in. When the liquid hardened, they would cut away the skin over the channels—leaving nothing to hide their mark on this, their first priestess.

Drima's vacant eyes were half-closed, lashes obscuring her dilated pupils. The gods were attentive for any sign of wakefulness. Although they knew much of human anatomy, the mind mystified them. Human science did not hold a full understanding of their own minds, so the gods needed more data to come to any conclusions of their own.

It made full control and use of their new captured race complicated.

"She'll be complete within the day," a god said.

"More will join."

One god floated closer and stretched its fingers to caress the smooth skin of Drima's stomach, now tattooed from within with curving, black lines.

"The timing is appropriate. We need our most loyal subjects to reach out into the cities below or we risk a revolt."

"No." The god next to her moved its arm, letting one twig-like finger touch her chin. "The first to truly be ours should be treated with honor."

"Hardly. She is still human. She's part of the system and considering her as more is senseless."

"Serving the higher interests sometimes requires considering the success of the machines."

"Agreed. We send the priests and priestesses who follow her to investigate the areas. It will be a strong way to begin our converting in the under-cities."

"That *is* the clergy's purpose," said the dissenting god. "It is time they begin. I see no purpose in waiting."

"It is the will of the mass," the other two said together.

Drima's eyelids fluttered, and a whimper escaped her lips, but she soon drifted back into unconsciousness. All but one of the gods floated from the room out into the central chamber, letting the door seal behind them.

# CHAPTER 5

"How long have we been here, do you think?" Ladair asked. She was lying on her back across her bed. Her head lolled gracefully over the edge, and her doe eyes fixed on Jaisa. Her dark hair, the vivid colors of her minimal clothes, and the dusky brown of her skin were the only breaks in the expanse of stark white bedding. Similar dots of color scattered over the long room, with its evenly spaced beds. The other Companions dotting the room, most like deactivated dolls, had collapsed, ceasing movement as soon as the drones demanded nothing from them. Yet their costumes still screamed with color and glitter.

"Long enough for you to be able to ask that question and me to answer." Jaisa looked down at the heavy mirror in her hand. Green eyes stared out at her from a pale face and hair currently colored a vivid blue hung straight to her chin with long locks mixed in, twisted with ribbons. The length meant nothing as the machines could alter that. The image held few traces of the woman she had been when this whole thing had started. She tucked her knees up under her on her bed, falling naturally into the graceful pose of a Companion. She didn't feel like an aunt or a wife anymore except when sleep overcame her defenses.

She couldn't afford to feel like her old self. That way was only madness.

That wasn't her existence. The gods had chosen this façade of a life for her.

"Time used to mean so very much to all of us. I haven't even thought of it," Ladair said, rolling over to watch Jaisa. "It doesn't have much meaning, does it? At least until they auction us off. But I still wonder, how long have we lived like this?"

"Five months, maybe six?" Jaisa was growing adept at ignoring the wringing sensation in her heart. This time, she almost managed not to think about where she would have been right now if the gods had never arrived. She almost didn't see Rick's smile.

To avoid the despair that threatened, Jaisa focused her eyes on the blank white wall behind her friend. Their quarters were more intimate now; the room housed around twenty of the prospective Companions. Ladair and Jaisa had secured beds in the corner farthest from the door and the black presence of the drones. Tavar slept near them but was often occupied entertaining or cheering other Companions.

Ladair propped her head on her hand, peering over at Jaisa as she spoke. "I hope you won't be angry if I ask you a question."

"What question?"

"You may not like it."

"If you thought I would like it, you wouldn't have suggested I'd get angry. What question?"

"Why don't you choose to serve the gods and be a priestess?"

Jaisa watched the fall of Ladair's short, black hair, which was streaked cosmetically with bright purple. The other woman's eyes gazed through her. Jaisa felt a little offended—as if she stood no chance of being bought—but also struck by the word "choose." The idea of her life being something she controlled and directed was frighteningly foreign. "Choose?"

"We have choices." Ladair's enhanced lashes fluttered down, shielding her eyes from scrutiny. "We can cause our own deaths, we can submit, or we can walk the priestess's path. And I want to know why you haven't chosen to be one of the 'gods folk.'"

"Why do you ask that?"

"Most of the other Companions who were less than perfect-looking have already chosen that life."

Jaisa winced, but Ladair was right to be honest. Lies served no purpose.

Ladair went on. "They measured their chances and chose. You are still alive, so I know you don't want to die. So, why don't you choose to serve them? It would ensure your survival."

"Too many have already died," Jaisa said with a smile. She wanted to lay her hand over Ladair's and offer comfort. Instead, she clutched the mirror tighter in her hands.

"I don't understand."

"That was the first thing you said to me, and now you say it again in the prettiest words." Jaisa sighed and scooted toward the edge of her bed. "I couldn't live with myself if I chose the life of a priestess. I will not work for my death, but there are some things I cannot do, and remaining on the Earth just isn't worth serving them. I don't think I've fully decided if I'm willing to sacrifice what it takes to stay in this world."

Ladair looked down at her hands, and when she spoke again it was soft, barely above a whisper. "Too many have already died. I still believe that."

Jaisa inspected her friend's perfect face. If Ladair believed so firmly in life—why risk going to auction? Why expect Jaisa to bend where she would not? "Why don't *you* become a priestess?"

Ladair laughed. The sound was deep and sensual. It was the laugh they had been encouraged to use, but Ladair had made it her own as Jaisa never could. "Do you want the truth?"

"Only if your fingers won't go numb from it." Without thought, Jaisa's fingers clenched, an automatic response to the tingle of nanites she half-expected any second.

"My life isn't as vital as yours. I don't matter."

Jaisa lowered the mirror to the bed. Her brow knit. "Now it is my turn to say I don't understand. Why would you say that?"

"You matter." Ladair glanced at the other Companions, a silky lock of her synthetic hair slipping down between her breasts. "You've spoken out to the gods, stood up to the drones... and you survived. People watch you."

"All that means is that at some point, I'll step too far and they'll take me down."

"No. You won't let yourself. Because you know that all of us would see you die and that it would affect everyone here. You'll tread carefully because different still means death, but someday it won't. I'm just a face, but you have something more inside you."

"Hush." Jaisa's eyes flicked to the drones at the edges of the room. They didn't move.

"It is not a traitorous thought," Ladair said. "If you were a traitor, you'd be gone by now. You aren't, but you're not the same as the rest of us, either."

"I will not serve them."

"Neither would I." She smiled, her eyes distant again. "I wonder what death feels like? I think it would wash over you, like pulling a blanket over a bird's cage."

*There is such a softness inside her. How has she kept that alive? If I let myself feel anything at all, I start to fall apart.*

Jaisa looked up at the sterile room and found quite a few eyes rested on them. Gazes fell away at Jaisa's look.

Tavar smiled and nodded. Was he also just another "face," as Ladair had put it? He was brave and kind and seemed to know where the allowable boundaries were well enough to still be alive. What good did that do any of them? They were alive but nothing else. No way to fight and no way to resist. It was so useless, it sickened her, and she broke eye contact.

The things Ladair said were nonsense.

Yet outright dismissing the statement proved beyond Jaisa. Could her little actions, her little near-rebellions, be so obvious to the others?

No, they were all fools if they found something to respect in her. She hadn't stopped anything from happening. She couldn't really be important. It made her feel both better and worse.

Jaisa looked back over at Ladair and found her grinning.

"You should ask for red hair tomorrow," Ladair said. "It would flatter your skin."

"Now that is constructive advice. I will." *Rick liked red hair.* Another thought followed, softer, almost without her noticing. *Does Tavar?*

Tavar mattered. Jaisa hadn't realized until just then that he did. And he wasn't the only one who did matter. Ladair was right; all the Companions mattered to Jaisa. But that didn't mean that Ladair understood the inner workings that had kept Jaisa alive.

Living on for them might not be something she could do. Not with Rick, Evie, her mother, and everyone she'd known before on the other side of the scale.

Ladair slunk through the empty white hall as she did every evening after her required dance training. She'd have to go through a cleansing wash for the sweat covering her, but first, she took advantage of her few moments of free time, searching for a window. Without the window, the world outside took on a mythical sheen.

*The sun rises in the east and sets in the west. But what is east and what is west? I need the sky, the wind... Humans have caged humans for ages. This slavery is nothing new. All I ask is to feel the wind on my face—to know that it is still free and with it, that freedom exists.*

Was God up there still? The true God? To kneel in prayer was forbidden. To speak in worship not of the new gods would earn her death. But out under the sky, perhaps she would be enveloped in God's love.

She ran her jewel-studded nails over the white wall, but

the surface remained smooth and seamless. No windows. No way out. No hope.

"Soon," Tavar said.

Ladair jumped, his smooth voice freeing a sob of panic from her throat. She forced her hands away from her hair. Even after six months, being bareheaded made her feel shameful, and add that to being in a man's company without a proper chaperone? But this was the only world she had.

"I didn't mean to startle you." Tavar slipped into her view.

And she'd spent hours dancing with this man and learning the instruments the gods were introducing to the words. The dances left her entwined with others, men and women, as each movement set was designed to mimic both dancing and fighting, but also to culminate in a baser act. It was hard to be shy with any of the Companions, least of all Tavar, who had always been as gentle as allowed.

Of all the people in the compound, Jaisa and Tavar interested her the most. She wished there had been more time to study them—to know them, to understand. But Jaisa kept to herself, quietly brooding, always on the verge of a fight, and Tavar flitted between everyone, never settling long enough for her to get a proper feel for him.

How many more would have died without their strength and encouragement?

Tavar gave her a sheepish smile and clutched one of the gods' wind instruments in his hand—a wind instrument, with pressurized buttons down its length, slightly larger than a flute and made of a translucent metal. Of all the Companions, he was one of a few who had truly taken to creating music. She'd bet that was the reason he'd been allowed to take one out of the training room.

"Do not worry about startling me." Ladair ducked her head in acknowledgement. "What do you mean *soon*?"

"Soon," Tavar said, "we will be outside these walls."

"One way or another," Ladair said.

"Either way, we won't be here."

"Nothing will change."

"Have hope." He twirled his instrument between one hand and the other. The air passing through it made a low noise, quiet but plaintive as it moved. "Change can be small. I am waiting for the touch of sun on my skin. You?"

"The sky." The sky as it had been, without the bars the aliens had put in place. Unfortunately, she couldn't close her eyes without seeing the webbing of the gods' great black ships reaching out across the heavens. "Before I die, I wish to see the sky."

*I've been a caged bird all my life. This is no different. Oh, to close my eyes and fly to the heavens.*

She shivered and wrapped her arms around herself. Was the only freedom she'd ever experience in death?

Tavar peered into her face, waiting for her to go on.

"They will choose soon," Ladair said. Did the Chosen have the sun and sky? This thought plagued her—that the Companions' futures would be with people nothing like them. The gods had reformed the Companions, and she understood what they had become, but what had the gods created in the Chosen?

"Yes." Tavar bowed his head. His beauty shocked her as his pale eyes flashed up out of his sculpted features. Her body had no response to that loveliness—it was distant as the heavens and just as vast.

"You will be selected," she said.

"None of us have a guarantee."

Did he not see the divinity in himself? How like Jaisa. "I've watched you, and you will be chosen."

"Ladair, what would you even look for to know that?"

Part of her wanted to reach out and touch the instrument he held, or hold up a mirror, but if he didn't already know himself, she would not be able to reveal anything to him. "Not all with eyes can see."

"What do you mean?" Tavar asked.

"Sight is not everything—the world is a puzzle we fit together with our eyes, ears, and hearts. It's always about how you put the pieces together."

Tavar chuckled and turned to head back to the sleeping chamber—then he ran a hand through his thick, black hair and stopped. His hand lingered on his bicep, moving in little swirls before he spun to face her.

"I don't know what to wish for," he said. "To be selected at the auction or not."

Ladair nodded and watched him go.

Once Tavar was out of sight, she sighed and slumped against the wall. *I shouldn't stand like this. The drones won't like it.*

But her body refused to be sensible.

*Everyone talks about how much everything has changed, but life has always been like this. All I've ever done was train to please. I never made it to the husband my father planned for me... Will I make it to a Chosen?* Tavar's spoken doubt crept into her own thoughts. They were all alone in this new world—and alone was no way to live. *Do I want to live at all?*

She pressed her palm to the wall and shoved herself off. The structure held her, sturdy and permanent but not comforting. These were the new bars to her loveless cage.

*At least Daddy loved me. No one loves me here. No one ever will. I've been caged since birth, and I will be caged until I die.*

Ladair smiled and drifted down the hall.

*If I could fly free, even for an instant, I'd give my life willingly.*

# CHAPTER 6

T he contents of Jaisa's stomach lurched as her eyes communicated to her body what the next test would be.
Every bite she had eaten that morning surged up, and she
curled over. Retching was her body's reaction to the sight. Her
mind was better trained, so as soon as her body finished, she
stood back up, rearranged her so-called dress, wiped her mouth,
and turned her eyes back to the mating couple.

The machines made short work of her mess and cleared
out of the room. Jaisa remained, quivering and doing her best to
hide this betrayal of her body. She trained her eyes on what she
was meant to. At the center of the room, a couple writhed on
the floor, not lying on a bed but on a black mat laid into a carved
hole in the smooth, tile-like floor. Not even a wall of glass separated her from the horror.

The couple were not both human.

Jaisa knew what being a Companion would entail, but at
least the Chosen were *people*. She'd never imagined having to be
intimate with a metal killing machine. No wonder her body had
rebelled.

*I'm next. Can I do it? Will there be a second chance, or is this it?*

The black drone's body certainly moved as a man might.
And the Companion lying beneath him moved mechanically
but as trained. She did not glance up at Jaisa or to the door on the
other side of the room through which she would be able to flee if
she managed to pass the test.

Jaisa's mind fluttered on the brink of panic. By now, she understood the consequences of most of her actions. This was new. Obviously, the gods wished to divide those who would be able to fulfil their functions for the Chosen from those who would not.

Without knowing what the result would be if she failed on her first try, either to commit the act or to pretend enjoyment, she kept envisioning a black finger coming toward her, perhaps even from the same drone she'd just—her mind refused to think it.

Sometimes there were second chances, but usually, there were not. *Will I be judged on my actions standing here and watching as well? But of course I will.*

It was an ingenious test. Companions were meant to give physical pleasure. Like any whore from the world before, they needed to perform regardless of how they felt.

The woman beneath the drone had her eyes closed. She appeared relaxed, with a trace of a smile on her face. It was impossible to know what thoughts went through her mind. Did she enjoy this? That could not be.

Again, Jaisa's stomach turned, and Jaisa bit down on her lip. There was no other option. She had to do this. If she failed here, she might as well have died on the first day.

*Failure is not an option. Not only would I die, but everyone here would see me break.*

Jaisa would fight. She might not be able to fight the gods or the drones, but she could fight her own emotions to a standstill. Tamed but not broken—this wasn't a matter of simply not speaking. She'd have to choose to obey and continue to do so. At any cost. Someday, she might strike back, but only if she lived.

*The others watch me, that's what Ladair said. And if I fail now, I'll be giving up any chance of them seeing me succeed.*

"You will disrobe now." A second drone at Jaisa's side stepped forward.

Jaisa looked up at him and smiled. Her hands unfastened her loose dress. It pooled around her feet. Her numb fingers struggled with the few clasps of her undergarment. Her eyes refused to move from the drone's single red eye.

"Will you be my partner?"

"I will." The drone's face formed into hers.

"Can you..." Jaisa paused and tried to coach her voice to be deeper, more like they wanted. "Could you wear another face? I would prefer not to see my own face."

The drone's red eye blinked once. "There is no directive against permitting this request."

"Thank you."

Its face had already gone blank. Even that was better. Anything was better than metal flesh wearing her own face.

The other couple rose. The woman looked dazed with her eyes opened. She looked at Jaisa as she departed. Jaisa nodded her encouragement. She tried to say with her eyes that no one would blame her, that they were in this together. Once the woman left, only the smell of sex remained to show they had been there. Even this was being cleaned away.

Air burned in Jaisa's lungs as her body refused to exhale.

She pictured the drone reaching for her. Its hands would be as cold as steel, and they would touch her. Again and again, she imagined the black twig-like finger stretching out to stop her heart. She could almost hear the thump of her corpse hitting the floor.

Jaisa stared at the drone and stepped out of the pool of fabric at her feet. If it reached for her, she would scream. The sound barely remained within her throat, and the drone had yet to move. If those arms lifted, and those fingers came to her, she had no doubt her terror and disgust would break free, and she would be dead. She took another step back. The drone had finished forming the parts necessary for the interaction to follow.

*Breathe in. Breathe out.*

She propped a hand on her hip. Just one more breath and maybe somehow her heart would slow, and she would be prepared.

*Breathe in. Breathe out. Don't think about it.*

Her eyes fluttered closed, and she allowed herself a rare indulgence. In the depths of her mind, Rick came to meet her. He smiled at her, and his face was his own. It must be done, and she would do it with his strength. She imagined his smile as he sat across the bar with a drink while music played too loud to talk over.

After the space of a breath, Jaisa opened her eyes and went to the drone. She lifted her arms and brought the drone to her. She pressed her lips to its face that wasn't a face. Imagining warmth, she slid her arms over its chest. Music stolen from hidden spaces inside her filled her ears. With a smile, she stroked the back of its head.

"Shall we?" She knelt and motioned it to her.

Then, and only then, did she allow herself to close her eyes. To see it coming toward her might be too much. It was best not to risk it. She had to stay strong. So she waited, and it came to her. She could not find the music from the world before. It was too distant. In the silence left behind, her weakness swallowed her. The drone was cold, and when the illusion of warmth slipped away, she floundered, alone in her mind, shivering.

Rick was gone.

So she opened her eyes and gazed at the truth.

And over the drone's shoulder she saw another human. A man this time, whose name she could not recall, waiting at the side of a drone. He watched, the onset of panic shining in his eyes. *If I fail, he fails. If I panic, it will push him over the edge, and I will be responsible not just for my death, but for his. Breathe in.*

Jaisa smiled and pressed her lips to the drone's shoulder to keep from screaming or spitting in its face. Fear and disgust was written on her fellow human's face. So she moved her eyes back to the drone. *If I fail, he fails. Breathe out.*

And then at last, its weight left her, and she stumbled to her feet. She moved away from the drone and toward the man, already naked. Jaisa extended her hand. She pressed her palm on top of his arm and forced a smile. If she could force smiles for their captors, she could give one to this man.

She ignored the tingle of the nanites warning her against touch.

On the other side of the door, she stood with the others who had come through this most recent test. They hadn't been given clothing, but that didn't matter. Their skin was hardly a revelation to each other. Her legs had no trouble holding her. She looked down at her hands, and they didn't shake. Jaisa stepped away from the door and touched the shoulder of the woman who had preceded her. The woman wept softly.

"Hush." Jaisa knelt and held the other woman. "There is nothing that cannot be borne. What can this be but the last of their tests? You have passed, and soon we can be out of this place. Soon this will seem like only a nightmare."

"Do you believe that?" Tavar asked from the corner of the room. His voice was firm and rang out with hope in a room filled with tears.

On lifting her face, she found Tavar's eyes on her. They both knew the answer she needed to give. If there had been a way, Jaisa would have thanked him. These people needed hope, and by speaking their doubts aloud, he was helping her to soothe them.

"I do believe. This nightmare is almost over." But it wasn't true. Rick was gone. Ethan was gone. Everyone was dead and that would never end. It would never be better until they could rise and fight.

But there were others now. She'd find the strength, for them.

# CHAPTER 7

T he music ran through Tavar's veins. Back in the "good ol' days," he'd called it the lightning in his veins. But that had been before his divorce, before the accident, and before the end of the world. Now, with his fingers slipping over and plucking at the strings of one of the gods' new instruments, the music felt more like a wave that flowed out from him, reaching over barriers and embracing those around him. He'd always preferred stringed instruments to all others. Somehow, his hands always knew how to move, and this was the closest they had to a guitar; longer in body and slightly more resonant in its notes, it created a sound he found soothing.

And with the auction coming within a ten-day—the new gods' version of a week—each of the Companions needed a hug, a hand to squeeze, and a shoulder to cry on. Tavar did his best to provide that without ever breaking the no-touch rule.

The drones at the back of the room watched him periodically but made no effort to stop him from playing. This continually surprised him. With how much they condemned anything from the world before, he couldn't believe they allowed a former musician to continue with his trade in any form. Yet thus far, he'd been encouraged to learn the new instruments along with all the other Companions.

In any event, it had been years since he'd performed sober, years since he'd looked into an audience and cared. So maybe this was all new enough to please the gods.

Out in the room, other Companions practiced their own skills. Most practiced whatever skill they had the most talent for, while a few worked on the skills they lacked. Tavar played for all of them.

Ladair and Jaisa were paired on the dancefloor between several other dancers, performing one of the calmer dances taught to the Companions. These were not the fight dances that Tavar preferred but movements that seemed reminiscent of a May Day ribbon dance. It should have been beautiful, but the undertone in the air was panic, and that permeated even the most perfectly performed movement.

A couple swung by him, smiling but leaving a panicky sweat scent on the air behind them.

*Many of us are about to die. That's a simple fact.*

*But even more... What happens to those who are picked? What is outside this compound?*

Tavar kept his worry away from his fingers and watched his friends twirl. Of the women in the compound, Jaisa and Ladair were the closest to friends he had. Ladair asked nothing of him but had a softness to her that the gods hadn't stamped out. Jaisa was the opposite. Without words, she asked for everything yet seemed indomitable. What sort of Chosen would select them?

They would likely be worrying about the same thing, so if he could, he would provide them with a brief respite.

Tavar played for them, watching Jaisa's green eyes and Ladair's brown ones, until both showed no worry. Then he played on. Give them a moment of peace—sometimes distraction is the only peace.

When the drones stepped forward into the room, signaling the end of the practice period, Tavar's fingers ached. Ladair turned to him with her shy smile, and it had been worth it. A feeling of peace filled him.

Companions began to file from the room. Tavar turned and replaced the instrument he held on a rack, which then retracted into the wall. He wouldn't be practicing more that day.

When he turned back to the room, Jaisa and Ladair waited a few feet from him.

"Grab something to eat with us?" Jaisa asked.

"Is it that time?" he asked, a little surprised. He hadn't heard the telltale chime.

Jaisa nodded, and her hair, then an emerald green bob, slid over her face. He resisted pushing the strands back from her eyes.

"Shall we?" Ladair asked, glancing nervously at the drones.

Tavar nodded again and started walking. Jaisa fell in step on one side of him with Ladair beside her. After their dance, both women looked flushed and damp with sweat, but as usual, Jaisa wore the look proudly, while Ladair hid behind lowered lashes.

"Thanks for that," Jaisa said. "Music used to be everywhere—I took it for granted." She glanced down at her fingers, although Tavar didn't know if her nanites had activated or if she just expected them to. "Now... well, it's amazing how refreshing it is to escape, even for a second."

The three of them walked down the hallways in an easy silence for a few moments.

"Do you think you'll be able to play in the auction?" Ladair asked, briefly looking directly at Tavar.

He shrugged. "We don't really know what it'll entail."

"No," she said, slowly and thoughtfully. "But we know that people will be choosing us—thus, standing out will be the key."

Tavar ran a hand over his bicep. His mind clutched at her words, tilting toward a realization that he couldn't yet name.

"Not all of us will be picked," Jaisa said. They all knew it, but her bluntness was a knife cutting through the tension in the air. "We all need to show our best selves to get what we want."

And there it was. What did he want? Being picked and surviving would be a start, but it would also matter who chose him. Because leaving the compound wasn't just an end, it was a beginning, too. He eyed Jaisa. "What do you want?"

"To make sure as many of us survive as possible," Jaisa said.

"So many wish to live," Ladair said. "But since the first day in here, this hasn't been living. I want to be free."

Free. That was something none of them would ever be again, but he kept that to himself. Still, it was an idea that dug into him. Freedom was relative—and would depend on who purchased them. The question was, how to control who it would be. How to advertise, without the gods knowing, that he wasn't a convert.

Living was only the first step. To get the rest right, he had to prepare properly for the auction.

As the door shut behind her, air entered her lungs in a rush, filled with perfumes that nearly gagged her. Alone for the first time since she'd first woken in the white bed six months before, in a white metal room barely six feet deep and maybe five wide, Jaisa stared in front of her into her own reflection. It wasn't a face she would have known a year before. Over the past few months, she had changed. Diet and exercise had slimmed her cheeks, and the gods had removed every tiny scar. More than that, something behind her eyes had transformed.

She looked dangerous, reminding herself of a spy from one of the action movies Rick had watched.

Her natural hair, once a deep chestnut brown, was colored as red as partially dried blood, and curled at that. Once blood had meant death, but now death was silent and still. Blood was *life*. She touched the wild, red curls on her head.

*Today, I'll probably die. But I'll protect them. Live or die, I'll be strong—strong for those like Evie, who can't be.*

She pushed the doubt back. If she died, then she died, but there was no point in giving up.

Today was the day of choosing. All throughout the building, she was sure the others were altering and re-altering their appearances. They would be trying to be unforgettable. Jaisa just wanted to be herself; she'd rather die that way than in costume.

All over the world, or the sky, or wherever it was they were, there would be complexes just like this one, and all of them were filled with people beautifying themselves. How many perfect faces were swollen this morning with last night's tears?

Jaisa ran a rod over her hair, taming her flyaway curls into ringlets. *I will be what they have made me. Why pretend?*

The room's display offered her all varieties of temptations from the extensive closets available to all Companions. Each offering was alien, foreign, screaming that it had come from the gods' grace.

Her naked flesh was pale and firm. As her face was altered, so was her body. It was a sensual body without flaw, and as she moved, she felt none of the self-consciousness that would have troubled Val.

She ordered a short, red tunic, simple and comfortable. Clothed, she returned to the mirror and inspected herself. With a swift movement, she tied her hair back away from her face. She did not even command the machines to do it for her. A few curls fell free, dashing across her porcelain skin.

*Rick would have loved me like this.* This thought, too, she discarded. She couldn't let grief weaken her.

Today was a day for strength. All the other Companions had tossed fitfully in their beds the night before, and Jaisa had watched, wrapped in her blanket. All of them were scared. *I will walk among them, and I will do whatever I must.*

A few days ago, they had learned the statistics. Worldwide, there were twice as many people waiting to be selected as there were elite waiting to bid on their desired Companion. Which meant that many of them would die. Since the training facility they were in wasn't the only one, who was to say that any of them would make it? *If we're all cracked and weeping, none of us will survive.*

Jaisa emerged from the dressing room. The drones waited outside, and as she expected, she was the first to emerge. The drones all looked over at her, taking on her face as they always did.

*How beautiful my face looks, and yet so cold. How do they make it look so emotionless?*

"You are ready?" a single drone asked. She thought there might have been a tone of disapproval in its voice. Could machines disapprove?

"Yes, I'm ready—unless you have a demand for me." Jaisa moved one bare foot behind the other, presenting herself in a pose that after so many months felt natural.

"You are not as expected," the drone said. Its red eye blinked. It was consulting with the main computer for protocol.

It turned away.

Jaisa grinned and sauntered to the center of the room, where she waited for the others. One by one, the other Companions trickled into it. They were images of extravagance.

Some were dressed as eroticized harem girls, while some wore little more than lingerie. The only thing forbidden to them were clothes of the now-dead modern world, but it didn't appear these women and men would have been tempted by anything so understated. A few had brilliantly dyed skin, unnatural blues and greens. The goal was to stand out, and alone, each of them did. But together, they were a mass of glamorized beauty.

Of all of them, only two truly stood out amid the mess of color and glitter. One was a girl who had dyed her skin the unholy black of the gods. She wore not a stitch of clothing, but a large red jewel hung on her forehead, suspended by a golden chain. Her hair was pulled back in a slick ponytail, also dyed a matte black.

The other was Tavar, who had shaved his head clean. He was clothed in loose, white garments, which but for fine silver traceries could have been the outfit he'd awoken in on that first day. A cosmetically added scar traced from one cheek down to his chin. He met Jaisa's eyes as she inspected him and nodded at her.

He, like her, had been as much of a leader as was possible in a world of nanites who watched words and actions. She could only be thankful the nanites were not programmed to care about thoughts. Would Tavar be as dead as she if the nanites had sensed unacceptable thoughts as well?

As she was studying him, wishing she'd tried to get to know him better, Ladair made her way to Jaisa's side. She jingled as she walked, bells hanging about her ankles and dangling over her hands. Like an Arabian goddess.

"I could not sleep." Ladair ran a hand over her midnight-blue hair to smooth an errant lock.

"I don't think that any of us slept," Jaisa replied. "It doesn't show. You're perfect."

"We all are," Ladair said.

This, Jaisa assumed, was her way of saying perfection was irrelevant when it was a common commodity.

Once all of them had gathered, the drones led them through a doorway that had not been there the day before. The door opened upon a place in the complex that Jaisa had never entered.

A large garden, complete with trees, ponds, cultivated streams, flowers, and fluidly shaped patches of grass welcomed the Companions. There was even a fountain hidden from view that made a lovely musical sound. The bright colors were staggering after months in the parched white of the complex.

Jaisa's foot pressed into the damp grass, sinking into the waxy strands. She stepped out in front of the others. *Real grass, green trees... If I tried hard enough, I could even imagine I was home —that this was my Earth. The sky looks like ours too... Are we still on the planet?*

"Where are they? Where are the Chosen?" Ladair asked from behind her.

# CHAPTER 8

There was no sign of the gods' Chosen anywhere in the garden. Jaisa looked over her shoulder at the other Companions as they hovered around the edges, some still filtering through the door.

Tavar marched straight out into the garden, lifting his face to the glass-tiled ceiling, as if he believed the Chosen might have been watching from above. It was possible—they would have no issue seeing through the frosted glass that obscured the sky.

"I thought…" a woman's voice said.

They would all panic if they stood there and worried. Wherever the Chosen were, freaking out here only brought the drones' touch closer. Words wouldn't call the others, only action. And maybe Tavar had the right of it. Jaisa looked away from them and walked into the garden. It even smelled as a garden should: pollen, cut grass, moving water.

"We have this place," Tavar said. His voice sounded musical, steady, and smooth. "It's beautiful. We have no control over the rest."

"Maybe they're watching us remotely," a man said.

Jaisa bent and picked a flower from beside the grassy lawn. It was like no flower she had ever seen before. The colors moved over its petals in waves. She twirled it in her fingers as she turned back to the others. A few were moving out into the garden, but most were hanging back.

Maybe the other Companions needed words, after all.

"If they *are* watching us, standing there isn't likely to grant you your life," Jaisa said. "Feel free to do as you like, but I'm going to explore this place."

The garden welcomed Jaisa as she made her way toward the sound of water splashing. The glistening spray of a fountain showed through slender trees and glittering branches as she approached. After pulling back the branches, she stepped onto a dainty marble courtyard. The fountain stood proud at the center, but she stopped a few paces back.

The fountain twisted in the shape of the aliens' ships, and water sprayed out from it in patterns like the webs that had covered the sky. A soft mist of cool water freckled her face and hands, little droplets between her breasts as she stared at that symbol of domination. She was about to turn away in disgust when she heard a gasp from behind her.

Ladair moved past her over to the small pool's edge and trailed her fingers in the water. She lifted her hands under a jet and cupped them, letting a pool gather in her palms.

"It's lovely."

"It's an affront," Jaisa said.

"They've made the garden theirs. What else?" Ladair shook her head, jingling bells in her hair. "Did you think they were leading us to the world we knew? That world doesn't exist anymore. I believe them, and you should, too. This exists now. I intend to enjoy this moment. Soon I will rejoin my family."

Rejoin her family? Did she intend to die? That couldn't be. She was the one who'd spoken of the sanctity of life.

By then, another Companion had joined them, so Jaisa didn't dare ask. As this man drifted over to the fountain, she leaned closer to her friend.

"You've survived this long," Jaisa whispered. "Don't lose hope."

Ladair trailed a finger in the water. "Today is different. Me living means another woman dying. Life is sacred—all lives, not just mine. I leave this in God's hands."

Jaisa didn't miss that Ladair was referring to God in the singular. "Don't worry. You'll be chosen."

"If it is God's will." Ladair lay back and closed her eyes.

After waiting a moment and failing to find anything to say or any way to calm the clenching in her gut, Jaisa walked away. Ladair was just scared, but she'd get over it. She'd try. She had to. Yet the garden no longer seemed friendly. It was *their* garden, and Jaisa had been a fool to expect joy. They were in the gods' garden, and they were little more than colored birds to decorate it.

And decorate it they did.

The crowd had dispersed and was making the garden into a stage. One girl rested against a tree, her harem costume arranged around her as she tied together long strings of flowers. Half a dozen men were practicing a style of weaponless fighting the drones had taught them. Another group composed of both genders explored the garden. A few with the accidental foresight to dress for the water had gone into the streams to frolic.

Jaisa placed one hand on her hip, and her mouth curved in a tentative smile. Well, they were all beautiful birds.

She wandered around, observing the others in their play. Even those who simply reclined with their faces turned to the leaves were achingly perfect.

Jaisa looked at the few who stood close to the door. She walked over. At the center of the group, a young woman, no more than fifteen, wept. The others parted and allowed Jaisa to reach out and stroke back the girl's powder blue hair, ignoring the tingle of nanites from touching her.

"You're being foolish," Jaisa said. The remainder of her frustration with Ladair spilled over. "Don't you want to live?"

The girl—Harilis, yes—looked up and did her best to smile, even as she sniffled. "What do I do?"

"What did you intend to do if the Chosen had been here?" Jaisa said.

"I don't really know."

"And you?" Jaisa addressed the rest of the small group.

One said tentatively, "I thought we would sing or dance. That we'd do what they taught us."

Another hugged his arms around himself. "Maybe we would answer questions."

"Or just stand there."

"I never learned how to swim," Harilis said.

"But all of you know how to dance," Jaisa said.

The crying no longer bothered her as it once had. People had to cope, and there was nothing productive to do. Why not cry? This time, though, it wasn't time to merely cope. This was the time to push through. They could do something—they could stay alive.

"If they had been here, you would have shown them what you learned. So do that. Dance, sing, or just stand around, but for the sake of your lives, don't just stand *here*, huddled like there's a finger ready to descend."

Jaisa grabbed Harilis's hand, spinning her out and back in until the girl's hair danced out from her face. She partnered Harilis through a series of steps. When Harilis' face relaxed, Jaisa released her and swung about, her hands reaching out. She twirled with her head tilted back, experiencing the scents in the air and the brush of the other Companions' garments against her bare legs. The grass was slick between her toes. She laughed with her face tilted upward—laughed loud enough for the gods to hear her.

When she looked back, the reticent Companions had almost all joined the dance. Those who were not dancing made their way into the crowded garden.

*What did Ladair mean? She sounded like she was certain she wouldn't be picked. Why?* Jaisa stopped moving and stood in the whirling midst.

Slowly, she picked her way out and off to the side.

"There's no point in that," a voice said.

Jaisa turned to see Varlece, the woman who had dressed as a god, resting against a tree. Her black-painted legs were folded under her at just the right angle to seem both casual and sensual, while also showcasing how long her legs were. "Not all of us will make it. Let the ones who should fail do so."

"You mean let them die." *Ladair intends to die. That wasn't angst holding her back. She is intentionally giving up. Leaving it up to her god was simply a way to avoid calling it suicide. That's why she's sitting there alone.* Jaisa's hand moved to her heart, where a sharp, sympathetic pain jabbed her. *I don't want her to die. Please don't let her die. Who am I even asking?*

Varlece grinned. She had colored her teeth black, too. It was perfectly horrid. And she would survive. This was what the gods wanted, this sort of filth to populate the world.

"If they're meant to survive, they will on their own." Varlece shrugged her black shoulders. "The same number will die with or without you. You are just damning people who made the effort all on their own. These idiots are not the ones who deserve to live."

That this woman might live and Ladair would die was the final blow. *This world doesn't deserve to have Ladair... and yet, she must survive. I can't lose her.*

Jaisa spat at the other woman's feet.

Varlece laughed at that. "How unattractive. Perhaps now you should coach yourself to dance."

Jaisa had already turned away. Her lips curved up into a rather joyful smirk. "Weren't you the one just cautioning me to let those who were meant to die perish?"

The garden in front of her was even more beautiful to her now.

*I got to spit at the gods and they didn't even know.* Her footsteps were lighter as she lifted her face to search for cameras on the domed ceiling. What felt like the sun warmed her skin.

# CHAPTER 9

The room in front of Neriso made no concession to his entry. The low chatter of voices and rustle of clothes remained constant as the Chosen who were already seated made tentative advances at friendships. It was the first time the Chosen had gathered. Despite the huge number of people, the space didn't have the deafening roar typical of large assemblies. Stations had been set up with viewing monitors, seats, and control panels, which all floated in the gravity-free areas of the room. There were enough stations for all of them and most of the people had settled in.

Still, many of the stations remained empty—optimistically, one-third of the seats were filled. Neriso smiled slightly at the conspicuous absences. There were enough places here for the almost two hundred thousand Chosen, but many of the lowest-ranked Chosen, the Rank Ones, would be absent. The fifteen-credit minimum price tag on a Companion equaled nearly half their annual allotment.

Which meant most of those present had not only qualified to be the gods' Chosen during training but were the minority that had a rank better than One. These people were the best of the best according to the gods. And, as a Rank Five, he was the best of them, which gave him the flush of pride and confidence he needed to enter the crowd.

Neriso walked along the gravity pathway to one of the stations. He would need to learn to navigate the gravity-free space. For now, most of the humans confined themselves to the gravity panels, but the gods flowed by in the empty space. To please them, gravity-free travel would be a skill worth learning.

The gods did not currently wear human faces and, as a result, each of their single red eyes appeared menacing. He discarded this observation as meaningless. He wouldn't gaze into a snake's eyes and decide it was evil, though his initial impression might be of menace. The evil intent existed only in his perception of the biologically different appearance and knowledge of its ability to do harm. Classifying differences by fear was easy but hardly accurate.

The gods did not mean him any harm.

Neriso took a seat. A man reclining to his left appraised him and then returned his attention to the video feed on the screen in front of him.

Neriso didn't stop to speak to anyone. There was no reason to waste time studying the Chosen in the room until he knew who would be important and who could be left in the fog of irrelevance. It would be impossible to tell by conversing which of them were Neriso's equals—or even those who at Rank Three and Four would be working directly with him. He only knew the ones from his training facility, and since each facility produced only one Rank Five, he had yet to meet the others.

He touched the viewing screen, and it woke. He programmed in a few parameters: gender, age, and height preferences. The main screen showed all his options, too many to peruse, but he navigated through the living images of the Companions. They were more... ornamental than he had expected despite being exactly as they had been described. Like fantasies come to life, there was no reality to the Companions. Neriso wanted more than just beauty.

Neriso brushed past woman after woman. As one of only fourteen Rank Fives selected by the gods, there was a certain weight to his choice. Everything he had must be better than what anyone else had. *I could have any of them.*

He wanted a woman, not a doll. They might be intended

only for sex and entertainment, not for love, but there was nothing saying he couldn't enjoy being around her. Someone boring, stupid, or predictable would never do.

"Wow," a woman said from beside him, obviously impressed by the Companions on her screen.

After the first woman spoke, many of them made small asides and comments. Neriso had his attention directed to one woman or another for a good thirty minutes.

He sifted through women who fulfilled every fantasy he'd ever had. Women who were so beautiful, they hardly seemed human at all. A few times a face stood out to him, and he moved the woman's image to the side panel for future consideration, but even these didn't hold his attention long.

"This is impossible," Neriso said, letting his annoyance color his voice. "How do I pick one out of all these indistinguishable creatures?"

"So wait till the rest pick and then choose from the leftovers," a spectacled woman to his right said with a casual shrug.

*She doesn't know who I am.* Neriso shook his head. No, he needed the best one. Companions were to be their visual status symbols. He would not stoop to picking through the dregs.

"Playback, 17653," a man said to his left. There was laughter in his voice mixed with awe. "Had her selected for ten minutes now on the side panel. Bold and reckless... but I can't look away."

Neriso typed the number in.

A woman with scarlet hair and an Amazonian stride appeared.

At first glance, there was nothing special about the redhaired woman. Her beauty was underwhelming amid the rest of the Companions. But the other Chosen's description wouldn't leave him; "bold and reckless" certainly stood out. And the fact that people couldn't look away sold him on taking a little more time watching this woman. Neriso played back five minutes, but he didn't need even that much time. From the instant he saw her in motion, he knew why the other man had spent so long with her in his sight.

She was something special. A fire burned in her that made her real and distinct.

He sat back in his seat, his eyes glued to the screen as a god floated by in front of his station.

The careless twist of the on-screen Companion's red curls seemed indicative of the rest of her. Green eyes stared out from a white face, and pale lips curved into a smile as she danced. What was interesting was that she seemed to be leading the other girl, whose eyes were glistening with tears. As the other's tears faded to a smile, the redhaired one spun away. Neriso tried to decide what made her face beautiful.

"Hardly as attractive as the rest, if you ask me," a voice said from the side.

And yet they were *all* mesmerized by her. Neriso's eyes never strayed from her.

She stopped dancing, the cascade of whirling limbs obscuring her even from the endeavors of the camera. Then she reappeared moving away from the cluster. Her feet were bare and unornamented.

Her face darkened.

Neriso changed his view and found that she was facing a seated woman painted as one of the gods. Her naked reclining body was perfect, but something in the coldness of her stare was unsettling. The redhaired woman spoke.

The fantasy goddess smiled; her teeth as black as her skin.

At that, the redhaired woman spat and turned away. Neriso held tight to the side of the screen. He half-expected to watch her die immediately, but it was not a real god she had spat at. Whatever the drones were capable of understanding, they did not understand this. *She dares to stand up to their image. She mocks them, and they are blind to it.* It would be dangerous to have a woman like that.

Bold and reckless.

But wasn't a woman capable of skirting that line capable of other delicate decisions? Capable of watching his back? He would have many enemies in the guise of friends, those who wanted his status and would do anything to get it. A clever woman could help fill in for his blind spots—and he knew that he must have them, as small as they might have been.

The smile on her face transformed it, lit her up. There was a spark in her green eyes that had managed not only to survive, but to thrive. Her eyes lifted, and she appeared to meet his gaze, a challenge in her expression.

Bold, reckless, and peerless.

*That is the woman—the only woman.* He touched the screen and told it to replay from the moment of her appearance.

As he followed her actions a second time, her brazen confidence reinforced his choice. With every movement she made and every word she said, she proved herself to be more than the others. And all of her fellow Companions watched her as if they knew.

Choosing her was dangerous. But she could be taught to accept the gods—she was already at least pretending as much. Obedience could be learned, but the other talents she had were unteachable. His finger pressed down to place a hold on her. When the bidding began, he would win her. He would bid whatever required.

He would hold that flame.

# CHAPTER 10

The Companions all huddled in clumps of shivering humanity. Jaisa sat on her bed, wishing she could hug Ladair. But the other woman seemed lost somewhere inside her mind and quietly muttered to herself. Tavar sat between two women on the bed to Jaisa's right. All of them had gravitated to their white beds or in close groups beside each other on the floor, their backs against the featureless walls. Only Varlece stood. Her face was still black, and from her white garments, hands blacker than the night emerged.

Her decision to emulate the gods had separated her from all of them. Even her old friends kept a sizable distance. This left her smug-faced with the space of two empty beds on either side of her.

Jaisa was certain the priestesses would be proud of her. She was also certain that someone out there would bid for Varlece's audacity. From the triumph in her eyes, Varlece had no doubts, either.

Ladair continued murmuring. Jaisa caught only the low sound, but the words blended. It reminded her of the way a next-door neighbor's TV sounded through the walls. It made it easier not to think because she found herself almost forced to figure out what Ladair's private chant contained.

"Even a caged bird can sing" was the only bit Jaisa made out.

A god surrounded by drones entered the room. Jaisa shut

her eyes against the rush of unbidden images the god brought. Beside her, Ladair continued murmuring, as if not concerned with the drone who'd come to deliver their fate.

*It's like the whispering of the dead.* The chant entered Jaisa's thoughts unbidden and tore through her walls, the whisper sounding one moment as if it had come from Rick, and the next as if it could have been Ethan or Evie.

Many of the others were on their feet, and Jaisa stood to join them. This was the end.

Ladair remained seated until Tavar moved between them and helped her stand.

"The day of your choosing is over," the god said. Its voice was no less mechanical in this language than the last time she had heard it. This was probably not their native tongue, either. "Those of you who are desired have been purchased."

Jaisa tugged at a blood-red curl. She held her breath and leaned closer to Tavar and Ladair.

"Ten of you have been shown to be exemplary," the god said. And then he called out ten names and ten prices. Jaisa was not surprised to hear Varlece's name in the mix. Nor that Tavar had made the list. He was special, and anyone with eyes could see that.

What surprised her were the amounts listed as their purchase costs.

The drones had informed them how the bidding worked. Each person's bidding started at fifteen credits. Most purchases would not exceed that amount.

The same credits would later be used to purchase other things like house decoration, house expansion, servants from the Half-ranks and Rankless, and transportation. With Rank Ones making only fifty credits a year.

Varlece had sold for over two hundred credits, which was more than ninety percent of the Chosen would earn in a year—only a Rank Four or Five could possibly have had so much to bid after just six months. Even a Rank Three would only make two hundred credits. Tavar had brought in only slightly less than

Varlece.

The others listed had multiple but fewer bidders and didn't go nearly as high in price. Among their number was Harilis. Apparently, the weakness her tears has shown was attractive to someone in the world above. Though Jaisa suspected that her purchase was as much or more to do with how beautifully she'd recovered. She wanted to hope that someone out there had saved the girl because she was so young, but Jaisa had trouble putting that kind of faith in the Chosen.

And then, last on the list of exemplary sales, the god called Jaisa's name. She stiffened. To have been picked at all was enough of a shock, but to have been in some sort of demand was unthinkable. A tendril of pride wound through her, but this reaction died swiftly under a clenching of nerves.

Who had bought her? Why?

The god went on, its inky flesh parting for a moment to show a flash of bone where its head was, which then flowed into a moderate resemblance her face. "Jaisa, you managed one hundred initial bids. No other Companion obtained such a substantial number."

Tavar took in a sharp intake of breath beside her, but Ladair didn't stir, didn't even seem to hear. Jaisa stepped back, her head spinning.

The number was unthinkable. One hundred Chosen had bid on her? Why? And what did it mean? The number pressed on her like a weight. Whoever had won such a battle would be expecting superior spoils. She didn't even know what her new owner had seen in her, so what could he—or she—be anticipating?

The god looked at her. Its eye twitched about in its head. "When we chose the prospective Companions, you were almost discarded. Your face has flaws. I am pleased to see that my judgment of your desirability has proven to be correct."

Jaisa lowered her eyes. To be spoken to so personally by the god was too much. Half of her coiled inside to strike, to show it what she thought of its judgement. *Someday I will judge* you. *We'll see how you like my flaws then.*

"You will come with me," the god finished, motioning to Jaisa.

"And the others?" she asked. "Have they been chosen as well? Won't you say their names?"

"The drones will continue with the less important names." The god briefly glanced at Tavar and Varlece. "Other gods or I will return to escort the remainder of the exemplary Companions to their transports."

The message was clear. Only ten of them were worth the gods' personal attention.

*Another weight to carry. I don't want their red eyes on me.*

Jaisa turned her head to Ladair, but the other woman's face was blank. There could be no goodbye with death looming. So Jaisa trailed the god with her hands clenched in front of her. She passed through the familiar hallways of the complex and followed it to a door that had not existed before: a splash of green set in the white walls.

The god opened the door.

Jaisa stepped out into the sunlight.

Unable to process the sunny world in front of her, Jaisa stopped. Frosted glass lay underfoot and composed every building within sight, as well as roadways and walls. Dusty purple shrubs lined the walk, dotted with blue flowers, and off in the distance, a forest of burnt orange surrounded the edge of the city. The air smelled fresh, as it might after a rain, but different in a way she couldn't label.

She tilted her head to the sky, hoping to find reassurance there. The sun remained, but the blue sky she'd hoped to see was riddled with black lines and slightly too bright a blue. Even the atmosphere over the planet was not the same since the gods' arrival. Yet it was Earth, her Earth, not some strange alien planet, not a starscape. *We've been here all along. They aren't taking us anywhere... They're taking over.*

The god had moved a few steps head, giving her a good view of its rippling face, a smooth skull visible under its flowing outer shell. *Could I kill it? If I just had a weapon, I doubt I could resist trying.*

"Does the new world please you?" the god asked.

Was it serious? As if any fancy buildings would ever atone for the fact they had killed billions. They had killed Rick. "Is this where I'll live?"

"No. This is Seventh City. You will live in Fifth City." It motioned to her. "Come."

"You won't transport me?"

"No. Our transport has an unacceptable fatality rate with humans. Your hearts have difficulty with the reassemble."

*And I'm worth too much to risk now. More important than however many innocent lives they ended on the day they arrived here.*

Jaisa followed the god across the cool blue walkway until they came to a wide strip of deeper azure with several gray floating ovals. These hovering objects ranged in size from between a semi-truck to a commercial jetliner.

"This is your transport." The god motioned to one of the smaller ovals as a rectangular hole opened in its side, forming steps down.

*Like a tongue flopping out... and I'm supposed to just walk into the gaping mouth.*

Jaisa turned back to where the god had stood a moment before, but it was gone. She stood alone in the clutter of alien vehicles, on a planet she no longer recognized.

Her heart hammered, and her mouth felt dry. Boarding should have been so simple—walk into the doorway. But that black hole was so deep—so final. No more other Companions to think about, no more pretense at fighting. Just a person who owned her, and an Earth she didn't recognize, and a sky covered in alien spider threads.

And if she stepped on that ship, it was the final movement of her surrender. She had the choice to die now, fighting, and join Rick. Join Ethan and Evie. Or she could live. But she had no choice now. The Companions weren't with her, but she couldn't so easily throw over her choice to be strong for them.

A tingle began in her hands, and without further debate, Jaisa walked toward the black entrance. Buried inside her, Val howled, struggling to break free. But Jaisa would be strong—she'd seek an opportunity. She'd help the others survive in this alien world. She'd find a way.

Ladair stood facing the wall, trying to see through its solid surface into the world beyond. All those who'd been selected had been led out by a drone—after the lucky ten were seen out by gods. More than half of the Companions had made it alive out into the world.

*When I die, will I see the sky? Will I fly free?*

The floor shivered with the impact of the drones' feet. *All the compound's drones must be here.* Whimpers and muffled tears filled the room, but they were heavy and fell off. Despite the noise, a lingering silence dwelt around Ladair.

*I chose this. If death is the only freedom for me, then I will take it. Please, don't let me bend, don't let me cry. I must face this bravely. Out there, someone is able to live in my place. May they enjoy this captivity as I could not.* She pictured the blue sky and sunbaked drive outside her father's house. Tried to recall the rumbling laugh her father and brothers shared.

She lifted one of the useless scarves of her outfit and covered her hair, wrapping an end to cover her face. Best to go into the afterlife as decent as possible.

She heard a drone approaching and turned, her shoulders squared. Behind the drone, other Companions crumpled. One woman's mouth moved in a scream that Ladair's ringing ears didn't hear. Another woman howled as she tried to run. A man attacked the drone. Both fell to the floor, dead, before Ladair met the drone's red eye. It approached her.

Would the gods see these deaths? Watch from the safety of their ship as their rejected toys were disposed of? Ladair's hands rested at her side, open palms welcoming whatever came. Her eyes closed.

*I'm coming, Father. I'm sorry. I wasn't strong enough to bear life's burden. Hopefully, God will understand.* The sky in her mind rippled with the summer heat, and beyond it the baked cement steamed.

The drone's touch was chilly. With it came a crash of agony that started as a pinpoint and spread out, encompassing her everything. She fell beneath the pain; even as it ravaged above her, she sank into the velvet darkness. Air brushed her exposed skin as she fell.

*I'll fly.* The darkness was complete, but as she toppled into it, she regained some focus, floating under the waves of pain.

# CHAPTER 11

L adair woke with a scream. Her chest burned, and the lines of the world were blurry. Yet even disoriented, she recognized things were wrong. Arms—warm and human—encircled her. She kicked out, throwing herself away from this potentially deadly human contact.

On the cold floor, she recalled her last moments, the pain and the blackness. The room around her was the same, littered with bodies where they'd fallen after the drone's touch. The only differences were the men, living men, kneeling on the floor with the fallen Companions, and the open door behind them, leading from the chamber into the outside world.

*Who knew it was so close?*

Through the open door the blue sky mocked her—riddled with the black lines of the gods' ships. The door might have been open, but she was still here. Trapped in their web.

*I was free. I was dead.*

She sucked in a breath to assure herself that she was breathing. Her chest ached with a heavy pain, impossible to ignore. Her fingers moved up to where the drone had touched her. There was a burned patch—rectangular. She had seen nothing similar on drone victims.

"Why aren't I dead? Who are you?" she demanded in the gods' tongue.

"You're alive," said the skinny, beak-nosed man who'd apparently been holding her. His skin was a sallow pale color, sunburned over the cheeks. His words took several moments to sink in as her brain struggled with the language. They were not speaking in the language of the gods.

"Stop. You mustn't use words like that." She blinked against the fog of her eyes. These were ghosts of the past. They didn't exist. *Is this my afterlife? Why does it hurt so much?*

"I cannot understand you." Impatience filled his tone, and he glanced back at the door several times. He had not held her back as she struggled away, but now he grabbed her shoulders.

*He is speaking English. That isn't possible.*

Ladair rubbed her hands over her eyes, trying again to clear the impossible vision in front of her, and tilted her head. When he didn't disappear, a smile crept onto her lips. Could it be that somewhere, somehow, life went on? Were there still birds who flew free? No, that was an impossible dream. Better to learn the truth than live in fantasies.

The room around her was littered with Companion corpses, but she was alive. Breathing air that came in through the open door—a door that led out to a world under the sky.

*And these men... can they lead me into that world?* She looked from the skinny man in front of her to the others, barely taking them in. Her eyes were too dazzled by the idea of an open door.

"English? What are you, then? And what am I that is not dead?" Her English was slow and heavily accented. She'd studied for many years in school and kept up the habit of speaking with her brothers, one of whom worked in the USA on a visa. *No. He doesn't work there. He* worked *there; he is dead.*

The thin man adjusted his glasses on his beaklike nose and looked pointedly away from her. Over among the vividly arrayed corpses of her fellow Companions knelt a gawky, freckled preteen who ogled her with no shame. Next to him knelt a Black man, who even on his knees, towered over the others. Last in the group was a muscular man in army fatigues, white skin more tanned than burnt, whose nose had obviously been broken before.

Except for the preteen, they all appeared to be U.S. soldiers. She recognized the uniform from the movies. The invasion of their eyes on her exposed skin stripped her confidence away until, shaking like a small child, she crossed her arms over herself and shrank away from them.

*Men like these are dangerous. Father says... No, Father* said. *Will they rape me? Kill me? Why save me?* Every breath she took sent jabs of pain outward. It made thinking clearly impossible. *Do I trust them?*

The man with the broken nose eyed her hungrily, occasionally glancing away.

She met his gaze when he looked again. He could keep her safe from the others, and the hunger in his eyes told her that he might even be willing to. The gods had trained her to use hunger like his, but she'd chosen to die rather than do so. *They saved me. Why save me if they mean me harm? Yet if he can protect me, turning away the assistance would be insane. I know nothing of this world.*

"You *were* dead," the big guy said. His voice was deep and gruff but sounded kind.

"By all the statistics at my disposal," the beak-nosed one said, "you should still be dead. We attempted with the others." He motioned around him with one arm. "Your resurrection is a miracle, given how we must assume you died, but it's what happened, and we don't have time to explain."

Ladair shivered and shook her head. None of this was possible.

"We've got to get going," the man with the crooked nose and hungry eyes said. "Come on."

Ladair shook her head. She couldn't even explain to them for fear of the nanites in her blood. She'd spoken in English earlier, or thought she had, but that was impossible too. "I can't."

The preteen boy leaned forward. "They'll explain it all later. You can move and speak freely now. When you died, the nanites did too."

Ladair stared at him, not quite able to believe his words. After so long without hope, accepting this was too great a leap.

"For Christ's sake!" the beak-nosed man said. "You're not

under their surveillance once you've died and come back. Now, please, who are you?"

She stared at him. Her mouth formed "Ladair," then stopped. *I have no name. That is the worst death of all.*

"I go by 'Riley,'" the beak-nosed man said. "Full name Joseph Riley." He motioned to the others in turn. "This is Richard Connor and Jayden Benjamin. The kid is Louie."

"'Jayden' is fine," the giant said. "We're not in the military anymore."

"Connor," said the man with the broken nose. He spoke slowly despite the obvious nervousness of all the men. "You're safe with us for now. We seem to be invisible to the machines in the undercity, and we've successfully avoided the uppercity machines. You should be as well. They have trackers in the people they caught, but once your heart stops, you're safe. But we gotta get out of here before that door closes. Can you walk?"

Her eyes raked over Connor. From appearance alone, he was nothing but a brute—big muscles, weapons hanging on his belt—but his words were gentle. And despite how his gaze kept dropping to her body, he was making an effort not to look. And after all, she *was* dressed to inspire just that reaction.

"What's your name?" Connor asked when she didn't respond. Something red hot boiled under his blue eyes. His smile was warm and encouraging. He had a wonderful mouth and a smile she trusted—her father had smiled like that.

She looked at Jayden, but he was looking at the corpse of a male Companion at his feet. Then to Riley, but he was avoiding her gaze.

*I'm not Ladair now. Naeemah. I was Naeemah; I can be me again.*

"I never thought I would give my own name again," she said. "Naeemah. I'm Naeemah." She glanced at the open door, and Riley and Connor both did a check. *What happens if that door closes? Can they open it? I can't. I never even knew there was a door. To think, the world was always that close.* "And we should get out of here. I'd rather not tempt fate."

"Do you have any *clothing*?" Riley asked, a slight sneer on his face as he eyed her current attire. His eyes seemed small and cruel beneath his glasses. "You'll need it where we're going."

Connor motioned to Jayden and the big guy went to stand in the doorway. *Like holding an elevator open. Will that work?*

Naeemah ran her hands over her outfit. The small swathes of scarves and golden bells would not provide warmth or cover. The only thing they could be useful for was fulfilling the fantasies of men. They would all be better off if she covered up some. She would be more confident in her safety.

She glanced at a doorway, heading farther back into the building. Were there still drones back there? The ache in her chest burned as her breath sped up, reminding her how easily death could snatch her. What if they came out and found her? Either way, they'd be back, and the Chosen and their Companions would fill the streets at any moment.

"There is no time," Naeemah said.

Riley tugged a decorative cape from the body by his feet. "Here."

"These are my..." *Friends.* She shook her head. They were dead. This was not a time for sentimentality. "Yes."

She stood and walked across the room, not coming in contact with any of the bodies with her delicately placed footsteps. She did not touch them until she removed a pair of silky pants from a woman with blue skin.

*I'm sorry.* Glazed eyes stared up at Naeemah.

Connor came away with a handful of fabrics, a pair of flat cloth shoes and a decorative blade, which might serve some real purpose, all of which he shoved at her.

Naeemah herself had taken nothing after sliding the pants up over her hips and was instead standing and staring at the doorway. She took the cloth and held the soft pile to her chest, causing another intense wave of agony.

*I'm free. This is my pain. I own it.* She made no attempt to brush away the tears that slid down her cheeks.

"We need to go *now*," Connor said. "If that door closes,

there's no telling how long it'll take us to get out."

"You ready, girly?" Jayden asked.

"The streets will have people on them any moment now," Conner said.

"And drones. Where're we going?" she asked even as she followed after him.

"Below," Jayden said.

"Oh?" Naeemah turned to Connor.

"Nowhere," Connor said. His smile was replaced by a cloudy expression as he touched the wedding ring on his hand. "We are going nowhere, and that is the only place we stand a chance of being safe."

"I'm hardly concerned with safe," she said. "After dying twice in less than a year, I doubt 'safe' exists. Nowhere sounds good." Her hand rested over her chest, where Riley had shocked her to start her heart. She had already died here once—if she wanted to live, it would be somewhere else. She rushed out the door, preceded only by Riley.

*Where did they come from? How was it that they seem to have escaped the gods?* She thought of the way Connor had touched the ring on his hand. Did he even know for sure his wife was gone? How could he, without the gods to grind them into submission?

*If the gods never captured them, they will have seen things. Things no other person has, and I am going to know about it.*

Outside, under the sun, the others let Connor lead them back, and Naeemah fell in behind him. The sounds of the others scrambling behind her was soothing. *They're alive. Truly alive, not some wraith like me. That means people survived the attack. Are there more?*

Nothing was said as they passed back through the city under the vacant eyes of the buildings. The strangely colored vegetation watched them move. The heads of the flowers turned after the group's movement as the city of frosted glass slept around them.

Connor led her into a tunnel with a gentle touch to her arm. She knelt inside the marbled blue metal and crawled. As they moved deeper, total darkness fell, enveloping her. *It's like a passage to the undercity, where I belong.*

Whatever future awaited her there, at least she could face it as Naeemah.

The world that rose to meet Jaisa's ship was unrecognizable. She watched the unearthly scenery as she descended toward Fifth City. Even the landscape of the old world had been wiped away —left raw and new. She could almost imagine this was an alien world, if not for the computer's assurance she hadn't gone off-planet.

Her eye caught on the world beneath Fifth City. But if she looked closely, wreckage poked out from beneath the glittering city built for the Companions and Chosen. Toppled buildings and buckled, twisted roads sank down beneath the new city. It reminded her of old sci-fi. There was a world for the rich, and below it a world for *the others*. Lean-to structures rose in the world below, and smoke streamed from half-erect chimneys.

It was not that world that awaited her but the gleaming, picturesque city that rested on top of it. Buildings of glass and marble were suspended in the air, for all appearances resting on nothing but smoke and slender white bridges. In places, large gardens of green lifted in gentle slopes to meet the white city.

And in it waited a Rank Five, who owned her. Neriso. No matter how many queries she input into the computer, she found no answers as to why he would have selected her. From her records, she appeared dangerous and rebellious. Surely, that was the last thing a Rank Five would want. *So why me? Is it a bizarre mistake? A momentary lapse in his judgement? For his moral compass must value capitulation.*

Jaisa was jerked out of her thoughts when the aircraft landed. The idea of actually meeting her owner made her innards clench painfully. Neriso was an enigma she didn't want solved. She might not have moved except that after a few seconds, a god appeared beside her. She recoiled automatically. The glitter of the gown she'd picked in-flight reflected the monster's blackness.

"Come," the god said.

Jaisa rose from the gray interior—monochromatic, like all the gods' creations. With a step away from the window, she monitored her breathing to stay calm. *I'm alone. Everyone I met is gone. Ladair...* She bit her lip.

On the long flight, she had researched her new "husband" and the other thirteen Rank Fives. She'd even looked into Tavar's purchase, though the thought of him belonging to another person brought on an uncomfortable jealousy. *He's not mine. He never was. And at least I know he's safe, but Ladair...*

She hadn't been able to bring herself to check. If Ladair was dead, hers might be one death too many. Yet as she was ushered toward her new future, Jaisa wished she had looked. *Maybe I'm better off dead than in this position. Maybe that's why she gave up. Somehow, she knew what it would feel like to live on after this last round of deaths.*

The god led Jaisa from the craft's belly. She had no time for thoughts. As she stepped into the crystal sunlight, Jaisa spotted her new husband. Neriso stood in front of a large, white building. He would have arrived just before her, as the Chosen and the Companions had ended their separate training on the same day. The building behind him was a massive structure of cold marble, softened only by a stream that skirted it and funneled off into glass drains.

Neriso looked to be a severe man, as strict as the home behind him. He had a neat appearance, with the hair from his receding hairline combed back, but his thin body had a flabbiness that came with lack of physical activity. After the steady stream of beautiful men she had lived among, she found him mildly revolting. His detached inspection of her didn't help his appeal.

*What did I expect, a man like Tavar? Maybe that they'd give Rick back? I'm a fool.*

"Neriso, this is your wife, Jaisa," the god said.

Her stomach, still a mass of clenched nerves, revolted at the voice saying her name, and she tasted bile as she struggled to hold her reactions in check.

"She's different today from when I last saw her." Neriso's voice was pleasant and heavily accented. The displeasure in his tone when he referenced her went beyond demeaning, but she had no choice but to stand and take the insult. That or die. "Hardly the same woman at all."

Jaisa could not place what language that accent came from. Despite the difference in pronunciation, she had no trouble understanding him. His words weren't comforting. If she displeased him, did he have the option to send her back? *Can he trade me in like a car that came in the wrong color?*

A fire burned inside her as she stared over at the man who was her owner, her husband. She had been taught her place. She was his slave, even though the gods' word for their relationship mirrored the human idea of husband and wife. She had no rights. Her purpose was to please him and oversee his household servants and social calendar. A shallow existence, especially with a man who appraised her like livestock.

"She will be as you bid her from now on," the god said. "If her appearance displeases, you need only bid her to change."

"Indeed." Jaisa looked up at her husband. With that one word, she dared him to do so. Her mouth curled upward. It was not a smile. *Order me to change. Tell me that you expected better. I could rip your eyes out before the gods killed me. It might even be worth it to damage something they care for.*

His gaze changed at her tone, focusing in on her eyes as if he saw into her mind and was dissecting her.

"She will suffice," he said, without removing or softening his stare. "Jaisa, you will go inside. This is our home now." Then Neriso's eyes left her and traveled to the grounds. "Take a look around while I finish out here."

"Yes, husband," she said. The command rolled around in her head, and her whole body tensed. But there was nothing to do about it. He had the right to order her. She walked up the spongy gray walkway, pausing only to dip a red painted toe in the stream that wound through the garden. The water was warm.

How different this was from her first meeting with Rick. A sad smile snuck onto her lips that she wasn't able to fight away. Oh, Rick had stared just as intently—ignoring his date, whom she later learned had been a blind date—as Val sang a country song she only half-knew on the smoky karaoke stage. She'd thought he was a creep, giving her his number while there with another woman. She hadn't called him. But he'd come back the next week, alone, and her first impression couldn't have been more wrong.

Was she wrong this time? What was it Ladair had said about her? That she judged from isolation, and with missing facts, only false conclusions would ever result.

Jaisa did as Neriso commanded and entered the building. Once inside, she stood still in the entryway. It was large and dark. Nothing like a home, the smell reminded her of a freshly purchased plastic container. Everything was a glittering slate color.

How odd it felt—being alone. She hadn't had to deal with the Companion compound alone even in the beginning.

*Where is Tavar now?* She closed her eyes and tried to picture a home that didn't feel so empty. The man her mind conjured wavered between two faces. Rick smiled at her from the doorway, big and comforting, but then her mind changed, and it was thin Tavar waiting on the stairs. *If he could speak of his past, what would he have told me? I don't even know him. How can I let him take Rick's place for even an instant?*

That didn't matter. Her fantasies would never be more than that. If the thoughts of a man she'd never know kept her sane, she would indulge them.

After a while, the door opened behind her, and Neriso entered, alone. He was so buried in thought, he didn't see her. Which gave her a chance to study him more closely—certainly not Companion material, but that was not a fair bar to set. Rick hadn't been, either, and she'd desired him. Neriso's eyes were deep set, giving him an angry appearance, even with his features relaxed. Dressed neatly, yes, but also carefully. He'd tried to present himself decently.

*To impress me? If he were the monster I want to make him, why would he care what I thought?*

"The god is gone?" she asked.

He jumped and his eyes flew to her, panicked. Shame rushed over her—no, he wasn't the enemy. Just like all of them, the gods had ripped him from his world, made him watch his loved ones die. Who knew how much of him was a mask and how much a man?

In any event, there was only one enemy. The gods. She had to keep that in mind. Even if Neriso had capitulated early in his training in order to earn such a high rank, he still hadn't really had a choice. It just meant he'd realized and accepted that sooner.

"Yes. V'shLir is gone."

*The god?* "You know their names?"

"Only a few. Those tied most closely to my work, as they helped in my education and training with the new technology they've provided." His eyes wouldn't land on her, and an awkward pause ensued.

"What work do you do? All the computers said was genetics." Asking a man about his work usually did the trick. From questions like this aimed at Rick, she knew more about weaponry, survival tactics, and military strategy than she'd ever wanted to.

Instead, Neriso recoiled as if stung. "This is my first day here. I've done no work."

*Is he afraid I'll judge him?*

She shrugged and motioned to the hallway that dipped down in front of them, then up the twisted flight of stairs. "Explore with me?"

"Yes." He relaxed. "I've only just arrived. Let's explore our new home."

"After you, husband."

Her chest clutched tighter at the sight of him striding into the house he owned—approaching the woman he owned. *Me, he owns me. This is it. Rick will never come home to me. This is what I get... but after all I did to get here, do I deserve any better?*

Jaisa took a few steps to his side and took his hand in hers. No negative emotion welled up at the touch and no nanites to censor her.

"You are not the sort of woman I ever expected to... marry."

"Well, this is hardly the sort of marriage any of us expected."

"Come with me, Jaisa. We'll see what sort of accommodations we are to share."

He took off into the dim halls, leaving Jaisa to follow. His pace was too quick, and Jaisa had no time to inspect her new home. He walked with an agenda, though Jaisa was clueless what it could be, given the only task they had to do was explore empty rooms.

Why the hurry?

*Is he always like this? So businesslike and cold?* She had no way of determining that, and the idea of living with a stranger hit her anew. He could be any type of man, and she had no control over it, no choice, and no escape.

"The kitchen," Neriso said with a certain amount of pride.

He pointed at an object in the corner she assumed was used in food prep. She glanced around the room and recognized enough of the panels lining the walls to agree with his assessment of the room's use.

"Am I supposed to cook?" she asked. She hadn't trained in that.

"Managing the house is your affair. That will include choosing servants. So whether you cook or not depends on your selections."

Selections? The word brought her full circle. She did have

selections to make, but he'd already made his. *Why choose me? Why not Varlece or Ladair... or any of the others?* His selection nettled her, and yet she couldn't ask him. The only way to find out what he really wanted was to wait.

Already, the waiting felt a bit like walking around wearing a noose as a necklace.

# CHAPTER 12

Naeemah gagged on the smoke clogging the air as they approached the end of the tunnel. After hours of walking, crawling, and climbing, her lungs ached and her chest felt abused. Exhaustion was taking over, and the men accompanying her didn't seem aware of her discomfort. Her eyes, used to the filtered air of the compound, teared up when hit with the smoggy air below the gods' decorative city.

Only Connor preceded her along the path. Halfway through the journey, he'd given her his jacket, leaving his shoulders and arms bare. He might not have been as massive as his friend Jayden, but Connor still looked intimidatingly large with only a tank top and army pants covering him.

Behind her, Louie jittered from one side of the walkway to another, seeming unable to calm down enough to walk a straight line. He kept trying to tell her about the things they would see, but Riley stopped him each time. The older man hushed the boy with a deftness that only a father could have —leaving Naeemah to wonder if the sharp-nosed man had once had equally bold-featured children. Jayden took up the rear; his dingy tank top and white smile were often the only parts of him Naeemah could see when she looked over her shoulder.

Then Connor's pace slowed, and he came to the end of the tunnel: a ledge overlooking a wide metal-walled hallway. Using one arm, he swung himself down to the metal floor below, his figure a blur in the smoggy air. Through her stinging, weeping eyes, he was only an outline of strength.

He extended his arms, and she jumped. Her feet slammed into the flooring, the impact jolting up to her knees with the force of the drop. His arms closed around her, supporting her and keeping her upright. The whine of machinery and a regular crash of metal on metal distracted her, and her lungs resisted drawing in the hot air. So she clung to Connor's strong arms, accepting his support as the changed world battered her senses.

Riley, Jayden, and Louie clomped down behind her. Each landed with practiced ease—even Louie, whose preteen gawkiness at least made his landing look awkward. That didn't make Naeemah feel less alone.

Riley's skinny frame hunched slightly, making his sharp-featured face seem predatory as he looked at her expectantly.

"So, this is where the 'Rankless' dwell," she said, using only one word of the alien tongue. She knew no word in English to express "Rankless," if there even was such a word. Her voice betrayed none of the rioting emotions inside. This place was horrid, like some afterworld punishment for the wicked. *And I am one of them—wicked and bad, fit for nothing else.* "And I'm a ghost in a world I never lived in and was never meant to see."

"Perhaps this *is* where you were meant to be." Riley brushed past her and despite the softness of his words, he clearly felt no empathy.

"Rankless?" Connor's hold relaxed, and he took a step away, shoving his hands in his pockets.

"I'll explain whatever you want." Naeemah glanced around at the underground passage. A patchwork of metal formed the walls and ceiling, and lights blinked from within a panel box on one wall. The grease on the manufactured stone floor could have been mistaken for bloodstains if not for the occasional drip of oil from the crack of the ceiling. "But please, let's go to our destination first."

"It's dangerous stopping here, Connor," Riley said over his shoulder.

"Come on then." Connor started down the tunnel to the

left, Riley falling in beside him.

Louie skulked after them, his preteen frame rail-thin behind the two older men—even in comparison to the slender Riley. Jayden clapped Naeemah on the shoulder and gave her an encouraging smile before taking off.

Pulling Connor's coat tighter around her shoulders, Naeemah followed.

They traveled through more dark hallways and past decrepit workers who ignored their presence. Each person working the machines in this undercity was caked with filth, dressed in rags, and hollow-eyed.

*Yes. This place is a punishment for the wickedness of human society. The world had been filled with corruption. Is this our atonement?*

At last, they emerged from the machine dungeon into row upon row of lean-to homes. Naeemah shrank away from the poverty. Connor proceeded ahead as she stopped, but Jayden dropped back to her side. His dark face was cheerful and open, the most reassuring thing in her vision.

"C'mon, girlie." He placed a hand on her shoulder and gave a slight squeeze, accompanied by a smile. "This ain't our stop."

Naeemah started again at his encouragement. Jayden had been nothing but kind to her, unlike the other men, but she saw none of the hunger in him that she'd noted in Connor and seen flashes of in Riley. Jayden looked at her much like her brothers had, and maybe given the situation, that was a saving grace. She covered what she could of her bare flesh with Connor's coat as they passed by the dejected occupants.

The air was clearer as they moved farther from the city, and Naeemah tilted her face back to the sky, looking for birds. All she found above her were fluttering orange leaves, occasionally parting to reveal a patch of sky. Nothing flew by.

They walked and walked.

"How far are we going?" she whispered to Jayden. Her eyes were getting heavy and moving her feet got harder by the minute. She needed sleep.

"Camp is just over two miles from the city."

Riley cut in, giving Naeemah a searing glare. "Quiet. We can explain more when we get there."

Naeemah returned her attention to the sky. The tree cover was thick, which she supposed was good. Theoretically, it would be harder for the gods to spot them. But even her few glances of the sky revealed the black webbing that the gods' network had carved over the Earth. This was their world. How could it be possible for people like these men to hide here?

"This's it," Jayden said, disturbing her musings.

The camp was practically heaven after the undercity, but still nothing with any true luxury. They'd erected large tents made of animal hide around the center of a clearing. The rubbery orange-leafed trees were dense all around, providing shade and protection from the worst of the wind. A stream murmured its soft song nearby, hidden just out of sight.

Naeemah touched a finger to one of the spikes surrounding the entryway—the long sticks were sharpened to a point and then sunk most of the way into the ground. A very basic perimeter.

"This way," Riley said. He moved over to a firepit, around which were several flattened logs and, to her delight, a jug of clear water.

She hurried over and drank, letting the cold water soothe the burn in her throat. It did nothing for the persistent pain in her chest. When her thirst was satisfied, she sat. The others were already seated, Riley on one side of her and Connor on the other. Jayden reclined across the firepit with his back against a log, and Louie sat cross-legged beside the big guy.

They all looked at her.

"What do you need to know?" she asked.

"Everything you learned about the aliens and their world," Riley said.

"It would help to know what you already know," Naeemah said. "What happened to all of you?"

"We were never captured," Jayden said.

Connor lowered his gaze to his knees, deftly avoiding even glancing at her. "We watched them destroy the old cities and build these new ones, burn out the old trees and plant these new... things. But we don't know anything about what goes on inside the city. Louie was part of the undercity, so we know a little from him. But nothing is really shared with the people of the undercity. That's why you're here—we need to know about the uppercity and the people who will be living there."

And so, with a clear voice trained by the creatures in the sky, she told them. She told them about the gods' Chosen and the purpose of her beautiful—former—counterparts. She explained the ranks, the Half-ranks, and the Rankless. She told them that death by the hand of a black machine should have caused irreparable damage to her heart—and that was probably why they hadn't been able to save any of the others. She explained the priestesses and priests and how they'd chosen fear or found love of their new masters. Without so much as a crack in her voice, she even voiced how she'd given her virginity to a black machine in a foolish attempt to live.

And then she said, "Today was the day of the auction. The dead Companions back there, like me, were not selected. We were all sentenced to die. Each of them had done so much to live, given up so much of themselves, and all for nothing."

"Better than to be one of us!" Louie said, with the conviction and blindness she'd only witnessed in young men.

*So like my brothers were—sure of everything. Not a shred of doubt. What would it be like, to think that way?* Naeemah smiled at him. "Is it? You're allowed to hate them. Even that freedom does not belong to us. We're expected not only to obey, but to love."

"Not you. Not anymore," Connor said. "Hating them is part of our lives."

"It *is* our life," Jayden said, sitting up slightly against the log behind him.

Riley sneered up at the sky. He didn't like her; that much was clear in the tense set of his shoulders. *Will he cast me out if I'm not useful? Or worse? There is worse they can do to me than ex-*

*pulsion. How can I trust these people?*

And what did they want of her? These men were warriors, and she was certain they meant to fight. But humanity had already lost their war with the gods. Three men and a teenage boy was hardly an army she saw as standing a chance. And then to add in one woman... she'd find out soon enough what they expected of her.

And if she couldn't work miracles, she'd have to face the consequences.

Tavar hunched over the digital display of the city, slowly plotting out the different neighborhoods. Was he even allowed to see all this? The display lay out over a large portion of the floor inside his new and completely unadorned home. Whatever projected the image remained out of sight.

Humming quietly to himself, Tavar traced a finger over some of the roads, trying to make sense of the new city's pathways.

"That's a beautiful song." The male voice from behind Tavar brought him immediately back into the gods' world. "We shall have to get you some of the gods' music. Though I'm certain you mean no disobedience, I'd hate for you to require punishment for a melody."

Tavar turned to see an older man—broad of shoulder and with a full belly to match. He wore a gray beard, streaked with black. The hair on his head didn't have any black left. Heavy features and a ruddy complexion could easily have seemed villainous if not for the gentle set of his mouth and twinkling smile in his eyes. Deep down, Tavar had expected something else of the Chosen—that they'd be frail, pitiable, or even weaselly. This man met none of those criteria.

The idea of being owned by another man did not surprise him. They were warned that these selections were entirely up to the Chosen's preferences. So, it didn't surprise him, but it didn't please him, either. Still, bedding a man would be nothing after the test with the drone. He supposed that was why the gods had done such a test—that cold flesh had been worse than going against his natural gender preference.

"I assume you enjoy music," the Chosen said.

Making no response, Tavar waited, his back partway to the projection of the city.

"I see you've found the city plan," the Chosen man said.

Tavar nodded.

The man sat down on the gray floor and waited with his hands folded in his lap. He clearly wished for a response from Tavar, but he had no idea what response was desired.

"You are unexpected," Tavar said, going with honesty, lowering himself to sit beside the other man he had to assume was his Chosen. His owner. "Are all the Chosen like you?"

The man guffawed and slapped a hand against his knee. "No. I'd return the question, but I've seen the other Companions."

"From what you paid..." Tavar let his voice trail until the man nodded, confirming this was his husband. "I would be shocked if you thought I was like the others."

"Rank Three, Ruiti," the older man said, patting his chest.

Tavar hoped he'd heard the right subtext. For Ruiti to be a Rank Three and have paid what he had meant this man had spent almost everything he'd had on Tavar. They'd have no servants, no fancy décor for the home... nothing. All Ruiti's credits had gone into Tavar. The question was: Why? And the answer had to be in front of him. He just couldn't read it... yet. Tavar reached out a hand, hovering over the city model. "Am I permitted to see this?"

"Anything I know is permitted to you. And I intend no secrets between us. That's the model of Third City, where we live—but most of the cities are similar." He pointed to a spot on a hill near the north end of the cityscape. "That is where our Rank Five lives, and in general, the ranks spread out from there, with the Rank Ones at the far edge of the city. The work-labs are mostly located in alternating patterns, keeping the types of labs close to those who work there."

"And the second level?" Tavar asked, pointing to the crowded network shown below the areas that Ruiti had indicated. He was just as curious how Ruiti would respond to the question as what his own answer would be.

"That's the undercity, where the Rankless work and live."

Tavar paused before questioning his new owner again. As much as Ruiti implied that he wanted openness between them, trust was a big risk. "Then what about the Half-ranks?"

Ruiti pointed to the southern corner of the projection. "There are labs over here that span both city levels. The labs in the uppercity are for certain types of experimentation, and most of the Half-ranks will live in the apartments layering downward."

Tavar stared, trying to imagine what the interiors of those buildings would look like. But if what Ruiti had said was true, he'd probably be able to see inside them. He wanted to ask Ruiti a bevy of questions, but fear of his nanites kept him silent.

Instead, he dragged his eyes away from the projection to the barren gray house. The emptiness was heavy.

"I have no budget to give you to decorate," Ruiti said. "Or purchase workers."

"You overspent on me."

"No. I spent exactly what I needed to."

Tavar kept his gaze fixed to the empty room. Wordless suspicions slid inside his mind. Ruiti had purchased him for a reason, and so far, what he wanted included sharing knowledge but no sexual component. Slowly, he turned back to his new owner. Ruiti remained seated on the floor, fingers dancing over the projection.

"You'll be the talk of the city," Ruiti said. "And in time, we'll make more contacts through word of mouth than I ever could have as a mere Rank Three."

Ambition. Or... Ruiti wanted it to sound like ambition. Contacts could be made and used for many different things, not just social climbing. But to accomplish anything, they'd need credits. He considered his response. "And contacts bring information. Perhaps you could 'rent' me out if it's allowed; we'd get credits and contacts."

"I don't intend to trade you. I need you here with me."

"Trading will be commonplace soon." Tavar stopped to weigh his words and thoughts. This wasn't about his desire; it was about getting power and connections—finding a way for humanity to rise again. "But 'lending' me to a Rank One who didn't purchase a Companion would be a great way to get an ally on your side. You may find it serves you to have me elsewhere."

Ruiti remained silent, but there was a sense of approval. They hadn't ironed out the specifics, but both of them seemed to understand the gist of what their lives were going to be. Ruiti wanted something more than just a bed partner—and armed with information like the city structures, Tavar might even be able to accomplish something to help humanity rise again.

Someday.

For the moment, he still had a very dangerous world to explore.

# CHAPTER 13

J aisa trailed a toe in the stream outside her house, watching as the green water-creatures shaped like tiny streamers gathered around her toenail. Behind her grew a tree with weeping purple leaves and a silver trunk. The silver bark peeled back in places, revealing an eggplant-purple interior. It had sprouted aided by nano tech and had grown fast enough for her to watch it shoot up in the stream, leaves folding out and spreading.

Jaisa pulled out a portable computer and rested it against her knees. A wave of nausea rolled over her, and she had to turn aside and lean over the ground. *I'm going to purchase slaves. How can I justify that? Even for my survival?*

In the training center, she'd had a reason to buckle to the gods' demands. But now, whom was she protecting except herself? Neriso and his "image" hardly counted. The Companions were out in the world and needed to either sink or swim protecting themselves. The only people in the world now who really needed her help were the Half-ranks and the Rankless.

And there was nothing she could do to protect all of them.

In fact, she was about to become a slave owner.

When she turned back to the computer, her hands shook, but the computer responded to her tentative motions, bringing up a list of options. Jaisa scrolled through, trying to see only the purchase costs and attributes. *But this isn't like buying a car or a piece of furniture... These are humans.*

She selected a few options from the Rankless, people who had experience with cooking and cleaning. They were probably older, more likely to be crushed by whatever cruelties lived in the world below. Then she went to the list of Half-ranks, who cost a good deal more, but she barely glanced at that. She didn't have to select anyone yet. A range of choices matching her desires would be brought to her to select from.

*Big and strong. It will be false, but a sense of security in my home would be nice... Plus, what says privilege more than bodyguards? It would look good for Neriso.* She selected appropriate boxes.

Then an option froze her: Prodigies. In order to be a prodigy, didn't one need to be a child? Jaisa swallowed hard. *If I can save a child from the world down there or from being used as a science experiment, I must.* She checked the box and shut the computer.

*I can't make any difference outside the system. I can't openly oppose the gods.* But if she worked with the system, maybe she could save a few. It wasn't fixing the world, but one step at a time.

Her eyes drifted closed. The sunshine licked at her skin like a kitten attempting to draw her attention. What would her selections actually mean? Who would come? Would there really be children? *Could* there really be children? Her mind whirled until the madness brought a sense of queasy dizziness.

Her computer beeped an alert. It startled her awake, though she couldn't recall having fallen asleep. All her worries flooded back as she gazed down at the flashing message. Her selections were approaching.

So soon? How long had she slept?

A honey-scented breath filled her lungs, and she relaxed her shoulders before turning her attention to the walkway. Bare moments passed before the drone and its "wares" arrived.

A new type of drone strode at the head of the group of bedraggled humanity. Rather than being shaped like a man, its upper body was comprised of more than a dozen black tentacles —like some monster straight out of gothic horror. The lower body was nothing more than a blob of black.

*Is that what they use to control the Rankless? Do all of its arms deal death?* She shivered at the thought. *At least I won't have to see one of those again. Its job will be taken by the tormented Half-ranks soon enough.*

As soon as people like her finished picking their house slaves, some of the stronger Half-ranks would be "outfitted into undercity enforcers." But what would that mean? Would their arms be replaced with metal tool-weapons? Perhaps a red eye linked to their foreheads to report to their masters? The only way to save any of them was to purchase them, and even Neriso couldn't afford them all—especially after buying her.

*If I weren't here... all of them could live.*

The tentacle drone approached Jaisa across the sunlit lawn. It led eight Half-ranks, six Rankless. Jaisa stepped over the stream, and then the individuals came close enough to make out. Emotions clogged her thoughts and she didn't know how she'd speak through the influx.

Little girls. Two of the Half-ranks, a pair of albinos, were actual children.

A tear slipped down Jaisa's cheek and she angrily shoved it away. She had no right to suffering, not with them facing slavery or worse. *They're so beautiful.*

Joy swelled inside her until it was hard to breathe. Until seeing them, everything in this world had seemed a burden to be borne. But to live for them, to help them and love them, sounded almost like a real life. And if she worked it properly, she could ensure that they had a real life, too.

The girl at the front was taller, thin in a natural way that children often get in their preteens. Her pale blue eyes had a wide set, which, along with her small mouth and pointed chin, gave her face a triangular cast. Her eyes were narrowed against the sun and every time she stepped into a shaft of sunlight, she winced.

*The sun is hurting her.* Jaisa's hand flew up over her heart.

The second, walking just a step behind the first, let her hair fall in a curtain over her face as if to hide, but unblinking pink eyes stared out in between ribbons of hair as she chewed on her lower lip.

*She can't be older than ten. Not too long ago, they both had families and lives—people who loved them as Evie adored Ethan. They need someone to love them, to take care of them. And I need them, too.*

Jaisa didn't glance at the other servants, but instead moved up to these two precious beings. Gently, she lifted their thin wrists, checking their markings, which would contain any information pertinent to their purchase. They had no names— their old ones had been taken, but without proper ranks, they hadn't qualified for new ones. When she owned them, she could give that back to them—if not their own names, at least the right to have names.

"You are proficient with two of the gods' instruments?" Jaisa asked the older girl.

"Yes. And I sing. Do you wish to hear?"

"I do, but not now, dear." A painful tingle bit into her fingers at the last word, but from the slight smile she received from the girl, it was well worth it. "I'll call you 'Lyra.'"

"And you." Jaisa stroked her finger over the younger girl's markings. "You're quite the prodigy. I've purchased instruments, and I hope the two of you will quickly become acquainted. I'll call you 'Melody.'"

Both of them were more expensive than she'd been expecting. Half-ranks ranged from five to ten credits in price. They were ten apiece. She gave a brief glance to the Rankless. She could have purchased all of them for the ten extra what the girls cost.

It didn't matter. This choice wasn't about math. For the first time since the gods had come, she was following her heart.

She motioned her hand to the two little angels and spoke to the drone. "I'll take these two."

Only twenty-five credits remained in her budget. She'd need most of that to get proper 'muscle.' And she still needed to purchase transportation for Neriso and additions for the house and garden. There would be nothing left to purchase any Rankless like cooks and cleaners. The girls would have to fill in there, but that was better for them than any of their other options.

She skipped the Rankless in the back of the crowd, a flush sweeping her cheeks. *Who am I to decide a person's worth? To say who will be saved? No matter what I do, I'm damning some of them, but I can't let it be the children. Can these others see that? Do they understand?*

Instead of dwelling on the questions, she eyed the glistening towers of muscle on the drone's left. One in particular arrested her gaze. The biggest of the bunch at around six-five, he still managed to be bulky, with rippling muscles that would have fit in inside a wrestling ring or on a romance novel cover. His face was lined with scars that along with his warm brown skin tone made it hard to fully place his age, thirty to forty? But it was his expression that had caught her eyes. A slight smile formed on his mouth, and his eyes flicked to the girls.

*He's happy they've been saved.*

"Him." She pointed. Then, noting no substantial difference between the others, she motioned. "And whichever of the other men I can afford."

The drone released the girls and the two men and departed with the others. Jaisa stared at the four remaining and realized that she owned them as Neriso owned her. Nothing was right about that.

She waved to the muscle. "Go explore the house. You'll need to be acquainted with our home and with each other. My husband will decide on names for you two."

Then she turned to the precious children. "Take the rest of the day to explore the house and the instruments. Tomorrow you will need to pick up other duties, but for today... go."

She watched them run off. A grin formed on her face. Giving them freedom would prove difficult going forward. There were strict rules on how to treat purchased Half-ranks. Even giving names had been regulated—they weren't supposed to have true names but labels that referred to their functions—but 'Melody' and 'Lyra' fit that requirement.

But other connections wouldn't be as easy. Touching them was forbidden and speaking to them discouraged. Finding ways around these rules would take a lot of trial and error.

It was time to start learning the gods' rules—and finding their loopholes. It was finally time to conform.

The crack of a campfire outside the tent was the only sound that disturbed the night. Connor turned on his side, trying to sleep. After hours of tossing back and forth, he was relatively certain that he wouldn't sleep anytime soon. Honestly, restless nights were better than the dreams he had when he did manage to drift off.

Before the aliens had come, he'd never had trouble sleeping. But the silence where all the noises should have been screamed too loudly to ignore. The absence of sound kept him up—gone was his wife's music playing softly through her headphones, the rustle of sheets as she turned in bed, and the even breathing while she slept. The lack of birds and traffic sounds permeated the hole that Rai's absence made.

Sleeping without her was more filled with her presence than the nights he'd spent with her. Given that, he should have anticipated not being able to rest with Naeemah sleeping in the makeshift tent beside his. He hadn't been around a living woman since Rai, and just the idea of that brought on a keen sense of guilt.

Rai wasn't avenged yet.

He lay there wanting to rush outside and into the city and take down the drones. Just kill and kill and kill until they took him down. But doing that would spoil any chance of getting any meaningful revenge.

So he tried to sleep.

Instead, he saw the faces of all the dead people in the—what had Naeemah called it?—the Companion Compound. His crew hadn't known what to expect within those walls, only that human survivors had been living there. He certainly hadn't expected a freshly dead army of half-naked beauties. After all the hope they'd had going in, all the hope of building up their numbers and getting people who understood the aliens' new society, to have saved only one was a crippling disappointment. Hopefully, she would be an asset, but no matter how amazing that one woman might turn out to be, she wasn't an army.

"And we need a fucking army," Connor said into the silence of his tent. *Screw it! I can't just lie here.*

He kicked off his blanket and stood. The blankets pooled at the base of the threadbare mattress they'd dragged into the tent. *Rai would want me to make the damn bed.*

Connor groaned, trying to force his dead wife out of his head. A distraction would prove more beneficial than anything else. And the crackle of the fire outside told him that at least one of the other four in camp was up. With Jayden on watch and patrolling the perimeter, Connor didn't have to guess who it was. Louie slept like the dead and Naeemah had been exhausted after her resurrection. Even if she wasn't asleep, which he found hard to believe, she had made it clear she felt uncomfortable under their eyes. No way she'd be leaving her tent.

Only Riley would be outside tonight. And that suited Connor just fine. Having been best friends for years, with their wives being best friends as well. He and Riley had an understanding of each other unmatched by anyone else.

Ducking down to exit the tent, Connor took in a deep breath of the smoky air. The waxy trees that surrounded the camp had an unearthly smell that he preferred to have covered by smoke. As expected, Riley sat hunched by the fire.

"Can't sleep?" Connor asked.

"I haven't even tried." Riley didn't glance up or move. The firelight flickered over his sharp features, and his reading glasses sat unevenly on the bridge of his nose, as if he'd been pushing at them. A book lay on his knees, but given that his elbows rested on it, Connor was certain his friend hadn't been reading.

Connor walked up to the fire before turning his head to gaze at Naeemah's tent. "What do you think of our new addition?"

"She'll be easy to camouflage for errands in the uppercity if Louie is right. We finally have someone who can walk unseen in front of the uppercity drones... even if she is only one woman."

"That's not really what I asked. Good list of facts, but what do you *think*?"

Riley chuckled dryly. "She's dangerous."

"Seems weak to me," Connor said. At least if they were going to only get one person, couldn't she have been strong? So far, they'd only managed to steal one thin preteen boy and a passive woman from the aliens. After all this time, they needed a bigger success.

"Her being weak is exactly what makes her dangerous." Riley sat up and for the first time looked directly at Connor. "We brought a beautiful, entitled, needy woman into our squad. Can you think of something more dangerous?"

"We need people. She's only one, but at least she'll be useful."

"I hope that's an accurate statement, Connor. I really do."

Connor turned away from Riley's serious expression to face the trees. With his back to the fire, the heat licked at his shoulders and cast his shadow out larger than life. "When we found this city, I had so much hope. Just knowing how to kill the metal men was enough. But more and more, it's obvious we're helpless. I didn't expect that."

"None of us did," Riley said. "And that woman doesn't help. I feel guilty just having her here. I couldn't save my wife... Julie is dead, and I can't do anything, but we saved *her*. I saved *her*. You want to know what I think of her? Nothing. I'm too busy feeling guilty for saving her instead of Julie or..."

Connor rubbed his wedding ring. He understood that. "Makes it harder to wait. I want to kill the bastards."

"I share the feeling, but it's a suicidal urge. We don't know enough, and we don't have the numbers."

And "the numbers" would be impossible to get if they could only gain one at a time. All it would take was one bad choice, and they'd be wiped out.

One woman wasn't enough, but it was all they had. Connor would figure out how to make it work for them.

# CHAPTER 14

The slate gray of the walls and floors boxed Jaisa in. Somehow, this color was heavier than the white of the compound—especially without the flashes of color from the jewels of the other Companions as they darted around. With her research open on a screen in front of her, she twisted, enduring the press of gray. Concentrating on the protocols for Melody and Lyra was proving impossible.

It didn't help that she'd seen almost nothing of Neriso since their first meeting. They slept in different rooms, and he worked early and stayed late. It was impossible to know if that was always true, as this was only their fourth day together. But that morning, he'd risen before her and taken his two guards, still unnamed to her knowledge, with him to whatever building he did his research in, with no words to her.

The idea of another whole day stranded in the house kept intruding on Jaisa's other thoughts. She'd been able to half-heartedly program in a schedule for the girls to follow, research some household acquisitions she thought might please her new husband, and read through a few messages. Most of the messages were invitations to parties and gatherings. To go, she'd need Neriso's permission—and company. He'd refused all her requests the day before.

She combed through the day's new invites, picked a few that looked the most prestigious, and sent a request to Neriso to approve their attendance.

While Jaisa waited, she signed up for a few training classes. It wasn't that more dancing and singing really appealed to her—but it would get her out of the house. Before she'd even finished, Neriso's refusals for each party arrived.

Jaisa groaned, looking up at the monotonous gray ceiling. *Is this really all? I'll go insane!*

Then, blocked by walls but nearby, came a trickle of music. Jaisa stood, gripping her screen, and followed the sound. She walked up a flight of stairs to the roof and saw Lyra and Melody sitting by the edge, practicing. Melody wore her hair loose and the white strands drifted on the breeze as she expertly used a wind instrument that Jaisa had never seen. Lyra strummed a stringed instrument with her head bowed to avoid the sun. The combination of sunshine, music, and the two sweet youths instantly made the world seem fuller and more vibrant.

Yet they both had their backs to the sun and they still squinted. Lyra's eyes watered. She'd have to get them a proper covering so they could be comfortable in the designated practice area.

Lyra's playing faltered when she saw Jaisa. Her blue eyes went wide, and her small hands froze. Melody followed suit, turning to Jaisa.

*They're afraid of me.* "Don't stop on my account," Jaisa said. Her fingers went numb, and she shook her hand as if to soothe the nanites. What had she said wrong?

The music restarted, but Jaisa's light mood had evaporated. She should have been allowed to give them simple commands... but how *simple commands* was defined would be up to the computer. *I can't even talk to them. They're terrified of me— because why wouldn't they be? How can I give them a childhood like this?*

*Must every command be sent through a computer?*

She sat down on the edge of the roof, staying on the opposite end from the girls. There would be no way to avoid some distance between her and Lyra and Melody. But the rules on Half-ranks had wiggle room based on individual needs and uses.

She'd have to get Neriso to allow her certain leniencies. Her fingers curled around the edge of her screen.

His previous refusals still showed on the interface.

If she wanted things from Neriso, she'd have to start making good arguments. Just sending her requests to him wasn't effective. And she couldn't accept *no* when it came to her girls. But what arguments could she even make?

They had to have a childhood, and that meant two things that they currently had none of: love and free time. Jaisa would never be allowed to show any love to them, but she could make a case for them being allowed to bond with each other. After all, children needed love to develop psychologically, and the two girls had been purchased as a team. Maybe she could even find a way to justify some extra attention from her with an argument of building their loyalty.

*I need them as much as they need me.* Jaisa tilted her head back to the sky. Just listening to the music had driven the gray of her new existence back. That was their purpose—to be entertainers. Maybe that was the key to finding a bit of time with them.

Jaisa tapped a finger on the screen. No way she'd send a request by the computer, but even so, perhaps she should draft her arguments. It would be easier to sway Neriso in person. Even then, she'd always found men were easier to sway when there was a physical relationship involved. As his Companion, Jaisa was certain she was meant to have such a relationship with Neriso, but as of yet, he hadn't asked for that.

The idea of sleeping with him to get what she wanted made Jaisa feel briefly dirty. But logically, their physical relationship was bound to happen eventually—she might as well get something out of it.

The music reached out again, carrying her in its gentle embrace. For a little while, at least, it could wash her worries away.

Neriso's bedroom curved on all sides and in the center floated a bedlike object. The surface, a slick plastic, was covered with a woven sheet. Jaisa lay across the soft fabric, staring at the ceiling, sweat still wet between her breasts.

Neriso's hand moved across her shoulder, gentle and tentative now. Rick's touch had never been so shy—sometimes tender, but never shy. She would not allow herself to pretend it was Rick's caress.

Getting Neriso in bed had been easy. All it had taken was waiting until he'd gone to his room to retire and then showing up at his door. And having done so, Jaisa felt for the first time as though he couldn't just send her back—or at least that he wouldn't.

Now was the best time to make her requests of her new husband. Now, when he had relaxed with her. But the swirling gray of the ceiling fascinated her, like watching clouds, and she lost herself in it. She imagined Tavar beside her. His hands would drift, memorize with a touch.

She shivered as Neriso's lips brushed her shoulder. But it was Tavar's full, wicked mouth her mind conjured touching her. That felt safer than remembering Rick.

"You're quite flawless," Neriso said.

*Okay. Time to talk now. Go for it. Be blunt.*

But she wasn't relaxed. This first bedroom encounter had unsettled her. Every touch felt like she was taking advantage of him—he'd been so nervous and awkward, and her mind hadn't been with him for a moment.

*I'm his sex slave, yet I feel as though I'm the one taking advantage.*

"This is what the gods intended I use you for." His tone was defensive.

When she glanced over, he had fully covered himself with the sheet, and she rolled on her side without an attempt to cover herself. She smiled. *If he didn't use me this way, what would happen to him? To me?*

"I'll get used to..." he began. "For you to say *no* to intercourse would be looked down upon, but perhaps it would've been better to grow accustomed to one another."

She shook her head, and he paused. Was he apologizing to her? Did he really believe he'd been the one to initiate this? "While I thank you for the thought, this is what the gods intended for me. We'll get used to each other. It was better to..."

"Get it out of the way?" He chuckled, little lines at the corners of his eyes wrinkling.

*He's just a man, after all, a man stuck in all of this.*

"That is part of your purpose here, but not all," Neriso said. "Your job is to maintain my image and my house. The gods have an advancement system for the lower ranks, which means in theory, I could lose my rank. It's important that we be leaders in all things. But the social aspect—the public portrayal—is beyond me."

"I'm your PR girl?" Her fingers tingled in reminder at the otherworld term.

Neriso's brow puckered in a glower. "I wouldn't use that word."

*No. I bet you are superb at using the right words. Is he just a man stuck in this? Becoming a Rank Five might take the kind of betrayal that it took to be a priestess. Has he sworn to love the gods as Drima did? I wish I knew how to see him, how to feel.*

"Why me?" Jaisa asked. "Seriously. I've seen the Companions the other Rank Fives chose. I'm nothing like them."

"You understand how to walk fine lines and how to lead. You must gain tact—the priests and priestesses are not blind to symbolism or tones, as the drones are—but I'm hoping you'll learn. I need you to see the things I can't, to watch my back."

*He's very worried about that. Is his situation so precarious? Or is he just paranoid? Better to use it.* "I'm doing my best, but you say *no* to every request I make."

"Not every one."

"Speaking of the Half-ranks," Jaisa said smoothly, seeing her chance. "I intend to make a few requests in regard to Lyra and Melody. If you want to say *no*, I'd appreciate the chance to speak with you in person to explain my reasons."

Neriso pressed his lips together. It seemed like an angry look, but she didn't know him well enough to be sure.

Well, he'd wanted someone with initiative. Jaisa pushed on. "If you wish me to take care of your image, then you owe it to me to at least know why I ask for things."

"In the future, I will await your reasons whenever possible," Neriso said. His voice was flat and cold.

She guessed it was better not to push him any further.

"You should go," he said.

She sat up. *Did I displease him that much? Maybe I asked for too much at once.*

He spoke again, softer this time. "We're not meant to be lovers. You cannot remain here."

*I could offer sex again, but do I wish to stay?* She hesitated.

"And we both have busy days tomorrow," Neriso said. "You'll need to look into training your servants and outfitting the house, and I have work."

He was right, and yet it stung to be dismissed. What had she expected? Arms to hold her? She'd always known this wasn't about love. She had what she wanted—a chance to give her girls a life. It was greedy to want more.

His fingers brushed over the back of her hand, and she forced a smile.

"Your work?" she dared ask again. If he would tell her what he did, it would be easier for him to feel close to her, to trust her.

"Cloning," he said. "My work is in cloning, primarily. You have clearance to know anything I know, but you must be careful of speaking any of it to one who doesn't have clearance. Our lives must abide by the rules."

*Is he making me a partner?* Jaisa grabbed up her flimsy garments and clutched them to her chest.

"I'll be careful with any knowledge I'm given, husband."

"Now go. We must both get to work."

Work, yes. But what he'd described as her work wasn't

what excited her. Keeping him entertained and happy was just what she had to do to give the girls a real life.

# CHAPTER 15

Crouching in the shadows of trees just outside the undercity, Naeemah felt more like a bird with clipped wings than ever. She did prefer her perch in the camp to the cage of the compound, but neither was freedom. Neither were the lean-to shelters and firepits she'd witnessed at the edge of the undercity. Feeling bad for her own circumstance had a hollow undertone when she stared at the rest of humanity—those allowed to live but not "favored" by the gods.

Beside her, Jayden crouched silently, his eyes moving slowly and constantly. How could someone so large be so still? She guessed he was watching for threats. He hadn't wanted to take her the few miles from camp back to the city, but the truth was, she needed to witness it herself. In the end, he'd only taken her because Connor had said that keeping her ignorant was more dangerous.

The Rankless in the city moved sluggishly through their filthy camps. Their movements had the abrupt edge of people who were exhausted and without hope. Between her and them was an invisible line, and on arriving, Jayden had made it clear where that lay. When she'd asked what stopped the Rankless from trying to escape into the wilderness, Jayden had told her that the undercity drones always found those who did, tracked by their nanites. Then they were brought back and brutally murdered.

So, the nanites would not let them cross, but scents of

human filth and decay wafted over just fine.

Luckily, they were at a sufficient distance to keep this from being truly nauseating—and to allow them to talk.

"The drones really never search over the line?" Naeemah whispered. She probably didn't have to whisper; from everything she'd been told, the undercity drones weren't as sophisticated as the ones in the Companion compound. They supposedly couldn't detect humans without nanites. "I can't understand how no one has found you guys."

"I don't understand all of it myself." Jayden spoke softly but not in a whisper. "You should ask Riley."

Naeemah gave Jayden an incredulous look. "Riley isn't about to take the time to explain anything to me."

"Well," Jayden said, pausing. She could almost see the scales tilting in his head as he weighed choices. But what choices? "We chose a camp spot far enough from the city that there'd be no visible sign of us, and we only built structures under dense tree coverage. Riley says we are undetectable from the sky. But ultimately..."

Naeemah leaned closer to him.

"Ultimately, I don't think they're looking for us. I don't think they care if a few stragglers escaped their hold. They assume that people like us will just die off on our own. Even Connor, Riley, and I almost didn't make it this far—and we're better trained and equipped to survive than most people would be."

"How *did* you survive?"

"Later," Jayden said. "That's hard to talk about." Then he glanced at her and offered an apologetic smile. He reached over and patted her knee before motioning back to the undercity slums. "That's where we found Louis."

"But Riley said that was a fluke."

"It was. We hoped to prove that thought wrong going up to your compound—or maybe that the drones of the uppercity would kill more gently. Less damage to the tissue means we have a shot at restarting the heart."

Naeemah shivered, a parade of remembered death dancing through her mind. "How many have you tried to resurrect?"

"Near one hundred, I'd say."

"So a two percent success rate?" Naeemah suddenly felt cold. There was a lot of weight in being the survivor, like she had to earn the right. She had yet to do so.

"Pretty shit. And we can't do anything more until we have larger numbers. Right now, any loss would be disastrous."

"Anything more?"

"Back before we came to this camp, we found a dead drone. Some poor bastard stabbed him before dying. But Riley..." Jayden winced there, and his mouth stayed parted, as if unable to say a word. "Riley studied it, and we figured out how to bring the drones down. We've done a few tests here, and our system works, but we can't afford to draw attention by killing a bunch of them until we have more soldiers."

"And I make a very poor soldier." It should have been Tavar here. He was strong, and he belonged in a group of war-driven men. None of this was right.

"Talk to Riley and Connor about that. You ain't supposed to be a soldier; you're a spy."

They faltered into silence, but Naeemah considered the statement. She'd worried about what they would do to her if she couldn't be useful, but all her training might turn out to be an advantage after all. If she could make it work.

She watched as a huge muscle-bound woman walked from the fire to a patchwork tent. Naeemah had a vague understanding of who had been picked for Half-ranks and Rankless from her research at the compound: people talented in one area but lacking in most others—people bent in body but with a talent for a profession, or mentally slow but physically strong. No one who was beautiful or brilliant made the Half-ranks, as those traits were reserved for Companions and Chosen. The Rankless were people broken in most ways already, people who in the world before would have been living on the streets or fully dependent on others. All they needed to be capable of was manual labor.

Naeemah knew all this, but watching them gave her new understanding. They weren't faceless; they were people with hearts and souls. People who been thrown into the lowest caste of a new society and were being ground down with no reward. Even the Companions were given some value.

"How can they live like that?" she asked.

Jayden shrugged. "No clue. It seems hopeless."

"But we'll try to help."

"We don't have the manpower to make a difference."

Naeemah chewed her lip. There had to be a solution, something to give her a purpose here. Without that, she'd always be vulnerable. A woman wasn't meant to be alone, surrounded by men. "You said you studied the drones you took down?"

"Yup. We keep them in a second site, away from camp."

"Can I see?"

"You'd have to get the okay from Connor." Jayden froze after speaking Connor's name, and his full attention focused back on the city.

The people out in the undercity camp stilled as well. Naeemah leaned closer—she hadn't noticed anything amiss. If she was going to survive, she needed to be more aware. Moving around a corner came a metal thing. It wasn't a man—it was a drone, but unlike the drones she'd seen, its form didn't even attempt to imitate that of a human. It still had a drone's flat face, with the single red eye and the constantly shifting features threatening to rise to the surface. But in place of a man's torso and arms, it had hundreds of tentacle-like extensions twitching about.

"What's that?" she squeaked.

"We'd better go." Jayden grabbed her hand and pulled her back.

Naeemah didn't need more prodding. She followed him, hunched low to not disturb any low-hanging branches. Jayden dropped her hand and forged ahead, not seeming to be aware of her anymore.

"What... What was that?" Naeemah asked when they'd gotten a safe distance away.

"One of the types of undercity drones. We'll show you the lab—eventually. You can see it all."

"Why not now?" Her frustration built. She'd never find a secure place among them if she didn't learn the true situation. She'd already spent too much of her life sheltered and helpless... and then exploited and helpless.

"It's not my decision. I smash things when Connor tells me to based on the information that Riley digs up. It's a chain of command."

"So Riley's in charge?" Her heart sank. Of all of them, he seemed the most averse to her.

"No, Connor. Riley's more like an advisor."

"Why Connor?" she asked. He didn't seem very stable to her, but none of them did. What he did seem was strong—strong and angry.

"It just worked out that way. And I'm happy not to have the responsibility. We've been through a lot, and he's the only one who never cracked under the pressure. He got us through." Jayden said this with a firmness that brooked no argument.

Naeemah tried to hurry, each root and stone nipping her feet through shoes that had never been meant to see the outdoors. Jayden's loyalty scared her. Not only was she a caged bird, but she was beginning to feel like a bird trapped with large predators she couldn't yet identify. She was not designed to be in the company of these men.

They'd saved her, but she wasn't safe.

One next to the other, Tavar set down the stones. All he knew as he worked was their pleasant weight and the fine sand-like texture of the alien dirt. He hummed gently in time, the rocks falling in perfect percussion. Occasionally, he would see his hands, dirt jammed under the nails, and they were almost the hands he remembered.

As he created, an old feeling of connection, a fullness, filled him. After his divorce, he'd settled into music as a second career. His first career had been chosen for him, as his father had owned a landscaping company. But before his divorce, he'd studied sculpture and painting and even dabbled in digital art. It had always soothed him to apply those arts to the grounds he'd tended. So as the rocks fit together to form a face, his mind settled into a calm nothingness.

His fingers fumbled with two blue stones, and in the vacuum of his mind filtered new thoughts, thoughts of the man who had purchased him. No one paid a massive sum for something unless they had specific intentions for it. For *him*.

A few days was plenty of time to come to some conclusions. So far, the limits of Riuti's touch had been a handshake and a few claps on the shoulder. Since the nanites wouldn't interfere with any touch permitted by his Chosen, this lack of contact seemed intentional. While he was not certain, Tavar suspected he had not been purchased for sex, at least not with Ruiti. Logic told him whatever Riuti desired of him, it was not straightforward, and it had everything to do with Riuti's desire to share knowledge and to use Tavar for connections.

It was too early to trust that Ruiti shared Tavar's opinions on the gods, but he was more and more hopeful.

At the sound of footsteps behind him, Tavar wiped his hands against each other, trying to dislodge the dirt, but also to block the view of his newly formed rock sculpture. Based on the scar and plain white tunic Tavar had selected during the auction, anyone who chose him would be lenient with references to the old world, but he wasn't desperate to push too far too soon. Especially not when otherwise things with Riuti were very pleasant.

"Beautiful." Riuti moved up beside Tavar and draped one arm across his shoulders. "You're talented with landscaping, I see. I think we will not need a landscaper to have an enviable house facade—this little outdoor patch will be yours. The blue is..." Riuti's pause dragged on just long enough to be clearly purposeful. "It touches the heart as well as the eyes."

Unsure if he had understood correctly, Tavar glanced from the rocks back to his husband, then returned to the picture he'd formed with dirt and decorative stones. The blue stones Riuti had referenced were the eyes, twinkling points of color in the lively outline of a small girl.

While making it, Tavar had only been letting the pain pour outward, and it wasn't until now that he fully realized what he'd created. Little Wendy. He'd named her after the character in the Peter Pan books, a little girl who chose to grow up in the end. Only his Wendy never would.

If talking about it had been allowed, the words would have burst forth. He couldn't remember the last time he'd talked about Wendy or that day. *Maybe it's better that I can't share those memories. That burden is mine alone.*

"I'm lucky," *I had nothing to lose*, Tavar said and did not say, choosing his words carefully to reveal without saying directly. "I have no one to blame but myself—the gods saved me from myself. I doubt I'd even be alive if they hadn't come."

He hardly remembered the aliens coming and couldn't remember what he'd been on at the time. It was pretty much a take-your-pick from an array of drugs, taken not as much from addiction as from a desire to die and an inability to muster the courage to use a handgun.

Beer and a car—beer in his system, a car he was driving—had killed his Wendy. Ended his life. All the aliens had done was remind him that there were other people out there. Other people who hadn't deserved to lose everything they loved or to die. He'd had to live because all those other Wendys deserved to see their killers punished.

Ruiti remained silent, seemingly letting Tavar process.

"Why am I here?" Tavar asked.

"Because I had money burning a hole in my pocket," Riuti said.

Tavar looked back at him, away from the rock portrait.

"And because I didn't want to be alone," Ruiti said. "I need someone with a brain to share my evenings with."

"Won't you get us in trouble if we don't share a bed?"

"I highly doubt it." Riuti chuckled. "Your job is to entertain me, isn't it? Well, you will. Truth be told, none of you Companions are my 'type.' When I need someone for my bed, I'm sure I can find an appropriate, *willing* partner among the Chosen."

"That's allowed?" Tavar finished wiping his palms on his pants, leaving a brown trail.

"Why not? Now stop the questions. Remember, I own you." The twinkle in Riuti's eyes made it impossible to take this comment seriously.

Tavar had never been more sure that this man would be part of any rebellion that happened. Humanity would rise. It had to.

All Tavar had to do was keep his ears open.

# CHAPTER 16

The girls flitted like pastel yellow butterflies across the pale city. Jaisa followed behind, watching them dash to and fro in their sunflower-print dresses with trailing yellow ribbons. Often all she could see were the wide brims of their equally sunny hats. When Jaisa and her girls had begun the daily walks, Lyra and Melody had been sedate, but slowly, their movements had grown bold—more childlike. Jaisa had also learned to take the walks early when possible, so that the girls wouldn't have to face the midday sun. Officially, these walks were to show off Neriso's beautiful possessions to the world. That was how Jaisa had presented the idea to her husband.

But Jaisa intentionally programmed in a very wide proximity requirement for the girls, so that they were able to dart across the pearlescent streets and stop to stare at the flying train taking other Chosen to the office spaces. They could whisper behind Jaisa or pause to smell a flower.

Jaisa, for her part, never asked more of them.

She wondered if they had any idea that she gave them liberties on purpose. Rationally, Jaisa couldn't justify why her girls should care for her at all—she was, after all, their owner. But she desperately wanted for them to at least know she was on their side. If only she could ask them if they enjoyed the walks, or if they felt it was an annoyance.

Jaisa strolled along at a steady pace, breathing in the clear air, tinged with the memory of rain and the scent of a foreign flower. She enjoyed the outings. Perhaps she was justifying them as being for the girls when, really, they were a way to entertain herself amid the lonesome monotony.

The girls came to a walkway that hovered over jade green water and they paused, staring down into their own reflections. Jaisa kept her pace steady and passed them. As the walkway came to the end, she could see a twist in the road, bringing her home into sight. The building no longer looked as stark as it had the day she'd first come to it.

Now there was a full garden, complete with climbing trees and a stream, and on the rooftop glittered a small arched building and crystal banisters. All of the smart crystals in her home were set to imitate the color that her girls wore, so that day they were a sunny yellow to match the garments Melody and Lyra had chosen.

The rooftop terrace was designed for gatherings. But so far, that was the one thing that Neriso had never budged on. He refused any gathering of people, making walking alongside children with whom she couldn't speak Jaisa's only pastime.

Jaisa turned back to the walkway to watch her two pretty prodigies descend. As the pale children neared the bottom of the slight incline, Melody tripped on a trailing ribbon of her gown. Jaisa lunged forward and caught the slender girl in her arms. Immediately, a tingle pricked her fingers. She held on to the girl despite the feeling.

*How often can I set off their warning signals before they decide I'm too much hassle and kill me?* Jaisa stared down at Melody as the girl scrambled to her feet. Jaisa's arms were numb by then, the electric sensation spreading up to her elbows.

Melody's wide pink eyes blinked several times before she turned and fled across the street in a flurry of sun-bright ribbons. The older girl, Lyra, dared a smile at her mistress before scurrying after her companion.

Jaisa froze. *She smiled at me.*

A warmth started in her chest and spread outward.

Jaisa grinned as she massaged feeling back into her arms.

She hadn't meant to help Melody. At least it hadn't been *planned*. Setting off the nanites might get her in trouble—but some reactions were automatic.

A camouflaged drone stepped out of her house and moved toward her even as the girls slipped inside the currently yellow gate that separated her home from the street. The drone had arrived in her home days earlier, exactly like the drones from the compound, only instead of staying black, it disguised itself to whatever stood behind it. Unless they moved, they were nearly impossible to detect, but the camouflage took a split second to change.

Currently, there were two drones living in her home—ostensibly for her "protection." And this one was for monitoring anyone deemed "at risk." And of course, the only person in Neriso's house who regularly seemed on the verge of irking the gods was Jaisa. She'd reached the gate to her home and had to walk past the drone. It would be trailing her for a solid day, making sure she did nothing further to displease the gods.

To distract herself from its loathsome presence, she went to the outer wall and pulled up a portable computer screen. Time to plan a party—something, anything, for a distraction.

The walks were good, but they weren't enough. If it had just been her, she could have accepted Neriso's constant refusals. But the girls would probably like to perform, to show off the skills they worked so hard on. Plus... wasn't this what Neriso had wanted from her in the first place? He wanted to be a fixture in society, and if she wanted to stay in his favor, she'd have to make sure it happened—but you have to be *in* society to be a fixture there.

She'd just have to make it a party he couldn't refuse.

Lyra's voice soared over the garden, from some cove hidden from sight. An immediate longing filled Jaisa. She needed to begin planning the gathering she'd envisioned to get both her and Neriso engaged in the new culture, but her feet wanted to dance. She waffled. Surely, it was all right to take a moment and enjoy the world. When her body tired of the movement, then she would sit and research the gathering she needed to plan.

Once her mind was made up, Jaisa moved a few paces far-ther into the garden until she saw the girls practicing by the lit-tle stream that ran through the gardens, Melody's toes tracing in the water. Jaisa let her troubles go. She lifted her face to the sky and watched the lines from the gods' ship pulse. Like a heart.

*Do they watch us from up there?*

Jaisa's feet moved in one of the dances she'd learned in training. The drone watched her from the gateway, its blank face reflecting her dance. It looked silly in yellow.

She dropped down to sit on the grass, and the girls con-tinued with their instruments, soothing her mind into a con-structive rhythm. She drew up an invitation list under the con-stant watch of the drone and the blink of its red eye.

After a few hours, she waved the girls inside. They would fix a dinner for her and Neriso. He would not come home to eat it. He never did. The man worked constantly, and other than the one-word answer he'd used to describe his work as "cloning," she had no idea what it was he did.

Jaisa moved to a bench under a tree with indigo leaves. It was the closest to privacy she'd get. She perused the direc-tory, looking for more people she needed to invite. But between searching for Rank Fives and important Rank Fours, her finger paused.

*Look for Ladair. I could find where she is, contact her. That would be better than any party with Neriso. But what if she isn't there? What if her name pulls up nothing?*

Jaisa shook her head to dislodge the thought, but as a con-cession to that silly part of her that believed she could still have friendships, she searched for Tavar. For a few minutes, she lin-gered on his profile, looking at his face. The smile on the screen relaxed her.

He'd always had that effect on everyone.

*I wish I could invite him.* She turned off the display. Why must her mind always betray her?

Jaisa kicked at a clump of dirt as hard as she could, sending a shower up to touch the leaves falling like a curtain in front of her. She parted the dripping leaves and walked into the house.

As she'd expected, she ate alone.

Around nightfall, Neriso entered the house. At the sound of his voice issuing a command to the guards, she ran to the top of the stairwell. Her fingers curved around the railing, gripping too tightly.

She heard the clumping footfalls of Neriso's guards. They now had names, just like her girls, but unlike her, Neriso hadn't kept the labels given to Half-ranks name-like. The larger of the two men, for whom Jaisa still had unrealized hopes, he called "Alpha," the smaller "Omega."

Sickening, totally inhuman monikers. But she'd seen no evidence that either guard cared. She would have to care *for* them.

Neriso entered the lobby area below. He looked small and breakable beside the rocks of men she had chosen for him. It was strange to think of him as her husband; even now, it was easier to picture herself at the side of the brutes who accompanied him. They looked crisp and clean in their outfits, where somehow, he appeared over-starched.

"Husband!" she called.

He looked up, expression clouded, distracted. His gaze passed through her, as if looking through furniture for something of import. Then his eyes focused on her, appearing slightly confused at her intrusion.

*Whatever it is that he does, his mind is always there.* She was used to that look and smiled in response.

His eyes drilled into her, seeking something. She straightened to take his scrutiny, her chin lifting. There was something intense about him that intrigued her despite everything else.

Alpha and Omega stood motionless at his side. Alpha's glower was deep and expressed in the lines of his face—she hadn't seen him smile since that first day. Not a flicker of emotion between them.

"Hello," Neriso said after a pause. "Do you need something, Jaisa? I must get to bed. Tomorrow is a long day for me."

"Of course. My apologies." She didn't sound apologetic, so she tried harder. "Unfortunately, I don't know when you'll be in again. I had to catch you now."

"I see."

Time to prepare for her party. Step one, convincing him to say *yes*. "If we're the first to call the fourteen Rank Fives together, they'll look foolish if they refuse. Plus, they'll be too tempted to compare what they have to what you have, and I feel that you'll compare favorably." Thanks to her, which she didn't need to say. "But I'll need your consent."

Alpha and Omega stared ahead, without averting their eyes or seeming to see anything.

"And if I don't consent?" Neriso asked.

Jaisa lowered her eyes in what she hoped was a demure gesture, but she didn't intend on accepting *no*. "Then I'll think of something else, of course. But it was you who said you'd leave our image to me. The fourteen will meet soon, and if the gathering is here, we gain an advantage."

"You're really quite clever, Jaisa," Neriso said. It didn't sound like a compliment.

"Marvelous. I won't need anything from you beyond your permission. We have everything in the house already for such a party. There's no need to be flashy."

"You do all of this social stuff so easily."

*Easy? He thinks this is easy for me?* She pushed the word aside and tapped her forehead with her finger. "It's all a strategy game."

"I was never much for games."

Time for flattery. "Which is why you wanted me on your team."

"Think of something else, Jaisa. We're not throwing a party." Neriso turned his face away from her, headed up the stairs past her, and walked down the hall to his room.

Why wouldn't he say *yes*? No, that didn't matter. Whatever his reasons for saying *no* were, she just had to convince him that he had more reason to say *yes*. The one thing he'd asked her for was status. Somehow, she had to work with that.

Alpha stepped around her without ever diverting his gaze to her. When she'd chosen him, she'd really believed she'd seen something more. Had that been imagined? The three men moved up the stairs behind her. The door slammed.

Only the drone's blinking eye watched her, and she melted back.

*Easy? It's like he's watching a different show than I am.* It wasn't *easy* being caged. She didn't have a choice. She'd never thought a party would mean so much to her, but sitting in the house alone and bored wasn't a life. It wasn't a life for her, and it wasn't a life for her girls.

She fell back on the bed, with a groan of helpless frustration. How had she thought she had any power? Even throwing a party was out of her control... and she certainly had no real hold on Neriso.

# CHAPTER 17

C onnor leaped to his feet on seeing movement at the periphery of the camp. Louie and Jayden were out checking the traps for game, and Riley was leafing through a textbook on robotics at the edge of the fire, so any movement sent up red flags.

But his heart didn't stop pounding when he saw Naeemah walking up from the river. Her long hair hung in wet coils down her shoulders, making water splotches on his old army jacket. It brought his mind back to many nights camping with his wife. Rai had always ended up in his clothes when she'd inevitably gotten cold. But this woman wasn't his wife, and the reactions his body had to her long legs where the rough pants stuck to her were inappropriate.

*Our job is to protect her and find out what she knows. Nothing else, and nothing else is appropriate. Get your mind back where it belongs.*

Naeemah approached the fire and sat down on one of the logs, extending her feet toward the flames. Jeweled rings and bracelets glittered in the firelight, and every time she moved her arms, the little golden bells jingled. He wished she'd stop wearing them. He'd have to make damn sure she did if they ever went into the city.

"I've been here long enough," she said firmly. "It's time for you to tell me exactly how you came to be in the compound to save me and what you want from me."

Connor glanced over at Riley. This talk had been a long time coming, honestly, but Connor didn't know how to start it. The easy part would be how they'd found her. But what they wanted? Even if they did tell her, how would they get her to believe that they stood any chance of standing against the aliens? Someone would have to take her to Riley's lab. That was where they kept all of their research, but more importantly, it was where they kept the carcasses of the drones they'd taken out.

But she seemed too soft for that. Having a woman in meltdown wouldn't help their cause.

Riley spoke before Connor could decide. "Louie told us they were keeping people in those buildings up there. He didn't know who you were, but the date you would be released was common knowledge among the Rankless. We hoped we'd find someone useful."

"Jayden says I could be a spy. Having a Companion on your side..." Naeemah stopped as her voice got thick. She was trembling.

What was she scared of? Even if she had no use whatsoever, they would take care of her.

"For now," Riley said, "it's more important that you settle into life here than go gallivanting in the uppercity. Connor and I will ask you a lot about how the uppercity works—as of now, we know very little. Anything else we might ask of you requires a level of trust on both sides that hasn't been established yet. We'll have time for the rest later."

"Trust does not happen by magic," Naeemah said, folding her arms. Her hair left wet streaks on the jacket.

"It takes time," Riley growled.

*Time.* Connor's mind slipped into the word. Too much time had already passed. He'd guess it had been nearly a year. Maybe a year. It was hard to tell, as somehow the aliens seemed to have changed the seasons—since they'd first arrived with their black lines across the sky, it had been a constant springtime. Riley said there were still real seasons away from the cities, but Connor hadn't seen it. Still, it had been something like a year, maybe a few months less, and yet none of his crew had moved on from the world before. How easy it seemed for Riley to say that "it takes time," but time didn't seem to have altered much.

Riley said something that breezed past him, and Naeemah responded. Her lips, now free of cosmetics, were a warm brown tinted with soft pink. Now that she was seated, the coat fell to her mid-thigh, shading the area between her legs. Her knees drifted slightly apart.

*Is she doing that on purpose, or does it just come naturally after so long playing sex-bot?* His guess was it was unintentional because there was an odd innocence to her when she was distracted. Like how she'd clung to him when they'd first entered the workers' tunnels.

"Connor? You should field that question." Riley cut into Connor's thoughts and slammed his book shut. The note of bitterness told Connor that Riley knew exactly where his friend's mind had been. And Riley clearly didn't want to have to answer her questions—she was Connor's problem.

"What question?" Connor asked, embarrassed.

"How did you survive the initial attack and not get captured?" Naeemah repeated. At least she pretended not to notice his distraction.

*Jesus, I'm more like a horny teenager than when I was a horny teenager. Okay. Time to get my head where it needs to be.*

He glanced at Riley, who'd shoved his hand into his pocket and was playing with a pair of pearl earrings he'd stolen when they'd reached the city, after the aliens had destroyed the base. It was a familiar movement, almost constant when Riley wasn't doing anything else. He'd stolen the earrings to remind himself of all the things he'd never given his wife, Julie, back when she'd been alive.

Connor thought it was not only morbid but self-destructive. No point saying that, though. They all got through however they could.

Naeemah gave a small, intentional cough, drawing him

back to her question about their survival.

"We survived..." Connor started and stopped, lowering his eyes to his own wedding band. "It was just a fluke. We had been scheduled for a vacation—a camping trip. But our truck broke down in some backwater forest, so we hadn't gotten back to the base by our scheduled report time. Riley believes the aliens had access to official records. So they must've assumed we were already back on base. We didn't even know until..."

Connor stopped, trying not to remember. There was a reason, beyond Connor's distraction, that Riley didn't want to tell the story himself. How could he talk about that first week without remembering? None of them talked about it.

"They showed us pictures," Naeemah said softly. Her accent was thicker than it had been earlier, and tears filled her honey-colored eyes. "I know what you must have seen. My father... his whole office, everyone just lay there, dead, slumped over their desks. But that was the easiest, a quick death. My brothers were harder to see."

Riley's glare had deepened, and he'd gone so rigid that he trembled.

"Anyhow." Connor avoided meeting her sympathetic gaze. *How do women do that? Just pull the emotion out, a little coaxing in their voices. I was doing just fine not remembering. I don't want her pity. Just spit it out, Connor, get it done.* "We doubt they've concerned themselves with a few strays after the initial attack, even if they figured out we weren't killed. At the time, we were worried, but five days after we came back, we made it to Olympia and were trying to find answers when—"

"Excuse me." Riley stood and fled from the firelight.

"You lost people," Naeemah said.

"There were five of us. One died when we got back to base, shot himself next to the corpse of his fiancée."

Naeemah's brow puckered and she paused. "And there are four now?"

"Louie wasn't with us then. Five days after the attack, the machines came. We were looking around the empty city, found a black robot, and Riley was pulling it apart trying to see how it ticked."

"A drone."

He thought he'd heard her use that word before. It fit. "Sure, call it what you want. We found one with a knife in a weak spot in its neck. We moved the body to a basement. The poor bastard who'd stabbed it had gotten electrocuted. We've found a way around that now, been able to take down a few of them. We lost that original one, though, when the machines came."

*Damnit. Don't think about it.*

She nodded. There wasn't a trace of surprise on her face. "You're avoiding describing what happened. I'm sorry. This must be very painful for you."

"Yes." Connor swallowed against a lump in the back of his throat. They'd been in the city next to their base, shortly after the invasion. It had been horrible enough living in an empty world after finding all their homes filled with corpses... then the aliens' machines had come for the leftovers. "We felt something like an earthquake, and three of us went up to investigate. Our friend, Casey, stayed down with the drone. But up top, we saw this flood of machines in the air..."

"And they leveled the city," Naeemah said. "They showed us pictures of it happening."

Connor nodded.

Naeemah's hand covered her mouth.

"Casey..." Connor started. He swallowed hard to clear his throat. "He didn't get out. I don't know how any of us did. We ran as the city fell around us."

"I'm so sorry. To leave him..."

"Jayden blames himself. Casey and him... they were close. I don't think Jayden will ever get over it. Riley has written out scenario after scenario in his notebooks, trying to find a way we could have saved him. He's found nothing, and he won't. We couldn't have saved him."

Naeemah scooted closer and touched Connor's hand. Her flesh held the chill of the river, but her soft, uncalloused skin sent chills up his spine that had nothing to do with cold. She could make him forget, soothe the constant ache of loss. Her touch screamed the promise. Connor drew away.

*I don't need to forget.*

"We can avenge him," he said. "Avenge them all. It's the reason we wake up in the morning. Question is, can you be part of that?"

And if she couldn't? Connor tried to dismiss the thought, but it wouldn't go. They weren't an operation set up to support civilians. Her pinched, angry expression didn't help.

Connor waited for the outburst as Naeemah tugged down on the corners of his jacket, arranging it over her thighs. Her mouth opened, then shut, as if her brain refused to form words in answer to Connor's question.

"How can I help?" she asked, forcing the words out on the second try. "I cannot see what part you want me to play. I'm no warrior. And I don't know how to get more people for your cause. Will you cast me out?"

"Why the hell would we throw you out?"

"I'm useless. I'll only die playing at soldier in your war. That isn't a woman's place."

"Death's the outcome for all of us." *A woman's place? Did a she just tell me what a woman's place is?*

"How you saved me—and the boy, Louie—it should never have worked. The drone's touch should have damaged our hearts. I'm afraid you're searching for a solution that isn't there."

"We'll find a way to fight them. That's the only reason to live. To get revenge." Connor closed his eyes, trying not to see the rotting bodies inside the commissary, with Rai's car in the deathly still parking lot.

Naeemah motioned outward with one arm. Her bells tinkled. "This isn't much of an army. Unless you figure something out, you're talking suicide, not revenge. And it would need to be soon. Right now, everything is in flux, as they get all the upper-city people settled and all the Half-ranks assigned. But as time goes on, their monitoring will only get better."

"Didn't figure someone who'd..." *give in to them would understand.* Connor bit back the words, but from her narrowed eyes, he'd said too much.

"Should I have died?" Naeemah asked. "We all asked ourselves that. If it was better to be caged, enslaved, ruled, and abused, or to simply not exist at all. Many didn't make it. They died screaming their real names or crying for those they'd lost. I made it through the gods' training, and so did many others. You have no right to judge any of us. You didn't go through it. You don't know."

"The right thing to do is to fight and die. Otherwise, you're living on the backs of corpses." *Rai died. Julie died. What makes Naeemah so special? That she's beautiful? She doesn't deserve better than my Rai.*

"You give this speech to the Rankless?" Naeemah stood, the movement of his jacket on her legs verging on showing everything.

Connor shook his head. "It's not the same. They're abused. You lived in luxury—"

Naeemah's voice lashed out. "Being *raped*."

Connor winced. She wasn't wrong. But it didn't change that she hadn't fought back. She'd let it happen. He would have died first. "Why not fight back?"

"Because it wasn't ever a *fight*." Her voice raised to a shrill screech. "Disobey and we died. Say something wrong, touch someone for too long, or even step out of line, and we died. It didn't affect them—didn't hurt them *at all*. Death wasn't a brave battle, just a pointless, painful suicide. I saw plenty of those, and in the end, after everything, that's what I chose. Maybe if I'd tried to be picked, I would be with a new master now, who could force himself on me whenever he chose, and the only way to remain alive would be to coo in pleasure for him. But I'm not *braver* because I'm here—I just couldn't live like that."

Connor twisted his wedding ring, hard, on his finger.

"Why save me if you feel this way?" Her lips trembled; all

the anger melted away. Her pain showed on her like a raw, open wound.

*Is it me she's defending herself to? No. I said what she fears is true herself.*

"My opinion isn't important," Conner said. "What's important is if you can help us defeat them, if you're willing to try."

"No one wants the gods deposed more than me. They took everything from me and then went on to take things I didn't know I had. I'll help you. I'll spy. Tell me how."

"You know the world they built above us, and you'll be able to spy up there in ways none of us can. We need you, but we don't really know yet. There's no point sending you up there blindly."

"I'm useless until then. And what happens to me if you decide I'm deadweight?" She pulled the coat tighter over her chest with one hand.

"Let's deal with that when it happens, Naeemah." What would they do? She was in danger in the camp, but that would be true wherever they sent her. *I should listen to myself—worry about that when it happens. But we've failed to protect so many; I can't fail her, too.* "For now, you're here with us. You'll figure something out."

Naeemah tossed her black hair and hugged her arms around herself. Then, with her head bowed, she stalked away from the fire.

What had just happened?

Steps in the doorway woke Jaisa from a turbulent sleep. Her heart leaped about like a trapped frog as she fought the fog of sleep. Her mind, before she controlled it, pictured a god. She bit her lip to keep in the scream.

Neriso, not a god, skulked across the room and sank down on her bed. A sigh escaped her lips, and she rolled on her side to face the door with one hand fluttering over her heart. His eyes focused on her, and it made her wish for his normal, distracted presence. His full scrutiny was disconcerting.

Realizing belatedly she must look scared rather than welcoming, she forced her face into a softer expression.

Their last conversation had been him refusing to allow her a party. It was entirely possible he'd come to wreak some further havoc upon her. Gaining control of the situation was her primary concern, but with only adrenaline drowning out sleep, she wasn't thinking clearly.

"I didn't expect you." Her voice sounded breathy and weak, unintentionally very close to the tones they'd taught her in training.

"You have no right to expect anything of me." The lash of his voice scoured her.

"Of course not." Jaisa quirked a smile at him and sat up. The cover slipped from her, leaving her torso bare. Nudity was a weak control method, but it was all she had. "You just scared me."

"I've never been good at parties," Neriso said, not even looking at her. "They're awkward."

Jaisa sucked in a breath. She also hadn't expected him to broach the subject. "You don't need to be good at parties."

Neriso looked up at her. There was no kindness in his gaze, but no cruelty, either.

Jaisa slipped from the bed and knelt by his knees. Her position showed her submission. Nervousness was better than what she'd thought had been coming after the chill of his gaze— she could handle him like this. She would take this opportunity. Was that at the heart of all his refusals? She imagined it was true that gatherings of people were a struggle for him. She lay a hand on one of his knees, adding a touch of affection to the subservience. "Navigating social situations is why you have me."

"And I'm not good with women like you."

"I am yours already."

Neriso snorted in derision.

"There will be just as many people like you, who are probably no better at parties than you are." Jaisa set her hands on his knees and tilted her face up to him. "Is that why you haven't wanted to attend the other gatherings?"

"I have work to do. It just hasn't seemed to matter, but you're right. This does matter, and I shouldn't let work distract me."

"It's easy to get distracted from the things you hate." *But what is his work? What sort of genetic engineering interests the gods? Interests them enough to make him a Rank Five?* Jaisa licked her lips.

Neriso turned his face fully way from her, now looking nervous. "I don't hate parties."

Jaisa laughed. She didn't know what to say.

"Have your party." He studied her, no longer judging, just taking her in. He touched her cheek. "I should trust you to do your job. You do know how to make a splash."

"I doubt the gods mean for you to be kind. Take me to see your work soon?" *Whatever he sees in me is more than is there. What will he do when he realizes I'm not what he believes? I can't let it happen—the girls need me.*

"I'll do my best. You aren't suited to my work."

Jaisa took his hand and kissed each of his fingers. He shivered at her touch.

"You're a rough man, but all we have is each other. I'll do my best for you. I can't expect you to offer any more." She took his hands and placed them on her chest. "If we aren't kind to each other, who will be kind to us?"

# CHAPTER 18

The undercity stank as much on Naeemah's second visit as it had on her first, but this time, the smells were less of the old machinery and more of human filth. Each factory, and they were almost at their fourth, made it worse. Connor and Riley walked in front of her, and out in front of them, Louie darted this way and that.

He seemed young for fourteen—more akin to the ten-year-olds in her village. Sending him out in front was a questionable choice, but Riley had explained in no uncertain terms that she wasn't part of the planning process. Jayden had kindly clarified that only Louie spoke the gods' language.

"I do, too," Naeemah had said.

"But you're an upperworlder," Jayden had replied. "These people won't trust you."

Thus, she stayed to the rear of the group, an addition that Riley tolerated only on Connor and Jayden's insistence. Jayden himself had been left behind to guard the camp.

Wearing her Companion garb again, in case it helped them connect, she felt even more vulnerable than usual.

The general purpose of this excursion was to speak with the Rankless and show them that Connor and his group were friends. They still hoped to be able to recruit the Rankless to their number. Naeemah knew that was impossible unless they found a way to stop the nanites, but she held her peace. They clearly weren't interested in her thoughts.

At each factory, they offered to help where they could. In the one they'd just left, a very large man had suggested that Naeemah's company would be a boon. Connor had shut the idea down immediately by saying, "She's one of us, and that isn't the operation we run."

Naeemah had felt momentarily safe.

Riley had looked unconvinced. As they headed toward a fourth location, Riley tugged at Connor's arm. He whispered to Connor without even a glance back to see if Naeemah could hear. She caught a few key words, enough to give her a good sense of what they were saying. From context, she gathered that he was espousing the benefits of whoring Naeemah out. This went on for a few minutes, and Naeemah found herself pulling the scraps of her outfit closer around her. The cold concrete ground reached up through the thin soles of her slippers.

Finally, Connor shoved his best friend away.

"Be a god damn gentleman!" he shouted.

She couldn't see his face, but there was a cutting edge of true anger in his voice that felt like a shield between her and Riley's cold whispers.

"We aren't gentlemen," Riley said, still in a low voice. He at least still seemed concerned with her overhearing. Even if his emotions drove his volume upward. "We're soldiers, and we are desperate."

"She's a human being. We are not doing it!"

That response didn't exactly fill Naeemah with confidence. If something didn't change soon, Connor might give up on her. What then?

Louie peeled around a corner and barreled in their direction, disrupting her thoughts. She could tell from the look on his face that something bad awaited them up ahead. Connor and Riley stopped, taking defensive stances, and Naeemah drew up closer to them.

"A crowd drone." Louie gasped, pulling to a stop and bending, his hands on his knees. "It just took out five of the workers up there...."

"Shit," Riley swore.

"We gotta go!" Louie said.

"Why not kill it?" Naeemah asked.

Riley scoffed. "Yes, let's start a war right now, when we can't possibly win. The more we kill, the more likely they are to notice us. Do you think we're ready for that kind of scrutiny?"

"I think," Naeemah said dropping her tone and glaring, "that if we want the Rankless people's support, this is how we get it."

Connor placed a hand on Riley's arm. "We need trust and loyalty. We need word of mouth."

Then, stopping any possible attempts at communication, Connor took off at a jog for the factory. Riley went after him. Naeemah's hand settled over her heart, which seemed ready to fly the cage of her chest. She had to follow. But this was her chance to prove she had uses other than... the sexual ones she didn't really want to face. Or being thrown out altogether. They owed her no loyalty and from the stories she'd heard growing up, U.S. soldiers were better at talking about protecting than actually doing it. Before her nerves or sense could get the better of her, Naeemah bolted after the men.

She ran out into a wide factory floor. Several dozen Rankless stood at workstations around the edge of the floor. A few abandoned stations and still machines took up the center of the floor. Another set of stations were also still; these were in a clump at the far end of the chamber, and in each, a corpse slumped over the desk. Their still bodies made a sort of semi-circle.

Naeemah gagged at the sight, seeing flashes of her fellow Companions strewn about the room she'd been revived in. But these were not the bodies of Companions. In place of bright fabrics and beautiful frozen faces, there was dirt encrusted flesh and features made horrific by the twisting agonies of death.

A blur of motion nagged at the corner of her vision, but Naeemah's eyes held firm to the bodies, fixating on one in particular. An older woman lay there, her hair white with age and her body withered and stooped, as if her shoulders had carried weight for years unnumbered. Her death-clouded brown eyes showed nothing but emptiness.

Naeemah shivered and took one step toward the bodies. What had they done to deserve such a death?

Then a piercing scream—the kind that could only come from pain—wrenched her attention over to the area where the blur of motion had been, where her compatriots were standing.

At first, she didn't see the source of the scream; she only saw the drone. The many-armed monster was still for a brief moment and then it burst into movement. Each of its dozens of arms, rather than wriggling as a squid's might, moved with purpose. At the tip of every tentacle-like appendage, a white mark stared out like an eye, and these were disconcertingly pointed toward the Rankless around the factory. Its flat face rippled occasionally, moving as if to form features but only making it halfway, leaving a mushed and monstrous imitation of a human face.

A knife stuck a quarter of an inch into the back of the drone's neck. As she watched, the blade fell away, sparks of electricity dancing off of it.

Connor rushed toward her, gloves she'd never seen before on his hands. On the other side of the drone, Louie lay in a heap on the floor. She only saw him for a moment before Riley's movement shielded her view.

Then Connor dragged her back, away from the room. The drone behind him continued moving, its limbs reaching for the nearby Rankless and the red eye on its forehead blinking rapidly.

*It's calling for help.* Naeemah's brain buzzed, and the sound filled her ears.

Riley scooped Louie up into his arms.

One of the Rankless fell.

Naeemah closed her eyes. *They're dying for what we did.*

Connor's grip wrenched her arm and propelled her backward. "What the hell?" he hissed. The comment was not directed at her.

"I don't know!" Riley shot back. "I don't control him."

"Who gave him those gloves?!" Connor cried.

Naeemah opened her eyes to find herself farther along the empty corridor toward the outside, still moving but slower.

"I don't know! He wasn't ready to start killing drones," Riley said. "He's a kid, Connor! I said this was a bad idea... If he dies..."

"What about the people back in that factory?" Naeemah asked, her voice slow and dreamy. Her eyes still buzzed. "They're dying. Why... Why not stay and defend them?"

"Killing a drone isn't a game," Riley spat.

Connor set his free hand on Riley's arm. "Because as soon as it was wounded," he said to Naeemah, "it called up to the aliens' ships. A load of drones is coming to that spot... and if we get caught, it's all over."

For us. It's all over for us. "But it's over for those people now. It's as bad as if..." She couldn't say it. *As if we'd killed them.*

Connor nodded, his jaw clenched.

A party roared around Tavar. Companions writhed at the edges, dressed in a way meant only to accentuate their nakedness. Some danced together, while others curled over the limbs of drunken Chosen. Half-ranks lined the walls, each with a wide silver platter covered with food or drink or pills.

Ruiti and two other Rank Threes sat at a table with Tavar in the dimly lit front room of the house. The Rank Threes stuck together, being the lowest rank invited to the party, hosted by Third City's Rank Five. All ten of the Rank Fours had come, but as this was a smaller gathering intended for the elite, only some of the hundred Rank Threes had been invited.

Tavar had a feeling that it was Ruiti's purchase of a Companion for such a high price that had earned him access to this gathering. The invitation was as much to get a look at Tavar as to honor his husband.

Certainly, Ruiti had every intent of showing Tavar off. He'd even taken an exchange of credits for Tavar to perform one of the Companion dances at the party. Tavar wasn't particularly looking forward to it. In the training facilities, the dances had all been sexual but had stopped short of touching, given the nanites. But he'd guessed the dances were designed to end in copulation. Not only had he been right, but that was exactly what Third City's Rank Five wanted as entertainment at this party. The programing in his nanites had even been adjusted prior to coming.

If that hadn't been enough proof, the Companions currently on the stage were.

*And I can't afford to disappoint a Rank Five or Ruiti. We need access to these circles if we're to have any hope of challenging the gods.*

One of the Half-ranks came around. A short female with a squat body, her face was covered by a butterfly mask. She offered a tray of drinks to the table. A pile of blue pills rested at the center. Tavar served each of the Chosen their preferences but picked nothing up for himself.

*No way this will go off well if I start drinking.* His eyes trailed the drinks as the Rankless disappeared, then fastened on Ruiti's brown drink. *I wonder if it tastes as much like whiskey as it looks?*

Tavar's hands clasped in his lap, and he pressed his lips together. *How will I make it the whole night? Just a little drink, just enough to dull the edge...*

Ruiti leaned closer. His hand on Tavar's thigh provided a welcome distraction.

"Why are you refusing our host's offerings?" Ruiti's mouth was close to Tavar's ear. "The others notice."

Tavar put his hand on Ruiti's chest in a suggestive manner. It was best everyone think that they were sexually involved. *How the fuck do you talk about something like this without mentioning the past? I can't exactly say, "Hey, in my past life, I was a raging alcoholic who binge-drank his way into every other drug.*

*I would've been dead within the year. Cheers, mate. Glad you purchased me now?"*

"With drinks, it is not the starting I fear, but the stopping," Tavar said.

Ruiti nodded and gave Tavar's leg a fatherly pat.

Tavar hadn't expected the weight off his chest to be so freeing. How long had it been since he'd made a decision and had it respected, supported? Far longer than the months that he'd spent under the gods' rule.

The surrounding conversation flourished, and he joined when he had something knowledgeable to say. Ruiti didn't want him playing the beautiful fool; silence was better than prattle. The current conversation circled around some project the gods had planned that would involve all of the Cities' Rank Fives in a collaboration.

"What do you think, Tavar?" a stern-faced woman called "Veis" asked.

Tavar's eyes widened. It was the first time any of them but Ruiti had addressed him directly. *As if I were a Chosen, not a decoration.* Tavar hadn't really believed it possible, though it was what Ruiti wanted of him.

"Any project that links the fifteen cities has value, regardless of the project itself," he replied slowly. Not having caught the entire conversation, he had to tread carefully. "We're building a community, and the common ground will bring us together."

"Ah, the social aspect from the Companion," Tyiv, another of the Rank Threes, sneered.

"The gods have not ignored the social aspect of human nature," Tavar said.

"He has you there." Veis giggled and drank the steaming concoction in her hands. She sounded like she'd already had enough.

Ruiti motioned to a stage at the forefront of the room. "It's time, Tavar. You'd best head up front."

Tavar smiled as he'd been trained, despite the sinking

feeling in his stomach. Not even Ruiti could protect him from all aspects of being a Companion. He was expected to entertain. Since Ruiti was not using him sexually, he needed to be seen at this, and later more, parties.

He skirted through the room of writhing bodies and perfect smiles and then headed toward the stage. The previous performers had vacated, leaving the spotlighted surface empty. Before he reached it, a woman ascended the steps, her hair in a long, blue coil, dotted everywhere with turquoise gems.

*She's going to be the first woman I sleep with in the gods' world, and I don't even know her.* Her hips swayed as she moved and long, thin legs revealed an olive skin tone. Despite her alluring movements, nothing enticed him in the situation. *But I'll do what must be done.*

Tavar climbed the steps as he slid past the crush of bodies. As he approached, she turned to him. He staggered back, nearly toppling down the stairs.

*She's half my age. She can't be more than sixteen. Only a few years older than Wendy would have been if she'd lived. I can't...* He glanced back at the table of Chosen where Ruiti sipped at some insane concoction. His owner didn't meet his eyes.

"I'm Zem." Her pouty mouth was painted a dark purple and drew his gaze as it moved. It seemed wrong for a child her age to be made up so exotically—like a child who'd gotten into her mother's makeup.

"Tavar." He circled her in the quasi-choreographed dance they'd been assigned earlier that ten-day. A dance he was now certain was intended to end with him violating this girl. It was bad enough that she was a child with her mouth painted like a whore.

*She's someone's daughter.*

She crouched as if stalking prey, her legs spread to display the shapely thighs to their best advantage. Her bare feet glittered with gold paint, etched over the lines of her bones. In fact, her whole body was painted with golden bones in place of clothing. Only a single, scarf-like piece of cloth wound from her groin to loop over her chest.

*Who the fuck bought a child? That's sick. Someone purchased her and then let her go out dressed like this in order to... Shit, am I just as guilty?*

Over her gold-painted shoulder, the rapt attention of many Chosen settled on them. Was her owner watching?

Zem lashed out with her foot, rotating so that the full length of her leg was revealed. Though Tavar's mind was numb, he'd practiced these dances enough for his muscles to know them. He ducked low as her foot arched high and brought his arm up to catch her slender ankle.

*Would it have been better if no one had chosen her? If she'd died?*

As the dance proceeded, the moves became dangerous. They each narrowly avoided blows that could break bones. Each exchange displayed the dancers and often left them in overtly sexual positions. They proceeded until the scarf that provided her only cover unwound in his hand—a slight tug that left her bare.

*I'd rather it be a drone up here. How can I possibly do this? I can't hurt a drone, but her? I wish they'd all stop staring. She must be terrified under that veneer, and they're all lecherously watching.*

She ran at him a final time, landing in his arms, her breasts pressed against his naked chest. The determined eyes that met his showed no fear. The stalking was done, the mock battle at an end. Time to begin the entertainment that Ruiti and her master had agreed to.

*If I refuse and walk away, will it just be me who suffers? I can't refuse to do this without dooming us both.*

She clapped her hand on the back of his head and then tugged him lower for a violent kiss, which ended with her teeth raking over his lower lip.

Like an animal, she pounced and put her mouth by his ear. "Gods' will must be done. I want to live." She sank down his body slowly, letting her nails trail over his skin.

*I've got to push past this, for her. Pretend it's someone else.*

*Anyone else.* He closed his eyes and Jaisa's image rose in his mind, her flashing green eyes and warrior stride.

# CHAPTER 19

Around Jaisa, the rooftop terrace glittered in the star-
light. Each jewel in the heavens danced over the tables
and chairs and was reflected on the mirrored surface of
the floor. Lyra sang wordlessly, her voice soaring with pristine
clarity. Melody plucked at a stringed instrument nearly as big
as her that made a deep resonating twang, carrying over the terrace. Their silver dresses were hooded to shield all but the most
modest glimpse of their pale faces.

The party was going perfectly. The girls seemed happy,
though Jaisa couldn't ask them directly. She decided for once
to simply let herself enjoy the evening—enjoy the little world
she'd built here where she could evade, if not escape, the gods'
control.

Already a few guests littered the floor. Their laughter and
speech was hushed. Neriso had stationed himself in one corner and discussed something intently with another of the Rank
Fives. Jaisa, clothed in the same twinkling silver as the rooftop
was, would have blended in if not for the fire of her hair. She
moved about the room with a tray and delivered glass goblets
filled with a sparkling drink introduced by the gods. Tiny braids
dripped like blood across her shoulder, the metal ends tinkling
with every movement.

She was glad for the distraction of distributing drinks. It
let her freely ogle the people present while enjoying the music,
without too many demands on her for unwanted conversations.

In the households of most Chosen, a Half-rank or Rankless slave would have performed this function, but her service made the party feel intimate, the guests important. They remarked how quaint and personal it was. She didn't have to explain that she owned no Rankless.

Her mouth was dry, and everyone looked oddly inhuman to her. Five of the fourteen had walked through her door, and she had greeted each personally. But after that initial moment, she saw nothing of them except their dispassionate profiles. Each of them had willingly signed over their species and their history. Other than a brief and pleasant *hello*, she could think of nothing to say.

Nor did she feel more bound to their partners, who all seemed like simpering, weak-willed children. *They are as beautiful as dreams and equally insubstantial.*

"The music is lovely," said Servia, one of the fourteen, and she seemed to mean the words. A dreamy expression crossed her face. Her features were sharp and her eyebrows heavy, shadowing her gaze; she didn't hold the dreamy expression easily. When those eyes turned to Jaisa, she winced away. "I'd nearly forgotten how inspiring and uplifting a nice song can be." Her eyes then flicked to the two Companions at her side. Jaisa knew that some of the higher ranked Chosen had multiple Companions, but she'd never seen the practice in person before. "Chilu, Mivshi, you should ask our hostess to dance."

Jaisa gave her best smile as the two golden men moved in her direction. She set her tray down on a silver table and offered her hands. Her eyes remained on Servia even after both hands were claimed by the other Companions. The woman's narrowed stare proclaimed her distrust. *Or is that how she looks at everyone? None of us trust each other. How sad. A world filled with traitors.*

*Yet she trusts the music. How wondrous my girls are to be able to reach over such a divide.*

"You have my thanks," Jaisa said to the Chosen. Neriso had altered the programming of her nanites for the night to allow basic contact. She almost wished he hadn't, that she could refuse this woman. "It'd be a pity for this music to go to waste."

Servia nodded once in a crisp, dismissive fashion and flashed a tight expression probably intended to be a smile.

Painted as gold as Roman gods, the men led Jaisa out onto the floor, and she twirled between them, flitting from one to the other. Mivishi's and Chilu's hands flowed over her like water. The touches were gentle and guiding, and if their charming smiles were a product of training, even Jaisa had to admit the effect was working. The fear that had mounted in her all day dissipated. Chilu's smile widened when Jaisa returned it, and his white teeth parted until it looked as though he might laugh. Mivshi watched her intently; she found his blue eyes on hers every time she glanced over.

So she danced. Whatever it was she was looking for in them, perhaps they were looking for the same.

*We are kindred souls, lost in this hateful world. Why not enjoy the moments we can?* She bent back over Mivshi's arm and let her hair sweep the floor. She stared up into his shimmering face. His eyes were a blue like the deepest ocean and their waters washed away the slime of shame and drowned the memories that haunted her in the depths.

Gold and red frolicked over the dance floor. Pure and powerful, their movements were free, even if they weren't. The flesh under her hands was real and warm. For the first time in months, the flame of desire licked at her. Chilu crushed her against him, and she tilted her face up to him.

*What would it be like to kiss him? No, not just to kiss him, but to choose to kiss him?* His blue eyes didn't shy from her. She spun away, but the warmth of him remained. The music and the physical touch awakened something alive inside her, something hungry. *Would Tavar's arms feel like that? Stop. Don't think about him. There's no point.*

The two men spun her to a stop facing the entrance to the terrace. Mivshi laid a hand on her back. There across the floor stood two newcomers. Had Mivshi and Chilu not stood like rocks of strength, lending her what they could, she might not have gone forward. But they were watching, and if she misbehaved, it might affect them.

Jaisa strode toward the Gods' Folk. Anger churned in her stomach, a wild rage that threatened to tip her over the edge. *Drima. What have they done to her? What did she let them do? She looks like the monster she is now.*

A vision of pushing Drima from the edge of the balcony played before her. *Control yourself. Please, I must get a handle on myself.*

"Drima, welcome." Jaisa lowered her eyes before the head priestess. "I didn't expect you or your companion. Might I know who it is I'm greeting?"

"It's *Priestess* Drima, Jaisa," Drima corrected. She spoke the new language perfectly, and her flawless face was the picture of purity and happiness. It was not the impassioned face Jaisa had last seen, but if possible, it was even more beatific. But where her plastic shell of a garment didn't cover, her body was a network of black lines. The gods ran over her body like an infection, making her revealed flesh asexual in its appeal. "My escort is the Head Priest Tristo."

"Welcome, Priest Tristo," Jaisa said as the music her girls played swelled on the air. "I hadn't realized that either of you were sent invitations, or I would have been more prepared for your arrival." Her gut sank, the awakened life inside her shriveling. This wasn't her world. The music had only disguised it for a moment. *This is the gods' world, and there is nothing I can do about that. I am not free, and I must not forget. I can't dance this away.*

"I trust it's a pleasant surprise?" Drima said. The flash of malice on her face left no doubt how pleasant she believed it was. "I recall you as a rebellious woman. Much must have changed for you to rise so high."

"May I offer you a drink?" Jaisa glanced behind her at the tray of drinks. Even a short break from this horrid woman would suit her.

"You may." Tristo's voice was an even baritone, and it

cooled any remaining heat from Jaisa's body. He was, if any-thing, more desirable than the golden twins—except for the black tattoos over his revealed chest. He was the visual mani-festation of what was weak in them all—beautiful surrender.

Jaisa turned and strode to her tray of drinks. Her girls were on a separate patio, and Jaisa took strength from them. She was all that stood between them and people like Drima. Jaisa had power—not much, but hopefully enough. She returned with the drinks to find Neriso speaking with the Gods' Folk. "Husband," she said demurely.

"You should go dance, Jaisa. I'll be happy to entertain our guests." Neriso lifted two drinks from the tray and handed them over to the priest and priestess.

Drima sipped and stared over Jaisa's shoulder in Lyra and Melody's direction.

"If you wish," Jaisa said, "but we have so much to catch up on." She couldn't leave Drima with the impression that she had something to hide. No, better to inhale the poison now than be struck by surprise later. "Priestess Drima and I went to the same training facility. She just asked after me. Certainly, you'll allow us to chat?"

"If you desire." Neriso's eyes were flat, but his lips thinned, and he pressed them together.

Jaisa took Drima's arm and led her away. The black mark-ings on Drima's skin pulsed—something was running through them. Jaisa stiffened but retained the physical contact. Upon her dais, Lyra lifted her face and her blue eyes showed briefly, watching the priestess with obvious fear.

When had she learned that fear? Did the girls have experi-ence with priestesses?

Neither Jaisa nor Drima spoke, but Jaisa could see the soft smile on Drima's face as they approached the railing overlook-ing the garden. The tame trees growing up to the edge of the rooftop were made wild as a jungle by the night.

"Your husband wishes to keep you away from us. I hope there's no reason, Jaisa. I hope you've put your unjustified rage in place and accepted the gods as our saviors."

"How could I go on living if I hadn't?" Jaisa could only hope having her back to the light would hide her expression. The little light inside her flickered. She couldn't even protect herself.

"No one is killed for not believing," Drima said. She sipped again at her drink—slow and unhurried. "But they *are* our saviors, and belief is rewarded. You could live, my old friend, but how could you be happy? And I want you to be happy."

"I'm overjoyed. How could I be anything else?" Jaisa closed her eyes and pictured a smile that she would never see again. Rick's image lent her strength. "I married a *wonderful* man." These words were hard not to choke on. It was not Neriso who counted as a husband to her. Lyra's voice carried on air scented of honeycakes, reminding her of all she had to be truly glad of. "I'm one of the most powerful people alive, and I can have almost anything I desire. I'm happy."

*Though I'd be happier if I could break this glass and cut your eyes out with it.* Jaisa's mouth curved up at the thought, and she leaned over the banister to hide the expression. But she couldn't even hold on to her rage. It would do no good to kill Drima.

"You haven't purchased a temple for your home," Drima said. "That worries me, my friend. We expect you to lead the way for the lower classes—for all the lesser people."

Jaisa winced. She'd never even considered attending a temple. They were optional. One of the few options that Jaisa had been given. "I intend to walk to a public temple. That way I can witness this world that the gods have built for us," Jaisa replied. *And, priestess, we were never friends. Someday, I'll show you how very much not friends we are.*

"Well, it is good that you have such an intention," Drima said softly. The tone of her voice didn't hide the clear threat. "You have made yourself such a lovely home. And those sweet musicians... Part of your duty to your household is to display piety."

"My girls?" Jaisa said reflexively before she realized how telling such a statement would be. She'd just confirmed the directions of Drima's attack.

"Don't worry. If you were deemed unfit to care for them, they would still find a lovely place in the world. They'd make lovely temple servants. I could take care of them personally."

*I can still protect them. I just need to go to temple.*

The thought didn't bring her strength. She didn't even believe herself anymore. Here she was, in her own home, with only herself and two girls to protect, and she was powerless. And the gods had a whole world of people suffering—girls like Lyra and Melody who hadn't been lucky enough to be purchased and were in the control of the temple. Even if she could keep herself and her charges safe, she was only protecting herself and those two girls. The whole world needed help—especially the underclasses—and Jaisa couldn't do anything except throw a party. How many people did Drima grind under her heel in a day? How many people still suffered without protection? Jaisa turned her head to look at the other woman. Drima stared out into the nighttime garden.

But she couldn't let Drima take Lyra and Melody. Not them.

"Most Companions are attending temple once every ten-day cycle," Drima said.

Jaisa wanted to protest that attending Temple was optional. But like so many other things in the gods' world, it apparently wasn't actually an option. She'd been a fool to think so.

Once again, there was no purpose in fighting. She'd already lost.

"Please, enjoy your drink. I should check in with my other guests." Jaisa turned around and darted across the room. Another trio arrived a few moments later; the Rank Five from Third was the only one absent.

She greeted them, but her mind stuck on her encounter with Drima.

*Must I continually lower myself to groveling on my knees to humanity's destroyers just to save my life? Now I must go to one of their blasphemous temples just to prove I'm not resisting. And all to maintain the system that put fear into Lyra's eyes. Will I be forever writhing beneath their black bodies and crying in pleasure?* Jaisa averted her gaze from the Gods' Folk for the next few hours. She talked, she laughed, she danced, and she avoided.

Finally tired of the effort, Jaisa climbed the few stairs up to a row of chairs and sat down. The others moved like jewels across the floor. Everything was a feast for the eyes. Even the fourteen were colored with the luster of booze and the gorgeous men and women draped over them like expensive garments. Lyra and Melody seemed lost in their music and rapturous smiles touched the corners of their mouths. How easily those smiles could be taken from them. The golden twins danced with five orange-taloned beauties. But at the back of this glamorous façade stood Drima and Tristo.

They were the hands of the gods in this world—Gods' Folk. And they could rip everything away from her so easily.

Jaisa regarded her drink. Bubbles rolled up the side of the glass, whizzing about in the pale liquid. Fizzle, pop, fizzle, pop. The hiss of the carbonation tickled her senses. The bubbles moved from edge to edge of the glass before finally joining the air at the rim.

They were so joyful, right until they met the air. They rushed forward, not comprehending their inevitable doom.

*Reluctant little bubbles. I wouldn't want to enter this world, either.* Fizzle, pop. *Would I hear their song if I leaned down? Does the gods' carbonation fizzle as ours did? Does it speak?*

Jaisa took another sip. All the joy in the room would evaporate as quickly as the bubbles. What of those who never got an escape? She kept thinking what Lyra's and Melody's lives would have been if she hadn't picked them—what their lives were before.

Then she'd think what their lives would be if Drima made good on her threat.

Memories of Ladair's pure faith in her from training returned. And she might not even have made it into this world. She hadn't had any power over Ladair's fate, and now it was clear how very little power she had over her own fate or that of her girls.

One of the five orange-taloned girls stripped off her dress and danced naked on the floor. Her flesh was a warm mocha brown, her full breasts tipped with a darker color. Jaisa downed the rest of her glass, and the bubbles collided as they headed down her throat.

After the party, Ruiti and Tavar took the central transport unit home. The speeding vehicle was filled with drunken voices and made it possible for Tavar to remain silent.

A laugh, too loud, more of a bray, jolted over the buzz of speech every so often, punctuating the journey. Ruiti talked with another Chosen, another Rank Three. His hands moved with more animation than usual, but otherwise, he gave no appearance of being impaired.

*How much did he drink? Is he faking?* Tavar tried to recall how many drinks Ruiti had gone through, but every thought of the party went back to Zem.

*I lived, made it through training to protect the other survivors, to honor Wendy. And now... I'm a fucking monster—we all are. The gods have won. We are corrupt beyond redemption. Can monsters even fight for a better future?* He glanced around the transport. Garish colors displayed intricate designs of every person —like some sort of slutty clown gathering, a circus of perverted freaks.

A bare-chested, glistening man shambled down the aisle.

*No, not clowns—drug-addicted whores, that's what we are.* There was a dreary quality to everything despite the glitz and colors. *This could be a back alley filled with drunks and wasted crack addicts for all the real joy.*

When the transport stopped outside their neighborhood, Tavar hurried away from the perfumed crowd. Ruiti's footfalls plodded behind him. As leisurely as they were, Ruiti obviously had no intent of catching up. Tavar didn't pause until he reached their garden. Once in his neat monument of stones, he knelt, hand on the earth.

Each pebble shone, gravestones that his imagination etched with names of those he'd never known. He found a stone and placed it amid the swirl. *For Zem. For the innocence she lost and the childhood she'll never have.*

"That was a grand affair," Ruiti said, stopping just outside the garden. The moonlight combined with the harsh glow from their house aged him—defining the wrinkles with shadows.

"Yes." Tavar stroked the newly placed stone.

"A lot of drinking."

*Is that what he thinks is bothering me? Being around booze? Logical. I can't expect him to read my mind.* "I expected the drinking."

"So?" Ruiti's hands remained by his side. He had been faking his drunkenness on the transport for the benefit of others.

Tavar clenched his fist. "No more children."

"I don't understand you. There are children. They mostly live below, but they exist."

"Not what I meant. That girl, Zem..." He weighed what words he would be allowed.

"Oh." Ruiti filled in the silence. "She's one of Licin's Companions."

*Third City's Rank Five bought a child? Ruiti couldn't have refused that offer. Still, I can't do it again.* "I thought Licin purchased that woman Calri. Isn't she over forty?"

"Yes. Licin purchased the youngest and the oldest Companions."

Tavar sighed and looked up at the twinkling stars. His hand moved to his chest, where once a network of scars had wound and crisscrossed—the only physical reminder of Wendy's death, now gone.

"Please," Tavar said. "No more children. Women, dandy. Men, sure. If some eighty-year-old Chosen makes an offer to trade for me—fine. But no more children."

Ruiti sighed. "You're both children to me."

"I'm twenty-eight."

"I can make no promises."

"Understood."

Ruiti paused, his ruddy face puckering in thought. "I realize you wish to help others. But it won't work like this. You have to forgive yourself first. If you don't see your own worth, you will never survive what comes."

He didn't know the things that Tavar would need to forgive. And Tavar saw that tree again and heard the crunch of metal. "My life isn't worth much."

"Then you'll throw it away too easily. You'll never be strong enough to lead in this new world. Did I really choose so badly? The only way to care for others is to care for yourself."

Tavar had nothing to say to that.

Ruiti walked into the house, leaving Tavar alone with his little tombstones. He stared at each monument to the dead and wondered why he'd been left alive when they hadn't been. The sound of Riuti returning didn't register with him until Riuti at his side. Tavar jumped and looked up.

Riuti held out a portable computer with the screen facing Tavar. On it glowed a picture of a Chosen and a Companion and an article. Tavar didn't bother reading it. Instead, he looked up to Riuti for an explanation.

"You're looking to make a difference... to help. I get that." Riuti nodded his chin down to the screen. "You knew her in training?"

Tavar returned his gaze to the picture. He almost replied with "no" until his second glance at the scarlet-haired vixen beside Fifth City's Rank Five. There, under the makeup and Jessica Rabbit cascade of hair, he recognized her. "Jaisa. Yes. We were on friendly terms."

"There's a contact we haven't been exploiting."

"She's just a Companion."

Riuti laughed. "Just? She's the Companion of a Rank Five. You want to make a difference? She has. Of all the cities, Fifth City treats their Half-ranks the best. And that is down to accommodations your friend asked for to help her household's Half-ranks. She made it the vogue to treat them almost like people. In some ways, she is as powerful as her husband."

Unspoken between them lay the idea that whatever efforts lay ahead, she would be an invaluable ally. But Tavar didn't want to use Jaisa. She deserved some peace, not more demands. He couldn't say that. Grudgingly, he replied, "I could contact her."

"She was the one who in the Choosing spat at another Companion?" Riuti's eyes sparkled.

Subtext being that Jaisa would want to help. Of course she would. That didn't mean she needed the pressure on her shoulders. Still, Tavar smiled at the implication. He wouldn't need to use Jaisa. If it came down to it, she would want to support any efforts they made. And he need not ask her for anything unless it became dire. "I'd actually like to speak to her. We were... almost friends."

"Wonderful. With a contact like that, I should be able to be more selective with what engagements I take on for you." Riuti paused, rubbing a hand through his hair. "Take what time you need."

"Give me a moment out here."

Ruiti stepped inside, and Tavar moved his little tombstones.

Later that night, Tavar typed a message. With no reason to expect privacy, there wasn't much to say. He wrote that he'd been purchased by a Rank Three—a fact she would already know if she'd bothered to look him up—and that his Chosen was involved in city planning and the general layouts of the cities. He commented on her Half-ranks and her wisdom in choosing such striking creatures. It felt dirty to refer to the two girls as anything other than human children, but in written form he needed to conform. After stating that he was doing well and sending well wishes, he sat staring at the communiqué.

It seemed empty. Tavar tapped his fingers, remembering his dance earlier in the night and the train ride with all the people who'd been no more than costumed performers. He couldn't send anything to her without something that was both meaningful and permitted, something that spoke to the ways that this new world was slowly breaking all of them. From what he recalled of Jaisa, she didn't see herself as strong. She might need help as much as the child he'd danced with... Only this time, he could do something other than cause pain.

Jaisa would be struggling out there with the eyes of the city on her—and yet she'd be unable to act freely. She needed to know she was making a difference.

He typed out: "I hear you are quite the trendsetter in Fifth City. I hope some of the treatment policies you used for your Half-ranks take root over here. It makes sense that they should have some rights—they are Half-ranks. I'm impressed that you sway an entire city."

Then to keep the tone light for the overseers who still stalked their every move: "Let me know what your next trend will be—I'd love to be ahead of the curve."

Before he could question the wisdom of it, he sent the message.

# CHAPTER 20

A change was needed, desperately. Jaisa sat in her room staring into a mirror. Tavar's message lingered on her mind. There was so little there—certainly nothing to pull her away from the necessity of her trip to the temple. She wondered if he had visited one... she couldn't imagine him believing. But it didn't matter what they believed.

It was time to dress... and she had to go to temple. Drima and her kind had won. All the little things that Jaisa had been so proud of and worked so hard on meant nothing—she'd never make any real difference for those who were suffering.

She'd never be free.

With one shaking hand, Jaisa touched her long, blood-red hair. How pointless the color seemed now. It made a claim to life, to true life, that she wasn't sure she could rightfully make.

She flipped her finger across the screen, requesting a change. Something short and brown would suit her mood.

A single word flashed across the screen: Denied.

She tried again, this time opting for grassy green hair. This two was denied. After trying three more variations, Jaisa was certain something was happening. She wasn't allowed to change her hair. Why?

Wasn't it bad enough she had to go pay lip service to her rapists, torturers, and conquerors and call them "gods"? She couldn't even control her own hair!

With a balled fist, Jaisa struck out at the computer. Her

hand ricocheted back at her, aching, but the screen remained unharmed.

Jaisa cradled her hand against her chest, seething. She needed to talk to Neriso before her trip to the temple. He would be the only one who could explain this. But first, she needed to be dressed.

Using the hand that didn't hurt, Jaisa ordered up a feather cloak and a white tunic, its plunging neckline decorated with matching feathers. *As if I'm a bird.* It would have been laughable if it weren't so depressing.

Jaisa strode out into the garden, conscious with every stride of Alpha's presence behind her, following her toward his master. Of all the decisions she'd made since coming to Neriso's house, the guard was one of the few she truly questioned. She'd seen no evidence of softness since the day she'd bought him. Her imagination must have conjured Alpha's fondness for the girls because now he was the image of rigidity and followed protocol in everything. Every misstep she took his eyes followed. *He follows me around like a prison guard tailing a criminal. Does he think I will hurt Neriso?*

Omega worked the edge of the garden, looking for imaginary intruders.

Jaisa forced a deep breath of the cold air into her lungs, in an attempt to calm the anger bubbling inside her. *I cannot afford to be angry. Not with Neriso.*

Without Neriso's support, she'd be dead. That was how little worth she held in the world. If she could get him on her side, maybe something could change—in the moment, she couldn't guess what. But as hopeless as things were, her angering Neriso would affect the twins as well as her. Yet in putting a restriction on her hair, he'd taken away the one avenue of real control she had. Buckling under completely to him might be her only option, but she couldn't do it. There had to be some way to retain the little control she had—to retain her soul in this world.

The upcoming conversation with him would be difficult.

The sun crested the horizon. Its bright light made the world look warm, though the morning chill remained over-whelming. Nothing Jaisa owned was meant for cold, and goose-bumps rose over her body. A Companion's wardrobe was in-tended to titillate, not be practical. But she couldn't wait to speak with Neriso until it warmed—he'd be long gone to work by then. She hugged her cloak of loose feather strands around her.

"A strange thing happened when I chose my outfit this morning," Jaisa said. She sat down beside Neriso on a garden bench. Her hand fell on his thigh.

He leaned closer and the heat of his body called to her. She wondered if his warmth could open up an answering warmth in her. Would his breath on her neck ever make her heart race? The slits in her short, white skirt parted, the fabric dropping to the side, revealing upper thighs—covered in gooseflesh. His eyes burned as they moved over her.

*If only his desire warmed me. If only I wanted him. This life would be so much easier, even have a modicum of pleasure in it.* Yet it was Tavar and Rick and odd mixes of the two who filled her dreams—the only thing they had in common was that she couldn't have either. Neriso was her only option. And he left her as cold as the morning chill.

Maybe he sensed it. Perhaps that was why he treated her with such clinical distance.

"Husband?" she said as sweetly as she could.

"Yes?" Neriso set his hand on hers and welcomed her as she leaned against his chest.

"I thought it was high time for a change. Last ten-day at the party, I saw some lovely styles to try out. Only when I asked to go blonde, my request was denied." She pressed closer to him, welcoming the furry fabric of his coat against her revealed chest. "Why can't I change my hair color?"

"Yes, I could've told you about that." Neriso stroked her hair.

"Please, tell me now, husband?" She resisted snapping.

What little power could be hers in the world came from him and he was limiting it rather than extending it. Anger wouldn't help—somehow she had to find a way to get him on her side.

"When you say that, it doesn't sound like a question." His arm moved around her. "This was a simple mix-up. It was the first ten-day after bidding finished. The fourteen Rank Fives were all given a gift directly from the gods."

"Yes?" Jaisa said. *What does a god's gift have to do with me? I didn't sell my soul to them to earn anything.*

"In order for all our Companions to stand out, we were allowed to pick a trait and reserve it. This service is now available to Chosen other than the fourteen. They just have to pay a great deal for it. But we were given the distinction for free."

"And you saved this hair color for me," Jaisa whispered. Her hair, which had been her sign to herself that her heart was still beating, that they had not stolen her life yet, now even *that* was theirs. *They own even my cry against them.*

*He owns it.*

"Yes," Neriso said. "You had your hair that shade every time I saw you."

"And now I must always have this hair." Jaisa touched the red braid that trailed down over her feathered shoulder. "What sort of things could you choose?"

"Anything unnatural in appearance. Servia chose that silly golden skin shimmer for her men. And Kilias reserved orange nails for his five girls. Do you understand? It's all very specific. Other women can choose red hair, but that shade is yours. I thought nothing of it."

"There was no need to tell me, I suppose." Jaisa lifted her head from his shoulder and turned her face to the sky so he could not see the expression on her face. She didn't even have the right to *know* about decisions someone else was making about her body. Had she been wrong? No. Somehow she had to make this privilege her own.

"More importantly, Jaisa, why did you want to change? I specifically chose a woman who was distinct. I don't need you to look like other Companions."

"I wanted to take a look at the temple." *Not a task I want to be myself for.* She could not hide her attendance from them, but maybe she could hide it from herself. She could bar her soul from traveling with her, and only her body would enter that black house.

"I need you recognizable to show our presence in temple," Neriso said.

"You want your wife to seem properly pious?"

"The way Priestess Drima looked at you gave me pause. I want it noted that you go to temple and pray. And that's what you intended to do, isn't it?"

"Of course, husband. I do wish you had *told* me that they were coming to the party." Jaisa stood and pulled away from him.

She had to remember he was as much their creature as Drima. One of the first to break, to bow his head to them. It was foolish to think she could win Neriso over. Not when she didn't understand him, when Drima and her cronies understood more about him than she ever could, isolated as she was.

"You invited all the other important human figures in the world. Did you want us to insult them?"

He flexed his jaw. It was an angry motion, and Jaisa did her best to push down her annoyance. Only angry retorts came to mind, so she bit them back. *I can't exactly tell him what I think of the Gods' Folk... or of him.*

"You should've thought to invite them," he continued when she didn't fill the silence. "I didn't know you would do your best to embarrass us the minute she showed up."

"We don't have the best history."

"Keep that under wraps, Jaisa. You'll go to temple, and when you do, you'll do absolutely nothing to hide who you are," Neriso said. "It doesn't matter how much everyone else at that party adored you if the Gods' Folk turn the gods from us."

"Of course. I'm sorry."

"And so am I." Neriso stood and kissed her forehead. "I'll

do better not to keep things that pertain to you to myself. You would have done better if you'd known."

"Will you come to temple with me? It'll be a relaxing walk." *Maybe a brisk walk will even keep me warm.*

"Why a walk? You could ride there."

"The walks are for the same reason as the hair, husband." To be seen, but the drones could hear words, so she didn't say it. Better the gods and their servants think she was doing all of this for another purpose. She would give them proper words. "Reminds me I'm alive."

"I have work. You must walk alone. Would you like one of my men with you?"

Jaisa smiled and shook her head. She didn't risk a glance at Alpha, who stood by the bench glowering down at them. *He could crush me like a bug.* "What would they be protecting me from?"

"Have a good day," Neriso said. "I'll be at work when you return."

Work. He was always at work. That must be the key, both to him and to having a real effect. It wasn't enough to just protect herself and her girls. She saw that. But helping the world at large meant seeing it, understanding it. Perhaps she could extend her influence over Neriso. The things he did with his work must have been making a significant impact on the world. Maybe she could affect those. Somehow.

Even if she came to understand him, he might never support her. But through his work, she could still access information and the more she learned, the more chance she had to find a use for herself in this world.

Jaisa took a few steps away from him. "Maybe tomorrow I can go to work with you?"

"Not tomorrow. Soon." His footfalls sounded up the path back toward the house, cutting off anything she might have said in response.

"Please, husband." Her voice was nearly a whisper.

He stared at her, cold and distant, then slowly, he smiled.

"Not tomorrow, Jaisa. But I will arrange a visit soon. There are things I'd welcome showing you. For now, take your trip to the temple."

Jaisa sighed and wrapped her arms tightly around herself, trying to conserve some heat. *Might as well start out now. If I put this off, I may never make it. Rick would laugh, knowing this is what it took to get me to church.*

The door to the house swished shut after Neriso and Alpha entered. Shortly after, Omega followed them in, leaving Jaisa alone in the garden. A tiny stream of music trickled down from the roof, where the girls must have just been beginning to practice.

This was one trip she had no intention of taking them on. If she could take on the horrors of the temple for them, she would.

*Off to church.* She pulled the edges of her white cloak around her shoulders and let the strains of music wash over her. The feathers of the cloak fell in loose strands around her, doing little to conserve heat. *How many times did I go to meet Rick after church? Sit there listening to the choir's last song from the parking lot. Every time we met that way, it was the same old fight. He didn't even ask me to believe, just to go with him, meet everyone and play nice for a morning.*

*I should have gone with him. Just to make him happy. Why didn't I ever give in? Not every battle was worth fighting and now that there are real battles, I can't even fight.*

Jaisa set out on foot across the marble city. The sunlight spilled out from the horizon and she followed, staying in the bright rays for the meager warmth they offered. There was an oppressive silence in the air. The gods' roads spread out in front of her and buildings loomed above, a gleaming ghost town. Wherever the people were, they were not on the streets. The hum of the train occasionally buzzed by or the whir of engines in the sky as the Chosen commuted to work, but there was not another soul on the marble walkways.

Strands of Jaisa's hair worked out of her braid and danced

in the gentle breeze. She leaned over a silver rail and looked down. A silvery gray mist obscured whatever was below the arched bridge she walked on. *We might as well be floating on clouds.*

She listened for noises from below but could hear nothing. *There are people down there. Most of humanity's survivors are down below that mist hidden from me. Those people I didn't purchase, they live their lives in that world I've never even seen. What are their lives like?* Certainly, they did not live in the elaborate prison she did. A stab to her heart told her that their lives were bound to be much worse.

*I'm lucky.* The words didn't fit no matter how she turned them. Whether she lived above in the gods' city or below, *lucky* was the last word she'd use for her life.

Other than the occasional Rankless servant, the inhabitants of the world below remained invisible. It was as if they didn't exist. As if nothing existed except the spotless beauty of the marble arches above. She watched the mist roll.

Was there anyone down there? Had they all been killed silently in the night? What if after the servants had been purchased, the rest of that world had been wiped clean? The thoughts darted across her mind, but she didn't believe them. Somewhere down there, the rest of humanity toiled, suffered, hated, and lived.

Lyra and Melody would have been down there. Others like them still were.

Jaisa leaned farther. Even the swirling mist that separated the world below from her view was beautiful. She lifted the long, white skirt she wore with one hand so that it cleared her knees. Tucking the cloth inside the golden belt hanging around her hips, she gripped the metal rail with both hands and swung herself up. Once her slippered feet were flat on top of the rail, and she had steadied herself, she watched the swirls of white.

Her new vantage point allowed her a vague image of the mist falling away in the distance. The mist appeared to topple off the edge of the world. The wind pressed against Jaisa's back, urging her to jump.

*Would I die? Escape this hell? But no. Nothing is that simple.*

There would be some sort of precaution to keep drunken people from killing themselves on the world below. If she fell or jumped, the mist would catch her, or some sort of netting below the mist would.

Jaisa strode along the rail. With the ghost street above and the mist below, she placed one foot after the other. Off to the side, she heard the train approaching. She waved at the tinted windows. When her eyes left the train, a drone's figure approached, silhouetted in the sun.

The rail was cool beneath her feet, and she suddenly found every reason in the world to watch the silver peep out from between her toes. The drone moved smoothly a few feet behind her, just close enough she could always see him from the corner of her eye.

When the temple came into view, a tall, black building amid the sea of graceful white, Jaisa turned to face the city once more. Her eyes settled on the drone, whose face was doubling hers. She extended her hand.

"Help me down."

The drone approached and offered its hand. Using the help, she swung down. The drone remained still. Its red eye flashed evenly.

"Is there anything else you need?" it asked.

"No. Thank you for your assistance. I'll go in now," Jaisa responded before entering the temple.

The inner sanctuary gleamed, and she stood in awe of the cold, alien beauty. The ceiling dripped with black columns, each studded with red and white. The floor was a clear black glass, the surface as slick as wet ice beneath her feet.

Around the room knelt people. Most, she noted, were spouses like her. The Chosen had no need to come here. They were represented by their pretty counterparts. She would bet that in the evening after work, the temple was flooded with Rank Ones and Twos who hadn't bothered to purchase Companions. Jaisa stepped farther inside the chamber as a priestess approached.

"Priestess," Jaisa said, bowing her head.

"Lady Jaisa." The priestess wore a shroud of translucent black. Beneath its flimsy folds, the form of her body was anything but hidden. Black metal circled her waist and decorated the flesh of her bare arms. This metal moved as the god's skin did. "Welcome to my temple. The grand priestess Drima said to expect you. I'm happy you've come."

"I shouldn't have waited so long." Jaisa averted her eyes to avoid gagging. Around the edges of the metal, the woman's bloody skin lifted. They had cut her open to pour in that moving metal, and she'd let them. *If I'd met Drima in the daylight, would she have looked the same?*

"Come. I'll show you around the temple and you can pick a regular time to visit if you wish." The priestess motioned with one mutilated arm. "I'm the premier priestess of this temple. Should you ever arrive here and I'm not present, regardless of your preestablished schedule, feel free to ask one of the drones or other priestesses for me. I'm always at your disposal."

"What name should I ask for?" *I must be more important than I thought for her to offer such a thing. But why? Can it really be just that I'm Neriso's Companion? My power doesn't stretch far in my own home, but I should see how far I can push it here.*

There were only fourteen temples like this one. There was one primary temple like this one for all fourteen of the gods' cities. The smaller cities, which didn't merit a Rank Five, all had temples, and each had their own priests and priestesses. Within the fourteen cities, there were also scores of smaller temples devoted to individual neighborhoods. This priestess would rank far above any of them except for the other thirteen priestesses of the primary temples.

"I have chosen a nameless path, so I have none to give." The priestess waved her hand for Jaisa to follow. They crossed the slick floor and through the echoing hall with its dim lights and columns of obsidian. Together, they entered a second chamber, the walls covered with screens. Each displayed a rotating set of images.

Jaisa covered her mouth to hide her expression of horror. These pictures were terribly akin to the horrible ones they'd been shown in training—death, destruction, and human frailty exploited.

"This room is a remembrance of how we were saved." The priestess touched the edge of one of the pictures—an image of a city crumbling as giant insect-like machines tore down everything in their path.

A few people knelt in the corners of the room. Jaisa imagined the impact of her foot into their spleens, their heads, or anywhere soft. They chose to be here, to kneel here, to worship. Her muscles tensed and she forced herself to relax before the nanites activated.

She told herself that no one had had any more choice than she did.

Images from the day the gods had arrived rotated with others of them setting up the new world—destroying the old. One of the pictures was of hundreds of frightened human faces staring up at a god for the first time. Feeling small and inadequate, Jaisa moved on. There were so many people out there who needed a reason to live on, so many people who needed help. But Jaisa had nothing to offer those faces.

Jaisa paused at a screen with both sound and picture. A newscaster sobbed with her makeup smeared over one cheek, crying out, "God help us." It was not the gods in black she was calling to. Jaisa pressed her jaws together so hard that it ached.

"Follow me," the priestess said.

The next room was larger and glass cups twinkled from waist-height pillars scattered around. In each cup, a few tablespoons of thick, black liquid waited. There was nothing else in the room but these glasses and a black flame in a chalice at the center of the room.

"We call this our prayer room," the priestess said. "Here the gods are kind enough to let us remember and even pray for those who were lost. I prayed for my brother here and asked that the gods contemplate redeeming his soul, even though he fell with the wicked on judgment day. They allow us this and evaluate our prayers."

"You're saying if I pray for someone I knew, the gods will consider saving their soul?" Jaisa touched the rim of a glass. A sharp netting covered the opening, and it stung her fingertip.

"Yes, it's marvelous! All you need to do is donate a credit to the temple coffers, and you will be allowed one prayer cup every five ten-days for the year."

"I pay you for the service?"

"Oh, yes." The woman nodded. Her eyes appeared vacant and soulless.

*Can someone be nothing but a void inside? If so, this idiot is in the running. I can't let it only be fools like this in power.*

*I'll bow down today, no matter how deeply I must bend. I'll reassure Neriso of my faith and pray that my true faith is rewarded. Lyra and Melody need me.*

"Then I shall. Request it of my husband. He'll agree to the expense." Jaisa pursed her lips and waved the priestess off. Once the other woman vacated the room, Jaisa drew in a deep, shuddering breath.

Jaisa waited, staring at the slush inside the cups. She would not offer a single prayer to the black gods. She would certainly not pray to them to save souls that *they* had damned. But this was a matter of appearances. When the priestess returned, she lifted one of the cups and brought it over to Jaisa.

"Thank you." Jaisa lifted the cup.

Once it had changed hands, the priestess swept off the cover, which melted and crawled up her arm, joining the rest of the black goo running in channels over her skin.

"I drink it?" Jaisa asked.

"Yes. Who will you pray for?"

"My cat," Jaisa said, tipping the glass between her lips. She hadn't had a cat, hadn't even liked cats, but there was no way she was feeding anything she actually cared about to this place.

The silence of the church unnerved her, and she missed the music her girls made. She hoped the black liquid wouldn't do anything to her... wouldn't change her or poison her. But it didn't matter. She had to drink it for her girls. She had to prove she was compliant. The bitter sludge clung to her mouth and throat. After gagging and forcing a wave of nausea down, Jaisa met the priestess' eyes. "My poor cat. I'm sure the gods knew what they were doing when they killed *billions* of people, but why the cats? I'm sure that was an oversight. And now I can't even buy a new one. Did you know, they don't offer pets?"

"Your cat?" the priestess said, her nose slightly curled.

"Of course my cat." Jaisa swallowed several times, trying to dislodge the slime. Why not spout their ridiculous party line? Mocking crept into her next words, but she did her best to shove her hatred down. "Everything else that the gods took, they have replaced with better than I ever could've dreamed. My husband is one of the most powerful men in the universe. My friends are either beautiful or brilliant, and I never have to wait in line again. I did hate lines. But my poor cat. I just don't see what purpose her death served."

The priestess bowed. No longer entirely vacant, she appeared disturbed. After asking pardon, she fled the room.

Jaisa touched the cups as she circled the rooms. The liquid sloshed inside as she stared into its darkness, which didn't even hold a reflection.

*No. I'll do better than pray for the ones I love. I don't know how yet, but I will.*

*I need to help those they left behind.*

# CHAPTER 21

Connor stalked around the edge of camp. At night, the rain sometimes came, and this night was one of those. The raindrops fell heavy, and the canopy of leaves over Connor's head made a pleasant pattering noise. If he closed his eyes, it almost sounded like rain on the roof of a car. The leaves were thick and answered the pelting with a metallic ting. Without warning, Riley fell into step with him.

"Not time yet," Connor said. It was only an hour into his portion of the night watch.

"I couldn't stay there. Naeemah tried to join me at the fire." Riley shrugged his skinny shoulders. "I've got a lot on my mind. Her simpering is just too much."

Connor leaned against the tree beside him and studied Riley where he stood streaked with rain. Riley had always been thin; he looked emaciated now. His eyes glowed with a feverish light from beneath his rain-speckled glasses. The close call with Louie had only made things worse. *He'll burn out if he keeps going like this.*

"How's Louie doing?"

"Ashamed. Shaken. Confused." Riley shook his head. "It's my fault he did it. We were going over the science of why the gloves work and how they stop the electrical charge from the drones. I guess he got it in his head to make his own."

"And if we're dealing out blame, it's my fault he decided to attack. I'm the one always complaining we need more people to fight."

Riley gave him a crooked smile. "Blame is easy to dish out." Then he glanced behind him toward where Naeemah would likely be sitting at the fire. "That's one thing about our Companion. At least she isn't doling out blame."

"I doubt the missus would mind you sitting in camp with a pretty woman." Connor twisted his own wedding ring as he said it. *Enjoying her company is no sin, even for Riley. Is he afraid it will be more? Would it? Doesn't matter to me if that's where her interests lie.*

"I'll be faithful to Julia until she's avenged," Riley snapped. "And even if I did intend to fool around with other women, I certainly wouldn't sleep with Naeemah. She's scared and looking for protection."

"Is it so bad that she wants a protector?" *Is it? Doesn't rub me right, either. My Rai never needed or wanted protection, but not all women can be like that. I doubt Naeemah was raised the same, either.*

"You looking to protect her?"

"My guess is she comes from someplace that didn't give her a lot of freedom. It probably isn't natural for her to imagine taking care of herself." Connor shook his head and moved back into the rain. Maybe the cool water would put out the fire that lit in his blood just thinking about the camp's new guest. Having a practically naked woman thrown in his face after months with nothing but men worked on his mental state and he couldn't stop seeing her that way, no matter how much cloth they draped over her. Connor didn't want to test his own theory about it not mattering.

It wasn't that he feared having sex with another woman after Rai. But if he did, it shouldn't be someone flashy, someone beautiful, or someone he could have feelings for. Better to sleep with one of the Rankless. At least then if Rai was looking down, she'd know she hadn't been replaced.

They turned at the edge of the camp to face toward the city.

Riley followed him with his hands plunged deep into his

pockets. The rain poured down, obscuring their view of the small camp just inside the forest, a few minutes' walk from the undercity, where all the Rankless people lived.

"She's a sweet girl," Riley said. It sounded like an apology.

"Maybe, but that's not all. If we let her grow into her own, she could be a real asset. There's steel in her. She made a conscious choice to die. That kind of backbone coupled with a face that could go to the uppercity... She's golden."

"For revenge, yes," Riley said. "For a lover? She's been acting like a whore for the better part of a year."

"Who's talking about sleeping with her?" Truth was, he'd never been one for 'sweet' women. He wanted them with backbone. That was why Rai had been so perfect for him; she had been as much a warrior as him in her own way. As long as Naeemah stayed sweet and passive, he could get his reaction under control.

"She's beautiful." Riley pushed his glasses up on his nose and splashed through a puddle after Connor. "And with the lack of decent clothes, a man would have to be blind not to appreciate her to some degree. That's as far as it'll go."

Naeemah's lips smiled in his mind, and he thought of her lashes fanning across her flawless skin. As much trouble as it was keeping her in camp despite her lack of even basic survival skills and the constant worry over the aliens or their servants coming for her, she was entertaining. And Riley had a point, even if he didn't know it. How could it hurt to appreciate her?

"She is a good distraction," Connor said.

"And nothing like Rai."

Connor's fists clenched, and Naeemah's image disappeared. "Rai's dead, and if you compare the two again... I'll avenge my wife. But she's not here, is she? She's rotting somewhere in the remains of the base under all of the damn alien flowers."

"Have you considered..."

Connor heard the unspoken words. *Have you considered that she might have survived?* "No. They destroyed the base and everyone on it. Just because we didn't see her doesn't mean she survived. Even if she had somehow made it past that, and even if she was somehow deemed fit for one of the alien 'ranks,' she would have fought them. She would have fought them to her last breath. The best I can hope for is she got a lucky knife in before they killed her."

"I don't think I could've given up hope in your place. Burying Julie and the kids took everything I have, but if I hadn't? I'd still be searching."

"Haven't given up." Connor growled. "I know she didn't make it, but that doesn't mean I can believe it."

*And that hurts the worst. Thinking that she could still be out there and still suffering, thinking that I could have saved her. She could be mourning me.* That's *a knife in the heart.*

The two men stood in silence under the trees and felt the occasional fat raindrop as it slipped through the canopy.

"I'm going to take Louie on a trip," Riley announced. "I can't stay here with him. I need to get him away from this failure... I need to get *me* away, too. We're just wallowing in an abyss."

"But I need you here."

"No, you *want* us here. But there are real reasons we should go, not just emotional ones. We're running low on supplies, and I need equipment. Hopefully, I'll unearth some sort of literature to help me study our machine men properly. I want to take the kid back to some of the ruins. Maybe there will be something to find."

"He's learning quickly," Connor said. He sighed and rubbed the bridge of his nose. "It would be good for him. It's funny, you doing all this studying."

"Funny?"

"Not in a laughing way, but all those years you put off going back to school and getting your doctorate... and now..."

Riley laughed, not an amused sound, but instead dry and caustic. "I'm finally the man Julie wanted me to be? Yeah. Doesn't seem funny."

"Do me a favor? Since you're leaving me to deal with Naeemah."

"Depends on what."

"Look around for one of those sari things the Muslim women wear." Connor rubbed at the bridge of his nose again. *Is she Muslim? I never thought to ask. I should. We should set something up for her, a place to worship if she wants.*

"Indian women, Connor, that's what *Indian* women wore. For Muslims I think you'd want a hijab. Is that what you want? A gift for Naeemah?"

"Yeah. Both? I don't know. I think she'd be more comfortable."

"You mean *you* would be more comfortable." Riley laughed, apparently more confident with the idea of her now that his plan to head out was in the open.

"No. She's covered enough for my comfort. I meant that *she* would be more comfortable. It's a simple thing to make her feel at home." Connor smiled into the darkness. He wanted her to feel at home... and had no intention of looking deeper into that desire.

Neriso's workplace was clearly not intended for Companions.

But she'd finally made it there. Neriso had been good on his promise of "soon."

The factory vents chilled Jaisa, blowing up through shafts in the floor. She'd expected something more like a lab of the old world. Instead, she found herself in a near-freezing hallway where the floor seemed to be a thick gel. With each step, she was afraid her shoes would simply sink through, and the lack of sound unnerved her. Not only did the blueish gel of the floors drink up the sounds of footsteps, but also of voices. Unless a person was within six feet of her, she couldn't hear them. So instead, she heard her teeth chatter.

Neriso walked beside her, keeping a leisurely pace, which

did nothing to help bring heat. Given the nature of the space, it made sense it needed to be cold; inside every lab room that lined the hall were chemicals and lab tables covered with odd specimens she couldn't identify. Jaisa hugged her loose robes close around her.

The Chosen men and women around her did not seem to notice the chill, but then they were not dressed like a Companion. Their clothing was sturdier and more capable of keeping warmth in. A man in a lab coat worn over long pants and what looked like a sweater breezed past, nodding at Neriso but not meeting his eyes. Jaisa rubbed her arms absentmindedly as she followed Neriso.

Three of the gods' Chosen watched her as she passed their lab. They paused their work, and one came to the door to continue observing her. From the blatant lust in the look, she guessed he did not have a Companion of his own. Jaisa endured the Chosen's gaze boring into her back until they rounded a corner. Few spouses bothered to stop by the labs. Not many cared enough, and not many would have the clearance that Jaisa did. She would come away from this place knowing more of its secrets than any Rank One or Two would ever hope to gain.

Hopefully, some of that knowledge would enable her to find another path. At the moment, she didn't really know how to move on.

According to Neriso, the rules regarding what the gods permitted a Companion to know were simple. They could learn whatever their husband or wife had clearance to know, but they could never speak of anything above a Rank One's clearance. When the punishment for doing so was death by drone, keeping secrets wasn't a problem.

She'd suspected as much.

So as she walked past the other labs, shivering and holding her arms, she tried to look like she deserved to know secrets. *I don't belong here.*

Neriso kept his focus ahead, explaining nothing and not seeming to notice the path they took. But at last, his pace quickened, and he glanced over at her every few moments, excitement brightening his face. The hallway had a slightly upward curve, and Jaisa wondered how many "floors" they'd already ascended in height.

She doubted he walked this way often. He was doing it for her, to show her the labs.

*He isn't so bad. If only that were enough, and I could be happy. But I need more.* She needed to be worthy of every life lost to the gods. Just staying alive wasn't enough. Something had to be done. As long as there were others like her, people out there suffering, something needed to be done.

*I can't help if I don't know what's happening. As they used to say, "Knowledge is power," and there has to be something here that will help me use what power I have.*

The hallway ended in a large, red door with white lines painted over its surface. Neriso stopped and held a hand out to a box on the side.

Jaisa stared at the door, which was twice her height and equally wide. *It's like a giant stop sign. I bet not many people come in here.*

When the red portal opened, Neriso hurried her through and as she'd suspected, the short hallway seemed empty. A dozen rooms shot off to the side with one blue door at the end of the hall. They proceeded past labs and a large empty office space she assumed to be Neriso's.

Neriso keyed a code into the door and entered. Jaisa slipped in behind him. Pristine white curtains divided off sections of the tiled room inside. Something living seemed to move within the tiles and she forced herself not to look too closely. Instead, she took in the room as a whole. It reminded her a bit of a hospital, beds sectioned off by flimsy fabric that blocked sight but nothing else. When Neriso pulled one curtain aside, Jaisa was not surprised to see beds inside the enclosed area.

She stepped up next to Neriso. One pale white hand flew up to her mouth as she stared down at the forms on the bed.

Her eyes presented a puzzle she could not solve. Each of the four beds contained the body of a woman hooked to wires and tubes. Each woman was identical to each other, and each was identical to Jaisa.

The women in the hospital beds made no movement aside from the rise and fall of their chests. Yet their faces, which looked like her own, pursued her inside her mind even when she turned her head away for respite. Not that Neriso's face did anything to reassure her—like a cat who'd given its master a dead rat on their pillow. *He wants me to say how well he's done.*

"I don't understand." Jaisa returned her gaze to the women. The women's faces looked vacantly upward. All four mouths hung slack and the hands, palm up, relaxed by their thighs. "What is this?"

"They're you, in a sense. We decided for a cloning project to recreate the spouses of the Rank Fives." Neriso's hand stroked one of the women's cheek, and his words poured out in an excited jumble. "They aren't you, of course—just empty vessels, useful for medical purposes and for finetuning human cloning techniques—but there's nothing inside. They'll be good for organ transplants, though. They lack thinking minds. We haven't found a way to make a fully functional adult brain."

Jaisa shook her head and stared down at her own body. It was a perfect replica. If anything, the specimen was even more perfect. Everything was fresh, unsullied by the world, and as Neriso said, it was vacant.

"How do they live without brains?" Jaisa asked. Her hands trembled, so she gripped them together to hide the revulsion that ran through her.

*This is the system I was trying to work with ... I can't be part of this.*

"Nothing lives without a brain, Jaisa," Neriso said. For a moment, his hand moved to the small of her back. "The specimens have brains. They're just unable to use them beyond basics like bodily functions. We keep everything moving about in them, but the brain doesn't respond. Eventually, they'll be shipped to the Eighth City and the doctors will use them to practice new techniques. Some will be used to test vaccines, amputations, any number of things, but that isn't the important part."

"No?" Jaisa reached out and touched a replica of her hand where it lay on the bed. The skin was cool. Jaisa remembered how cold being hooked up to an IV was. *They must be freezing.*

"No! Don't you see Jaisa? We created them. They're perfect, living replicas of real people. More than that, we were able to create them as adult specimens. We'll master the mind eventually, but the gods lack data for us on that front. Our brains don't work like theirs. Over in the Eighth City, they're trying brain transplants into some of our clones, but they've had limited success."

Jaisa shivered. Could he hear himself talk? Didn't he know how much like a mad scientist he sounded? "Brain transplants? Into me? Whose brains?"

"No, no, not you or any of the spouses. The labs have produced other specimens for that. It wouldn't do for another you to be wandering about."

"Whose brains?" Jaisa gritted her teeth and through sheer will alone kept her tone light. *Neriso is a monster.*

"Half-ranks. You know that, Jaisa. All of our experiments are done on Half-ranks."

Jaisa shook her head and looked up to Neriso. Did he not understand? Could he not see how horrible this was? Lyra or Melody could have been in that position.

"And there hasn't been a success yet?" She forced her lips to part and let the words out.

"Relative success. A few have woken up, but even then, too many connections were missing. None have been able to speak. A few have been able to scream."

"How terrible." Jaisa wrapped her arms around herself. What of the others? The ones who couldn't even voice their fear and pain? In her mind, she saw it, people trapped in bodies that were not their own, unable to control this new cage of flesh.

*They must be screaming inside, and no one can even hear them.*

"You're missing the point." Annoyance colored his voice, and Neriso stepped in front of her, his lips pressed tight. "They'll succeed, eventually."

"So, this is what you do?" Jaisa lowered her face and tried to get control. She looked at him through her lashes, hoping to appear thoughtful rather than ill.

"We're also in charge of all human reproduction." Neriso smiled. "I could show you over there as well if you like."

"You can't create working brains."

"No, we can't create working *adult* brains. We are doing just fine with babies. Most of the embryos aren't straight clones, of course. We're trying for some genetic variation so we're tweaking and crossing genes. Would you like me to show you?"

Jaisa pressed her teeth together to keep something she would regret from slipping out. When she was ready, she answered him. "Yes. I came here to see why our city exists."

She followed Neriso silently. The cold air from the vents brushed her legs, blowing her skirt. Too numb to notice, she walked unnoted past the eyes of the gods' Chosen. It was all she could do not to run back to those prone forms and rip the tubes from them. *This is what they're doing? Why did I expect anything humane?*

They passed a doorway guarded by two Half-ranks with metal plates replacing the right sides of their faces. The purpose of this metal was unknown, but it appeared painful. Jaisa paused and looked at them. The screaming in her heart grew, and she bit on her lip to keep it from coming out.

One of the Half-ranks met her gaze and a quizzical expression flitted over his features. She wiped at the tears that threatened her eyes and bowed her head to them.

"These are nothing special," Neriso said, glancing at the guards.

*They are less to him than a vehicle or a dog. How can he have forgotten so completely that he is human? And what that means?*

"They work here?" Jaisa touched first one man's face and

then the other. The force of her will was in her fingers. Her voice belonged to the gods, but she tried to tell these abused men with only her eyes and a single casual touch that she saw them. That they were not animals, and she knew how they had been treated was wrong.

"Some are servants, like Lyra and Melody, for personal use. But others are hired to suit their capabilities into regular work. The remainder we use for the betterment of mankind," Neriso answered as he pulled her around a corner.

"What would've happened to Lyra and Melody if I hadn't purchased them?" She held her breath and wished she could pull the words back.

"They would've had their minds studied."

"You can't mean that." *Of course he can.*

"The labs wouldn't take their brains out, if that's what you're wondering." Neriso chuckled. "Minds like theirs are too precious. They would've been hooked up and had their reactions studied to certain stimuli."

"And Alpha and Omega?"

"Probably outfitted to oversee the factories of the Rankless. We could get them upgraded with next year's credits if we chose."

"No." Jaisa forced herself not to gag. *Who is Neriso? He would pay to get Alpha and Omega tortured like that? Do I know him at all?*

"You already purchased them," Neriso said as they came to end of the hallway. "Stop worrying."

*What does that mean?* But this time, Jaisa held back her words, not wanting another answer that would haunt her.

After stepping into a small, dark room, Jaisa couldn't see anything. The moment of blackness gave her a chance to calm herself for whatever came next. Neriso's hands finished moving over a glowing panel, and lights flickered on.

And then one of the walls became a window, and Jaisa stared into a room of glass and metal. Encased in clear tubes were fetuses. They lay in their mechanical wombs connected to tubes and fed by machine.

*All these months, all this time, this is what he's been doing. This is what I've been helping him do.*

"I haven't seen a pregnant woman since before the training facilities," Jaisa said. *They're so tiny... What will their lives be like? These children won't even have mothers. No families, nothing, and all they will know is the world the gods created.*

"This method is better," Neriso said.

The grief that washed over her was sudden and unexpected. There was still a place in her that ached for a child. Odd, how that had meant so much to her in the world before but hadn't occurred to her in months.

It was the reason she had chosen to be in the city with Evie rather than at home with Rick. Seeing it now from a distance, the whole thing was painfully futile. She'd wanted a baby and because Rick hadn't, she'd been tearing their marriage apart. *If only I'd known that this was the future of mankind...*

"Women don't need to carry babies anymore." Neriso touched her back and motioned to the tubes as if showing her a fancy new car. "They're created here without all the flukes of nature, and then the church will raise them to be perfect contributing members of society. We need never bother ourselves with children, and we'll still get a next generation."

Jaisa smiled at her husband as a sane alternative to spitting in his face. Her hand rested on her flat stomach. His hand resting on her back nagged at her, making her long to twist away. To escape him.

*This isn't what I want. Not him and not this engineered future.* She'd wanted Rick's baby to have existed. Just to have carried it.

*Now I never will, and he wants me to be happy about it.*

"No wonder you're always busy. The future of humanity is in your hands." She did not add that he was mishandling it. Humanity would be doomed if all it had was men like him to protect it.

Who else was there?

# CHAPTER 22

The rocky trail hit a steep incline and Connor grabbed the rockface to the left to steady himself. On either side, the alien trees sighed and danced in the windless air. Clouds threatened in the sky, but they should reach the shelter before rain began if they kept a good pace.

Jayden had been certain it was time to show Naeemah the workshop and even if Connor wasn't sure he agreed, it was down to him to lead her to the place.

Naeemah's occasional stumbles behind him set off little flurries of pebbles scuttling down the hill. Connor shoved his hand against the rock edge to help push himself up the next section of the rise. Nothing but bushes' gangly arms extending toward the trail surrounded him. Careful of his footholds, Connor went to the first little flat space, just big enough to stand on. He turned and offered a hand to Naeemah.

"It's just over that rise," he said.

She took his hand and clambered up to him.

"Don't try to grab the bushes for balance," Connor said, helping her up ahead of him. "They aren't strong enough. Louie had a nice tumble down the hill."

"Why is Riley's lab all the way out here?" Naeemah asked. Her hand remained in his, soft fingers curled against his palm. His old jacket and a pair of Riley's old pants enveloped her, leaving little but a trail of hair from beneath a scarf she wore over her head and her hands, scratched from the climb, in view.

"If either the camp or the lab is discovered, we can move to the other. That's what Riley says. He likes the privacy too."

Her fingertips stroked his skin. The sensation, just a simple touch, scorched through him. *Stop it. Get to the lab. That's all we are doing.*

To his relief, she continued the climb without waiting for him. After the last shower of pebbles from her footsteps, Connor followed her.

The building was camouflaged, but not enough to hide it from someone who was looking for it. Naeemah was halfway through the brush toward the half-toppled house before he caught up. The rain began to patter—a heavy drizzle for now. Despite the oncoming storm, she didn't enter. The object behind the glassless window held her attention.

Without looking, Connor already knew it was a deactivated drone. Naeemah had seen them fail to take one down. Here was the proof that given the right circumstances, they could succeed. Jayden thought she needed that. Connor wasn't sure that more death could help smooth over her encounter with the undercity drone.

Connor hurried up the path to her. *What was Jayden thinking, asking us to meet him here? She's not ready for this. She's going to fall apart, and I don't have the time to deal with a crumbling woman. Jayden can deal with her.*

"It's dead," he said, motioning to the window. "You're in no danger."

Naeemah remained still, one hand over her heart, her wide eyes scanning the drone's body lying flat on the table.

"They have a weak spot right here." Connor touched the back of her neck. "That's a drone of the same kind you've seen in the upworld, but the others we have—"

Naeemah threw her arms around him and hugged herself tight to his chest. Her cheek pressed against him and her breath brushed through the buttons of his jacket. All of her, so close, so warm.

"It's okay," he said, awkwardly hugging her back.

"I..." she started as she pulled away. To his surprise, a smile covered her face. "That's the most beautiful thing I've ever seen. You killed it? With your own two hands? I mean, Jayden told me about it, but seeing one like this... it's different!"

"That one I did, but most were Jayden's kills."

"Others? Show me. Please?" Naeemah clapped her hands together in a childlike joy.

"Come this way." Connor showed her inside the house, ducking down under the partially collapsed roof for part of the journey. He went into the back room, where two more disabled drones were stored.

Jayden sat on a stool at the back of the room, sharpening a knife. He lowered and sheathed it as Connor entered. There was another drone on a table in the center of the room, and collected junk—like rations, cloth, seeds, and books—littered the floor.

"You seen any of my kills yet?" Jayden asked Naeemah, leaning back against the peeling paint on the wall.

She slid in and darted up to the table on which lay a crowd drone. Its numerous octopus-like arms draped over the side of the table and dangled toward the floor.

"As far as we've seen, there are four types of drones," Connor said. He picked his way carefully around the items on the floor toward her.

"I've seen a few," she said. "But I don't really understand why they have different drones."

"That one's used for crowd control," Jayden said, then he looked sheepish. He clearly had no idea what to say if he was rehashing old information.

"It can use each of those limbs to restrain or kill, but it doesn't have the mental capacity of the uppercity drones." Connor watched Naeemah carefully waiting for her to break down. But she just looked back at him with rapt attention. "The one across the room is a hover drone. It flies overhead and monitors the Rankless any time there are over three or four together at a time. It can't kill but has an instant relay to the other drones."

Naeemah leaned in toward the drone, her expression awestruck. "And the drones we had in training? Do those come down to the undercity?"

"Not often," Connor said. "They tend to be used for more delicate situations." He avoided mentioning that they also posed additional risks. If they were programed to see heat instead of nanites... they could be the army that wiped out Connor's little band.

"They die just like the rest. So, don't worry, girlie." Jayden winked. Then he set his knife down on a knee-high pile of books.

"And the last kind?" Naeemah asked.

"We call them 'herders.'" Connor looked at Jayden for help, but his friend just shrugged.

"What do they do?" Naeemah asked.

Connor's stomach churned just thinking of the herders. There was something inherently horrific about the figures of children killing. "They're three separate drones that work from a central system—kill one and you get the other two. But they're shaped like kids and are often used to 'herd' large groups or to converge on any threat that is trying to escape."

Jayden hopped over a pyramid of cans and crossed over to Naeemah and the table. "You're on our side now. Thought it was time you saw what that meant. We keep all of our drone kills here."

*All but one.* Connor approached, trying to block that memory.

"Have you learned anything about how they work?" Naeemah asked. She circled the table with the drone on it, gracefully avoiding the collections on the floor, her eyes hungry.

"Yeah, but it's all science mumbo jumbo," Jayden said. "You'd have to ask Riley. I just kill 'em. Damn machines. Gotta always be careful of the voltage, though—killing one could easily kill you."

Connor leaned a hand on the table, forcing himself not to avoid contact with the cold machine. "They all kill differently

—except of course for the heart damage being a constant. But the trick is, that they all *die* the same."

"We kill them," Jayden repeated. "It's what we're good at."

"Why store them here? This place is practically falling in." Naeemah motioned at the sunken rubble of the hall they'd entered from.

Connor winced, imagining the building falling. Screams echoed in his mind. Heartrending panicked screams and the taste of cement dust. Jayden clenched his jaw, his dark eyes accusing the walls. *Naeemah doesn't know. She couldn't have put known her words played so perfectly off of what happened to Casey. She's not doing it on purpose.*

Connor closed his eyes against the onslaught of memory.

*A red burst shot from the sky. As it crashed into the ground, the earth around it ruptured. The red beam, having struck, branched out to the sides, spreading carnage. At the edge of the city, a freeway overpass bent and broke. Concrete sprayed out and cars no bigger than specks flew into the air. The buildings began to crumble. Metal contorted, screamed, and finally shattered. Glass flew outward like flower petals in the distance. Connor's hands flew up to cover his ears. The city's scream was deafening.*

"If it collapses, we'll dig the fuckers out." Jayden turned and stormed out of the room. Connor understood it, though Naeemah cocked her head.

Connor gazed at the crumbling, slouched walls behind Naeemah. But the memory of that day wouldn't depart—it haunted him. The drum of rain on the roof transformed into the rumble of the city falling.

"You both seem upset," Naeemah said softly, her hand fluttering to touch his arm. "What did I say?"

"Bad memories. We were in a city when the aliens started reforming the world's surface. Our friend got caught in a building."

Naeemah let out a soft gasp. "I'm sorry. I should have put it together. Casey, right?"

"I couldn't have saved him—the building. It just…"

"No need to explain, Connor. I wasn't thinking. I'm sorry."

"Not your fault." He lowered his head into a hand, unable to block the remembered screech of metal.

*"We have to go," Connor said.*

*"Fuck that," Jayden replied. Pain etched over his face, he pulled at the wreckage with his uninjured arm. "He could be alive down there."*

*"We have to go* now," Connor said. He reached out and tugged Riley back. He pointed at the edge of the city where the mechanized shadow crept. Large, black creatures with spiderlike arms pulled down distant bits of city. "Or none of us is getting out of this alive."

Connor moved over to Naeemah. Life was different now. The elation from earlier had disappeared from her face and she stared at the drones as he'd originally assumed she would.

"You're sure they won't rise again?" she asked.

"Yes. They're out of commission."

A long silence stretched between them. Naeemah never removed her gaze from the drones. Her arms wrapped around herself as she rocked back and forth.

"I'll give you some privacy," Connor said, wanting to get away from the black machines and the woman in front of them in equal measure. It wasn't fair to dislike her—to blame her for reminding him of everything he'd lost—but he couldn't help it.

Naeemah flinched and flung herself at him. Pure terror boiled in her eyes. Her frail body shook. "No, please. I can't be alone with it."

Her panic pulled him from the pit his mind had fallen into. *One of these killed* her *only a few weeks ago. I'm an idiot trying to leave her. Just need to get a handle on myself.*

"I'm sorry," he said.

Her grip loosened, but her turbulent gaze remained on him.

"I'm trying to be strong, but I'm afraid. Afraid of everything," Naeemah whispered. "I never met anyone like you, Riley, or Jayden, in the world before. My father never would have allowed it. My only experiences with men were regulated."

Naeemah turned to face the drone. Connor set a hand on her shoulder. It was the only touch he dared without upsetting her, but he knew of no other way to show her that he was there.

"The day the gods came," she continued, "I'd just met the man my father wanted me to marry. I was at home talking to my father and eldest brother on a conference call. They were so excited for me to consent to the union, and I liked the man. Then... Now, I'll never get married. By everything I was taught, I'm disgraced, rotten, spoiled now and won't..."

"You aren't alone. We all lost the futures we planned. We're all in the same position."

"No," she said, her voice cold but not angry. Still staring away from him, she went on in a soft chilly tone. "You really aren't. You haven't done anything against your own beliefs. I can't tell you how many Companions I saw take their own lives. You had a life, a good one, and you lost it. I never had anything. I never lived."

"That means you can build a new life." Connor squeezed her shoulder, unsure what to say. He remembered the piled bodies in the Companion compound when they'd saved her. He could well imagine those were hardly the first bodies she'd seen. "We're a mess. All of us. Riley barely takes the time to sleep, he's so obsessed with avenging his wife and children. They're more real to him than anything; at this point, he doesn't even see me anymore. Jayden can't sleep more than two hours most nights without nightmares. And me? I failed everyone. I failed the people I swore to protect."

"You mean your wife. What was she like?" She turned her honey eyes to him.

Connor could almost picture her—but didn't want to. "Don't want to talk about that."

They fell into silence, both staring down at the black drone.

"I want to kill one." Naeemah's softness melted off to show the steel beneath. "For your wife, for my family, for all the Companions who didn't make it. I want to kill them all."

Connor experienced those words and her fierce expression as a physical sensation. The fire that filled her licked out at him, and Connor craved the warmth and danger. Not since his second date with Rai had he felt such an intense draw toward any woman—not just physical attraction, but a desire to stand there, washed in her strength and passion, to hear words as alluring as caresses.

But she wasn't Rai, and the last thing he wanted right then was a new woman. For the first time, however, he was certain of Naeemah as a soldier.

This was a woman who'd died and come back. And was still brave enough to fight.

"Stick with us and you'll get a kill," he growled.

"We need more than just drone kills," she said, voice dripping hate. "Especially if killing one drone is likely to shock one of us to death... we need more manpower to do anything. I want to kill the gods themselves. How do we get an army?"

He couldn't have defined it, but an idea stirred at those words. Naeemah had been shocked to death, and she'd come back. They couldn't rely on whatever drone miscalculation had caused that fluke... But drones weren't the only things in this new world that knew how to kill. "I don't know. Killing is what we do."

And killing doesn't build an army... unless it does.

# CHAPTER 23

The rubbery tree bark rubbed against Jaisa's palm. Tightening her grip on a branch above her head, she pulled herself into the arms of the tree and settled onto the thick limb. The bark stuck to her thighs.

For a while, she stared at the garden. Everything in it was foreign, but how long until it didn't seem that way? Neriso's work had made it very clear to her that a new and unacceptable normal was coming. There was simply no way for her to live with herself if she worked within that system.

The "church" made that clear. Neriso's lab filled with broken parts of Half-ranks made that clear. This world was designed to swallow her whole.

But just as she'd done with her girls, she had to find a way to work around the system and somehow make the lives of those in the world below easier. Her first challenge would be getting down to them. Neriso would never give her permission to travel the undercity.

Lyra walked the stone pathway below the trees, shrouded against the sun, spraying the plants. Melody would be inside, cleaning what the house's machines couldn't. The only thing in Jaisa's power to do for them was to stay out of their way as they completed their work. She had a few hours until she needed to go to the community center for dancing lessons with other Companions.

The only thing she was really allowed to do with her girls

were their walks through the city.

When watching the garden sway and Lyra walk grew dull, she leaned back against the trunk. Boredom seemed a small thing, comparatively—especially when held up against the tortured creatures in Neriso's lab—but the long days grated on them all. There was yet another reason to be glad for her girls; they kept her sane. The afternoon heat swelled around her, and her eyes drifted closed.

And she dreamed.

She stood on the railing looking at the mist below the city. It crackled beneath her, and a voice ranted, hidden within the overarching sound. But the words were distant and blurred. She knelt and leaned down to hear. Tendrils of white beckoned to her. It rose above its bounds, spilling over the rail and stroking her fingers.

The voices sang, and they screamed. They cried, and they laughed. And she knew them, but she didn't know from where. *I need to find those people. I need to know their words... What do they call for?*

A drone crept behind her. Its blackness reached for her. Its red eye blinked at her back. *If it gets me, I'll never see them. I must know.*

Jaisa leaped up, her bare feet curving around the metal rail. A swarm of red light filled the world above. The wind whispered against her face, dark and as cold as metal. She dove into the mist, away from the gods' eyes.

The white lifted to enfold her, and the air stung, hitting her like millions of ice crystals. Jolts burst against her skin, each a pinprick. But this was nothing to the cacophony of human sound. Children wept, and men laughed. There were so many voices and sounds that distinguishing among them proved impossible. She could only float on the tide. Somewhere, the refrain of a Christmas song struck, then hushed laughter.

Jaisa hit a net. It burned her skin, and her hair bled downward, away from her. She would bleed to death. But the net didn't hold. She plummeted through the blackness. Then she struck the ground.

The wrecked world around her smelled of cold iron and purified death. Jaisa looked down and saw that her foot rested on a skull picked clean. A scream rose from her chest to her throat, but when her eyes came up, a horde of people stood before her in a ragged mass.

Thousands of them crowded in front of her—people dressed in torn scraps with gaunt faces and vacant eyes. Jaisa took a step back. She didn't know what they would do. They watched her, but they saw right through her.

"A star," one said.

"The stars don't come here. No stars shine through that."

Jaisa looked up at the mist where it roiled above her—black and furious.

"No."

Jaisa knew that voice.

"Not a star."

Jaisa gasped. Amid the crowd of others were three people from Jaisa's past. Her mother stood there, her hands grey, and a hole gaped in her mouth where there should have been teeth. Holding on to her mother's arm, her sister stared as vacantly as the rest.

And next to Evie was Rick, whose smile had sustained Val when she'd been ready to break. Only now, he glared. He looked directly at her with such disgust, it shamed her. And it was his voice condemning her.

"Not a star. A traitor, fool, and coward."

Jaisa woke in the arms of her tree and knew, without a doubt, she had to go below. She would ask Neriso how to accomplish it. The how of it didn't matter. It only mattered that she view the undercity with her waking eyes.

She dropped from the tree and plucked a flower, leaving it on the doorstep for Lyra. Something pretty for the girl to hold, even if Jaisa wasn't allowed to hand it to her slave. Lyra and Melody had come from that world below, so even beyond the other reasons, Jaisa owed it to them to descend.

She'd have to convince her husband somehow.

Her goal of finding Neriso lasted all the way into the house, where she recalled that the last thing she wanted was to fight her way to the information. That was what it always came to with Neriso. No, better to keep him out of it as long as possible.

He'd forbid her from going. No. She needed to find her way around him somehow.

That on its own made things impossible. She walked carefully over the path that Lyra had trod earlier. Her walks with her girls were her only unregulated time. And because they were a regular occurrence, she could use them. After all, she didn't need Neriso's permission to change her destination.

Except she didn't really have any destination other than "down."

Jaisa sat on the bottom step of the stairwell and remembered falling in her dream. The sensation of the wind pushing her and the freedom of falling away from this world had not diminished. But she couldn't really get down to the undercity by falling. There had to be a way to access the undercity.

*No, Neriso can't help me... or won't. But he's not my only option.*

*Tavar. He's said his husband works in city planning. He might have a map.*

Jaisa went to the nearest computer screen and typed a query to him. Best the gods know as soon as possible what she intended anyhow. She couldn't hide. Any attempt to do so made her appear suspicious. And it would make her feigned innocence to Neriso more believable if she left a trail that she could pretend she thought he knew about. It would add weight to her denial that she had not purposefully hidden anything.

She stared at the screen and waited for his reply. Only a few minutes elapsed before she had a blinking notification.

*Happy as ever to help*, was all Tavar's message said, but moments after she read it, a map opened with a small digital picture of the entrance to the undercity.

Connor returned to the camp after a dawn patrol of the city. His thoughts were still crowded with death. He knew how to solve their problems. The only way to recruit people was to kill them first. The problems they had now were all because the drones did too much damage when they killed.

But resurrecting people would be much easier if less damage was done.

It would have been better if Riley had been around—He'd left at the worst time ever. Riley would have been able to tell him if his idea was genius or desperate and foolish.

But that wasn't whom he had. Maybe it was for the best. They needed to act, and Jayden was better at that. Riley always wanted to weigh the options logically, but Connor would go insane with any more waiting.

The camp was still dark, shaded by the trees. The only light came from the small fire at the center.

Jayden and Naeemah were sitting together, but as they spoke, their bodies leaned away from each other. Naeemah's baggy clothing slid across her body as she looked up at Connor. Her eyes were shielded and blank. Jayden took this opportunity to pat Naeemah's knee, a brotherly gesture.

"Jayden," Connor said, walking up into the light of the fire.

Naeemah looked up at him, a new warmth in her eyes. Something had shifted between them since the visit to the labs, but he wasn't ready to inspect the alterations.

"'Sup?" Jayden nodded.

Connor's shoulders relaxed as Naeemah's attention drew away from him back to Jayden. The relative "peace" of Riley and Louie's absence caused an inactivity that weighed on him.

When he'd been in this mood back in the old world, pent-up aggression demanding release, Rai had grinned at him. She had called his expression his 'ready to snap' face. Typically, she'd helped him through it either by starting a huge fight over nothing, giving them both an opportunity to break things, or help him work it off in the bedroom. But Rai wasn't around.

*Naeemah is.*

Distractions were a luxury he couldn't afford at the moment. He'd found a better, more productive way of releasing tension, a plan to get things moving again.

He wanted their opinions, and though he was sure that Jayden would fall behind any plan involving action, he was not so sure of Naeemah. She wasn't a killer by nature. As hungry for justice as she might have been, this idea might break their newfound trust.

"There are too few of us to make a difference," Connor declared. "From what Naeemah says, there are multiple cities, and we can barely do any good *here*. We need an army, and we need them to be outside the control of the nanites and metal men."

"You got a plan?" Jayden asked.

"Kill them."

Jayden's eyes narrowed. "Kill whom?"

"The people." Connor searched for better words but came up dry. So much hung on convincing them. His throat felt dry, and he kept glancing at Naeemah, whose face remained removed. She showed nothing in her narrowed eyes. *I'm not explaining this right.*

Jayden shook his head.

a smile curved on Naeemah's full lips. The glaze cleared from her eyes. "Yes," she hissed. "Better move fast. They'll keep a closer tab on everyone once the cities are fully running. Right now, they are still figuring out people's limits. As soon as the regular death toll in the city drops off, they'll notice every life we take."

"Hate to tell the two of you, but corpses make rotten soldiers," Jayden said.

"Yes," Connor said. "But we can bring them back. We did it with Naeemah and the kid."

"We failed on a shit ton of others."

"But everyone you've tried it on so far was killed by the

drones," Naeemah said, clutching her hands together. "That's not a gentle death. Louie and I were flukes. What Connor is suggesting won't damage people's hearts the way a drone's touch does—not if we do it right. Just stopping them, which should trick the nanites and make it possible to bring a significant number back."

"Not all," Jayden said, eyeing both of them and slowly shaking his head.

Connor nodded. "It's risky, but we have enough trust from the people to get volunteers. We need more manpower if we want to do more than just watch humanity die."

"So, who goes in to convince people to die for us?" Jayden asked.

"Naeemah," Connor said.

She nodded. It had to be her; she spoke the language and dolled up in her Companion gear, she would be a symbol of power they recognized. "We gather a dozen or so people. Then we bring them somewhere private, one at a time, to kill them. That way, if we have any mishaps, the others won't lose hope."

Connor was surprised at the cold practicality of her words. But it made sense.

"What's the plan after we 'bring them back'?" Jayden asked. "Too many people in the camp will draw a lot of attention."

Naeemah leaned back, her arms folded in front of her and a dreamy smile on her face.

"We split up once we have a big enough group. Jayden, you'll take the strongest and train them to fight and kill the drones. Naeemah will take another group and teach them what she can about the uppercity—whoever will pass best walking above and spying for us. When Riley gets back, he can train some with all that science stuff. I'll take the rest here—train them to fight and show them the backways of the city. We'll figure out a way to send groups to other cities and create a resistance force through the world."

"And the volunteers who don't cut it?" Jayden asked.

"There are places out there." Connor motioned to the trees. "They could support small communities without being noticed. The aliens are only doing their climate control in the areas around the cities. There should still be recognizable crops out there. As long as they stay out of sight, they won't pose a threat to us."

"Someone will need to teach them to hunt," Jayden said. But he didn't sound like he was arguing anymore. "Let's start tomorrow?"

Naeemah's eyes widened at the word "tomorrow" and she held out her hand, palm out in a gesture of caution.

"Fast is better," Connor said.

"To some extent, I agree, but we should wait for Riley to return," Naeemah said. "He knows more about their tech than any of us. If we start this without him, we're crippled."

"No," Connor said. "As you said, the longer we wait, the more noticeable it becomes. We have to act now." *Plus, I have to do something now, or I'm going to do something else I'll really regret.* "I see no problem with now."

"No waiting, then," Jayden said. "Let's get on this."

Naeemah muttered something in a language Connor didn't know, then pursed her lips.

"You can stay behind," Connor said. *Better if she does, for the actual killing.* "Once you've helped us gather them. You don't have to watch."

Something in his tone must have startled her because the look she turned to him was wide-eyed for a moment. She stood, and one hand rested on the curve of her hip. Wanting her was a painful prerogative, and from the sway of her shoulders and thrust of her chest, he would have bet that was her intention.

*Trained to be a whore. What a lovely world these gods are creating.*

"I'll stay the whole time," she said. "I cannot let you do this for me."

Connor turned away from her. The heat of her gaze scorched through him. *What does that woman want?* Well, what did they all want?

*Revenge.*

He could understand that. With revenge finally within arm's reach, the most difficult part was waiting.

# CHAPTER 24

The mist crackled as Jaisa's pale hand drifted across the railing out over the mist. She kept her breathing even in an attempt to control her heartrate—this was not the time to draw the attention of her nanites. The temple loomed behind her, its black spires arching into the sunny sky. A cold shiver traveled through Jaisa in its shadow, and she let the silent song of the mist distract her.

Yet the shade of the temple only stretched so far. And with each step, she drew farther away from that, and closer to something new.

The entrance to the undercity was nearby.

Neriso had signed off on her request to leave the girls at home and deviate from her usual schedule. But all she'd told him about was her intent to visit the temple again. She'd simply implied that she wished to stay longer than her norm. He did not know of her primary purpose for the outing and leaving the girls behind.

She had permission from him, but it might not be enough to gain her access to the city below. Denying that would be foolish. Her best hope was that there were no strong restrictions put on people *entering* the undercity. If it required separate permission, she'd be screwed. But she would know in a few minutes.

Now, she was free to ponder what she hoped to find. Luckily, she had roamed the city often. And Tavar's map covered this section of the city, so she knew the location of a passage. Someday she hoped to have the freedom to ask him how he had obtained such maps.

Jaisa was alone except for the traffic in the sky. The under-city was a complete unknown, which was why she'd decided not to risk Lyra or Melody there. *We're all facets of the world above.*

Slow and steady, her footfalls against the marble were casual. Jaisa cautioned her heart not to race. Keeping calm usually lessened how often she lost feeling in her fingers and toes and the risk that Neriso would be contacted.

*If I'm calm, they will not suspect.* So she lifted her face to the sky, letting the stress fall away.

When she looked back down, she saw the entrance ahead of her. Or, more accurately, she saw the building that housed the entrance. A drone stood by a one-room structure. The place had no windows, and its only door shone a pale silver in the sunlight. Around its walls grew flowers of a variety of alien colors.

*Do they sing at night as ours do? Or are such wonders not wasted on public buildings?* The flowers turned their bright faces to her as she approached. Their greeting was the only one she received.

The drone stood immobile beside the door. Jaisa set her hand on the flat metal panel that served as a lock. Her eyes remained on the drone as her fingers found the circular screen and keyed in her code. Not even a flicker of awareness across the drone's featureless face, just the steady blink of the red eye in its forehead.

The door slid open. Her heart thudded, ready for the drone to move to stop her at any moment. *Will it ask me what my purpose is or kill me without warning?*

Inside the doorway, a darkness deeper than any night welcomed her. Waiting to swallow her whole for her foolishness.

The hair on her arms rose. A cold wind gushed from the doorway's mouth. Her eyes fluttered closed, blocking out the empty blackness in front of her. She extended one bare foot and stepped down. A pressure pushed up on her sole, not a floor or any solid surface, but like a hand made of air coming up to support her weight. Then she moved the other foot.

Her eyes snapped open as the wind howled around her. Encased in the blackness, her toes wiggled on the invisible support. Briefly, she looked behind her. Her head spun at the view out into the bright daylight and the nightmare figure of the drone.

"I want to go down," Jaisa said.

She turned back to the blackness that, although it appeared to be without substance, held her suspended. Then she fell, but not the liberating freefall of her dream. She toppled as if through a thin liquid. The air shoved itself inside her mouth and nose. It pummeled against her eyes and into her nostrils, it bellowed in her ears.

She dragged her hands through the air to cover her ears against its song. As she passed through the current of the city, she strained to see something in the impenetrable darkness. The cold faded into heat that burned across her skin.

She landed on her knees and barely caught herself with her hands rather than her face. The ground was rough and unforgiving. Pain vibrated up from her knees as jagged little stones in the floor drew drops of her blood to stain the pavement. The air still hung on her like a winter jacket, and sweat broke out on her brow.

Jaisa lifted herself to her feet. The world in front of her roared with various machines that screamed, crunched, and buzzed. A patterned clicking came from her right, and a large gear steadily turned, moving a line of others that disappeared behind metal panels.

The drone from above had followed her and now stood close by her shoulder. Her instinct was to recoil, but she fought it. Jaisa set her hand on its arm before recoiling. Its skin, cold and slick, gave no comfort, and memories she preferred not to touch stirred at the intentional contact.

Jaisa moved into the world of machines and heat. She'd anticipated a dirtier space, but though the area jumbled mismatched metals together, there was no loose trash or filth. The air smelled of oil and gas—no evidence of humanity detected by her nose. Instead, the guts of the machine she lived on writhed in front of her.

This was the underbelly of her new world.

Jaisa pivoted, and her eyes found their goal: the irregular movement of humankind. She was too far away to get a decent view past the metal obstructions.

The ground bit into her feet, which, despite how often she went barefoot, had grown soft on the smooth surfaces of the world above. But she hated the men's boots and couldn't' afford to damage the Companion shoes, so she risked the pain. She rounded a large support beam and got her first view of the undercity inhabitants.

Ten people toiled at the machines, manning different stations. None of them paid her any attention. Jaisa appraised them. Slumped shoulders, tired eyes, decrepit, or broken by time and circumstance, they were not the creatures from her nightmare. They were living, breathing beings, covered in sweat and beaten down by their lives. But they were alive.

Jaisa didn't mean to smile, but she did. *These are real people. This is humanity.*

An old man looked up from his work at her. His gaze fixed on her smile and his limbs trembled. *What does he see in me? Is he afraid?*

"An angel," he said. His voice carried over the other sounds despite its softness. The force behind the words was enough to drive them like an arrow into Jaisa. A squeal of metal on metal rang out as his hands lost their rhythm.

Jaisa froze, torn between two impulses: shock at the old man calling her an angel and fear at the grinding metal sound.

The old man's attention broke from her as his hand scrambled to gain control of the device. But his arms appeared to be so weak, so thin. How could he stop that spin? And others glanced up from their work, panic rising to the surface.

*It has to be stopped.*

He grabbed on to the handle of the wheel, and his arms strained.

*He doesn't have to do this alone.* Jaisa crossed the room and fastened her hands besides his, trying to help. The bar burned across her soft palms. She gritted her teeth against the flare of pain. For a moment, she clung, digging her heels into the floor. Her smooth soles slipped, and the bar jerked from her fingers.

Her hands throbbed where the heated metal had touched her. She clutched them to her chest and looked in wonder as the thin old man stopped the spin.

When he looked up from the wheel that had now stopped, Jaisa stared back at him. His worshipful gaze had gone, replaced by something thoughtful. He was measuring her. Hope flickered in his eyes—and a new life.

But all she'd offered was a brief diversion.

Then his expression darkened as it fixed on the drone that trailed behind her. He turned back to his machine. *I wish I could be rid of the drones, but that'll never happen. They must be programmed to follow upperworlders down here. Why else would it have followed? And they're not going to make an exception for me.*

*My* wonderfully *unwanted guardians and* protectors, *here to keep the world below at bay.*

Jaisa glanced at her hands, reddened by the heat of the metal. She spoke as if to her hands, but the words were for the gathered Rankless. "Oh, I don't know how you do it. I couldn't."

Her voice echoed in the chamber, and each Rankless perked up at the sound. Some stopped their work to watch. A quick inspection showed that all the machines here were linked. So their machines would perform less than ideally as long as the old man's wasn't running.

"S'my job. I do it." The old man lifted his hands—calloused and dirty, bearing no resemblance to her pale ones.

One pale hand fell to rest on the white robe she wore. The fabric was soft and clean as no white object would remain down there. The other swept through hair as red as blood. She saw herself through his eyes—something beautiful. "Yes. We all have our jobs."

He grunted.

"I thought humanity was gone," she said, "but here you are. You're what remains of humankind."

"*We* are," a woman said, her left arm only a stump. "You's human much as we are."

"No." Jaisa folded her fingers in against her stinging palms. Her fingers began to tingle. The nanites had recognized this as a conversation—a forbidden one. "I'm what they created from the flesh of a dead society. You're humanity."

A loud crack resounded from above, filling Jaisa's mind with images of falling scaffolding. A screech escaped her, and she looked up, unsure what danger lurked there.

Clouds. Real clouds. And looking at the churning gray, she recognized the sound too. Thunder. *How do they keep us from hearing that? Does it matter? It exists. The storms are still there, hidden maybe, but ours, of our Earth.*

Jaisa stared up at the sky, watching with wonder as the dark shapes shifted overhead.

"Storm clouds!" Jaisa turned her eyes to the drone, though her words were really still for the old man. "It has been so long. Do they get rain here too?"

"They do," the drone replied. The red eye in its still-blank face blinked.

Jaisa grinned, lowering her eyes and turning back to the Rankless man.

She reached out to touch his grimy face, so beautiful and so real. Before Jaisa had time to realize she was going to, she kissed him. He froze. The contact was swift, but the tingle in her extremities eroded any other sensation. *To be here, to see real clouds and real humanity is worth anything.* She glanced at her hands as if the nanites would be visible, but all she found was reddened skin.

The drone's hand clamped down on her shoulder, hard. "Physical contact with the world below will be kept to a minimum. For approved practices, check with your computer system. This is your warning."

Meaning she would not get another one.

"Understood." With effort, Jaisa pressed her emotion away from the surface. She'd behave. She had to if Neriso and the gods were ever going to allow her to come back. "Might I ask one of them to escort me, so I don't get lost?"

The drone paused before it replied. "No. You will leave them to their work. Any questions you have you may ask through the proper channels."

"Understood." Jaisa's eyes swung back to the old man. Fear had him quivering. And she wasn't certain if that fear was of her or of the drone. She winked, hoping her confidence would put him at ease. "Let me help you restart this thing."

The old man looked to the drone, his eyes asking permission, but the drone did not appear to note him. That was understandable. From all she'd learned, the drones weren't programmed to waste time speaking with the people of the city below. Their primary purpose, after all, both above and below, was dealing death.

"You could turn that o'er there," he said, pointing a shaky finger, still not looking at her, his eyes fastened on the drone.

As she moved across the room to where he indicated, he turned and pulled at the main wheel. She found the lever he'd pointed at and leaned her weight into getting it started. Her feet slipped on the first try, so she had to stop and reposition herself. A second try got the lever started, slow and resistant against her straining arms.

Though the strength needed made her muscles ache, she managed. A light flared on, and the lever sank into the wall, the inner machine workings taking over her task.

Jaisa backed up and watched the other Rankless at their labor. When the machine whirred and clicked as it had when she had first descended, the old man looked back at her. Jaisa nodded at him, only to receive the same worshipful stare he'd started the encounter with.

*I'm nothing special. Why would he look at me like that? Like I matter? I don't deserve it. He matters so much more.* She smiled, the expression all she had to give him other than a moment's diversion. *If only I could provide real help.*

# CHAPTER 25

Killing people was far easier to plan when they weren't standing right in in front of you.

Naeemah brought a small group to their chosen spot at the edge of the city. Conner counted ten of them, mostly men.

They stood with their backs against a metal wall. There was no doorway within view from with someone could accidentally spot them. And behind Connor were the woods. It was a good place because as Naeemah had specified, there was a secluded area where they could take the volunteers one at a time. But it was also a good place because it gave the new recruits something visual to identify with. Even in the old world, trees and wilderness had implied a kind of freedom.

The defibrillator from his field pack hung heavy in the bag he carried. He had only a basic idea of the science, but from what he understood, a defibrillator could only start a heart that hadn't completely stopped. But the nanites shut off as soon as the pulse stopped. There should be time with the heart in what Riley called a "fatal rhythm" to restart.

Connor nodded at each of the Rankless in turn. They weren't healthy-looking people. In fact, one of the women looked like she was on the verge of starving to death. Desperation had brought them here.

*We are feeding on that desperation. Please let this work.*

The ragtag group of Rankless stared at him; their eyes

covered Connor in expectations. For the first time since arriving at the alien city, he felt himself panicking. These weren't trained soldiers with a solid conception of the situation. These were just people who'd already had their lives ripped away once. Now they were looking to him to give them a new existence, a better one. Each gaze wanted a new life from him. *If I do this, there's no turning back. These are my people. They'll rely on me.* Those expectations choked him, and the air he pulled into his lungs wasn't any good.

*What the hell kind of plan is this?!* The whole thing from start to finish was insane. Riley would never have agreed to murder people in the hopes of resurrecting them. *This is absolute, over-the-top idiocy. And for what?* The hope that no one would notice ten workers going missing at the same time? The hope that this drab needy pack of jackals could help them somehow?

Hope wasn't enough. The ten who gathered in front of him did not fill him with confidence. They appeared beaten down and only half-present behind their eyes. The majority were burly men, and women. All who weighed enough to out-brawl Jayden. The other recruits were one middle-aged man, one thin, wiry girl whose brain had barely been able to comprehend their plan, and two painfully ugly men who since finding each other were twitching in unison. They would improve without the alien rule, but even a vast improvement would not turn this group into an impressive echelon of humanity.

"It's time," Jayden said. If he was feeling any doubt, it didn't show on his dark face.

"We'll take you one at a time to the barrier at the city's edge," Connor said. "Naeemah?"

Naeemah slid out from behind them. She wore her full Companion garb, and as she stepped into the light, every volunteer turned to her. From where he stood, he could only see her long, shapely legs flowing from a breezy skirt and her long, black hair, unbound, cascading down her back, threaded with gems torn from costumes. She took the shoulders of the most muscular man. Her hands slid over his arms.

She had chosen the first.

"Come with us," Connor said. "The rest of you, wait here."

Connor walked ahead of Naeemah and the man. Her footsteps were light, as were the whispered words she granted the volunteer, but the big man's feet hit with thuds and dragged. *No surprise there. He's nervous and reluctant. We've asked him to sit back and let us kill him. That takes a ton of bravery.*

After a few hundred yards, they reached the edge of the city. Connor turned to face the couple trailing him. The big man's eyes flitted from side to side as if contemplating running. *He is on the verge of sprinting from us. Nothing I say will comfort him. Better get this over with. Any sympathy I show will only crack his control.*

"Sit," Connor said.

The man sat on the ground, and Naeemah sat behind him with her legs pressed against his sides.

"We need to suffocate you. This will hurt, but the pain won't last," she said in her smooth voice. "Be a man, and it'll be over soon. You can begin again with us—as a hero."

Connor knelt on one side of Naeemah and the man. Every second would be an agony of fear for that man. Jayden moved in on the other side. Naeemah tied his hands behind his back with a silk cord and then nodded at them.

Jayden pressed a drenched cloth over his face, chloroform. They didn't have much of it, but enough to ease the ten volunteers. Riley had found it in a city they'd passed through and judged it could be useful for medical procedures. *This is not what he meant.*

Once the big man slumped in Naeemah's arms, Connor held him down, in case he woke or managed to struggle. Jayden covered his mouth and pinched his nose. Naeemah held the man, her finger pressed against his throat. Her eyes were half-closed, and her mouth silently chanted.

They waited. And the wait felt endless.

"Now," Naeemah said.

*Now is the time for miracles. We've got to resurrect him... and if he doesn't come back, it's all over.*

Jayden leaned over the body with the defibrillator. Connor stood, pacing across the perimeter. Every time he turned around, Jayden remained, over the man's body. Naeemah knelt, hands over her knees, head bent in prayer. Her mouth moved in words Connor couldn't make out.

If this didn't work, the people of the undercity might never trust them again. Then they might never find a way to free humanity from the alien's clutches or to get their revenge for the people they had lost. Connor almost joined Naeemah in prayer but could not take his eyes off the man.

*Please. Come back.*

*It shouldn't be taking this long. Shit.*

Connor paced away and bowed his head. Naeemah was still praying. Were one person's prayers going to be enough? He folded his hands in front of him, but before he could form words, one gasping breath came from behind him. He spun.

The man rolled onto his side. Jayden stood as the man retched, while Naeemah moved closer to the big man and stroked his shoulder, cooing gently into his ear. Connor took in a breath he hadn't been aware of holding and allowed himself a moment of relief before turning to the next task.

He walked over to the edge of the undercity and stared at the invisible line. The barrier between the outside world and the city. There was no point in celebrating until they all made it over—alive. They had no proof that death alone killed the nanites. Perhaps it was the drone's touch specifically that deactivated them.

This gamble could still go against them. If they'd been wrong and the nanites were still active, the man would be dead after all, and they'd be no better than murderers.

*It's not over yet. He has to make it over that line. He could still die today, and if he can't get over it... Stop. No point worrying. I can't let him see I'm worried. This has to be hard enough as it is.*

Not only that, if a drone came, it might be able to process what had happened. If the aliens started actively looking for them, they wouldn't survive the day. The risk was huge, but to not take the risk at all just meant a slower death.

Connor squeezed his hands into fists and dragged in a deep gulp of air. *I've got to look. This is my plan. Even if it fails, I owe it to this man not to turn away.* He turned back.

Naeemah helped the man to his feet, and for a moment, he leaned on her. Jayden turned toward the invisible line.

"Whenever you're ready," Connor said. "Just step over there."

With one stumble as he regained control of his body, the man stared into the forest.

"This is where it begins." Naeemah's hand settled on his back, but her eyes were on Connor. She nodded, giving a smile of encouragement.

The man took one step and paused. His face paled as he hovered, right next to the line. His next step would decide it all.

Connor stood just beyond the barrier, his heart pounding, and his hands clasped in front of him. *Please, God. Please, let him cross safely.*

Naeemah nibbled on her lower lip. Jayden moved to her, putting an arm around her shoulder. Neither of them looked away from the man, but Connor anxiously inspected everything, as if a solution lurked within the rock and trees or in the curve of Naeemah's neck.

The man stepped over the barrier. Connor's eyes squeezed shut.

Rai glared behind his eyelids, her expression firmly labeling him a coward. Silence from the outside world. *He would've fallen by now if he didn't make it. Right? Damn it, Connor, look!*

Connor opened his eyes.

The man stood, both feet planted on the free side of the barrier. His mouth hung slack as he gazed at freedom and then at his feet and back again.

Connor steadied himself on a tree. *It worked. It fucking worked.*

Naeemah gave a laugh that was half-sob. And Jayden

hugged her. She hugged him back, the little bells on her wrist jingling as she moved.

"One point for the good guys." Jayden grinned and let Naeemah go.

"No time to waste. Let's keep it going," Connor said. He strode back over the barrier toward the rest of the group. Then without thought, he said, "Naeemah, stay here with him."

"Of course, Connor." Her gentle voice slowed his step.

*Rai would have told me to fuck off.*

"Connor?" she said.

The view of her behind him was lovely. She stood with one hand on the startled man's shoulder. He didn't appear capable of speech yet, which suited Connor. What did someone even say in a moment like that?

"What, Naeemah?" he asked.

"You did it." Her smile was a ray of light.

"We did." He headed away. There was a lot to get done. Not yet time for congratulations.

They brought another large man to the spot.

And brought him back.

Connor exchanged smiles with Jayden. This was working. He was excited when they brought out the third, this one a woman and heavyset. The challenge in her eyes reminded him of Rai. He let Jayden kill her and there was a new type of relief when she came back.

The fourth person they brought forward was a scrawny woman. She appeared half-defeated already, slumped shoulders and dull, sunken eyes. But Connor knew they could give her a new life. They could give her hope.

He held her hand as she died.

Then Jayden applied the first shock. She twitched. He tried again. And again. And again.

Naeemah gave a small cry, half-swallowed in her throat, as if she hadn't meant to utter it. She rocketed to her feet away from the woman. Connor stood, stepped away from the thin woman, and wrapped one arm around Naeemah's shoulders. He pulled her closer.

But he never looked away.

Finally, Jayden stepped away. He didn't look up at them.

Naeemah leaned against Connor. He felt her shudder.

*We killed her. Really, truly killed her.* Connor kept that thought to himself, though he knew they were all having it as they stared down at the corpse.

Then Naeemah took in a shaky breath and stepped forward. "What do we do with her?"

"What do you mean!" Jayden growled.

"We have six more people to get through," Naeemah said. "We knew... We knew..."

Connor continued her sentence as tears seemed to clog her voice. "We knew this was a risk. If we stop now, her death means nothing."

In his peripheral vision, Connor saw Naeemah nod. Jayden stood silently, stiff and resistant but not actually refusing.

"We get her out of sight," Connor said. "Then when we're done, we bury her and any others who don't make it."

The only snag was moving her body. Connor had handled a lot of death, but not death like this, not innocents who were dead by his hand. Naeemah and he moved the body out of sight together. When they returned, Jayden headed off, without a word, alongside Naeemah to bring their next.

Only one more didn't come back. Connor wanted to see that as an "only," but it was hard. Instead, he focused on what they did have.

By the end of the evening, they had eight new followers. By the morning, the number dropped to seven. A third recruit passed from the world with blood on her lips. But it was enough. They had the start of their army and a way to slowly grow their numbers. They had knowledge of how to kill drones and finally a way to get the manpower to start making a difference—to start saving people. That was enough.

They buried the girl who had died first, and the man who hadn't revived, followed by the woman who'd passed in the night, on free soil. Then, standing over the fresh graves, Naeemah took Connor's hand.

He looked over at her.

"Tonight, we go in with proof," Naeemah said. "More will follow us. And this time, we'll get to choose."

# CHAPTER 26

J aisa moved through the undercity.

Over the course of an hour, Jaisa peered at them from one part or another of a multilevel room—each level rimmed with metal fencing. Flashes of red hair reflected in the metal as she moved through all five stories. She walked, careful to stay an observer for the moment, behind metal crates or lines of workers carrying sealed containers. Her presence seemed to make many of the workers nervous, and she needed a better sense of the situation before acting.

She saw only Rankless in the workforce except for a few glimpses of mechanically altered guards. That would likely have been Alpha's and Omega's places if she hadn't purchased them. The idea of having perfectly functional limbs ripped off and replaced with metal, of having red flashing communicators installed in their foreheads or chests, was unbearable.

Yet it was the truth of the world she lived in.

She was here to somehow, eventually, make that better.

Jaisa gathered from bits and pieces she'd picked up that she wasn't the first person from the world above to enter the factory. But as far as she could tell from the workers whispers, she was the first Companion to walk among them.

As she made it from the fifth story down to the ground floor, Jaisa noticed one commonality in the people. They were all hunched, exhausted... hopeless. These were people who had given up. And why not? What did they actually have in their lives? At least Jaisa had her girls and some small freedoms and privileges.

These people had nothing.

On the ground floor, she came up to a station with a squat girl in it, red hair frizzy and freckles dominating her face. The girl's station was built into the floor, nothing more than a metal shell sunk four feet into the ground.

Jaisa approached across the factory floor, drawn as much by the fiery color of the girl's hair as anything else. The drone trailed her closely, and farther back, a drone she didn't recognize lurched after them. It had hundreds of arms and honestly reminded Jaisa of some monstrous octopus with legs.

Jaisa stopped in front of the station. Her white dress rippled down over the edge of the sunken metal.

"What is your name?" Jaisa asked.

"Don't need one," the girl said. She kept hold of the rope she needed to guide through the machine and sounded vaguely annoyed at being distracted from her monotonous task.

"Hmm," Jaisa said as she knelt beside the station. "I'll be gone in just a moment. There's no need to glare."

The girl lowered her eyes. Jaisa turned to some of the other factory girls, not wanting to bother the people she'd come to help. Twice more Jaisa asked for a name. Neither time did the girl she addressed give one. After that, she didn't ask. She realized that they didn't have names to give. They weren't people. The gods had made sure they didn't see themselves as anything.

Jaisa struggled with their silent resentment, hanging over her like a cloud. She could imagine what they must think of her —a strange upperworlder trying to connect with them, privileged and none too bright. She could see how out of place she was in this environment, the same as they did. Yet her pristine hands rested on the filthy ground with no hesitation, and her white gown was streaked with grease.

Hopefully, they could also see that she didn't think she deserved any better than they did.

"I want to help you. All of you... but I can't, can I?" Jaisa shuddered and wrapped her arms around herself, turning back to the girl. Her fingers would be sure to start tingling if she kept speaking, and the Drone would not give her another warning. Still, Jaisa braved a few more words. "What do you want?"

"A warm bed'd be nice." The woman shook her head, her dark eyes pinched with sadness.

*I'd feed and clothe all of them, but I cannot.* "It's not in their plan." *And I am as bound to the gods' whims as they are.*

"So bored," an older woman said.

Jaisa grinned, and the expression ran through her body, charging her blood. There was her answer, the thing she could do to give these people back a shred of their humanity. Jaisa had felt it herself, the pressing weight of boredom. And these people had to deal with hard, mind-numbing labor as well. Jaisa could not provide any less than her girls did for her. With a nod, she clasped her hands in front of her.

She began to sing, and as her song drifted out into the factory, she stood and danced.

Her voice was too small to fill the space, but it fluttered out into the din. She sang of love and of the world above. There was nothing impressive to the song itself, but music was not something that the gods would provide for the factories or the huts the Rankless went to at night to fall into exhausted stupors.

Across the factory floor, a girl closed her eyes. Her dirt-blackened forehead smoothed.

Jaisa felt separate from herself, watching the scene unfold even as she was an actor in it. The voice that echoed out was soft, but as it moved, it sped up until it matched her feet striking the floor in a distinct rhythm.

The expressions of people around the factory opened slowly, one at a time, some seeming to block her out for longer. It was if they were afraid to enjoy anything. That made sense; they'd all lost so much. *I'll come back.*

In her distraction, she missed the Half-rank foreman approaching until he was standing beside her. She only noticed when his voice rang out from behind her.

"Lady J—"

"No names," Jaisa said, interrupting him. If these people didn't have names, neither would she. *I'm no better than they are, no more human.*

The foreman moved forward until he was within arm's reach. He looked deadly and huge. He was half-machine himself, crafted in the factories above. The handle of an electric whip rested at his hip—Jaisa wondered how many of the workers had personally endured its bite. But she also saw the reddened flesh around his mechanical arm and the angry black that spread in the veins of his shoulder.

"This is no place for you," he said. Not kindly, but not abusive or angry, either.

"This is no place for any of us, and yet here we are." Jaisa touched his left shoulder, which was sculpted from black metal. "It must've been excruciating having this done. I'm sorry."

His human hand rubbed against his weaponized arm. "Couldn't do my job without it, lady."

The lady in question wiggled her fingers and then clenched and unclenched her fists. "I should really stop touching things. Bugs don't like it."

And the drone hovering close by reminded her that it was time to depart. Now that she knew something, no matter how small, that she could give to these people, it would be doubly wasteful to die.

Once the nanites had asked her to stop, doing anything against that might get her into trouble. The drone guided her back toward the portal to the world above.

Jaisa returned to the portal with her head bowed. Her feet were sore from the rough floors, and her limbs heavy from exertion. Both palms had blistered, and everything ached. Despite all this, the churning guilt inside her had halted.

*I did nothing to help them escape this hell, but at least I feel like I'm finally armed.* It didn't make any sense, but she'd witnessed the expressions on the workers' faces. The distraction, the presence of a little beauty and kindness, had lightened their burdens.

*I can't strike the gods, but I can do this. Singing and dancing won't solve anything, but why do I need to be the solution? I don't. Maybe just making life bearable for them is enough.*

She could give those toiling in the city below the strength to keep going. Hope was a precious thing, something that every person had a right to. Bringing hope would be enough.

*Maybe if I do it, others will follow.*

She couldn't feed and clothe them all. She couldn't resurrect anyone—but she could offer them the same hope that Lyra and Melody gave her. In the world before, music and distraction had been everywhere. That wasn't the case any longer.

If the best thing she could do was help the people of the undercity forget for a while, she'd do it.

When she came back to the spot where she'd originally descended, the workers were gone, and the little station appeared larger without the human presence. She lingered a moment, touching each station and imagining what it would be like to go through a day there. Each day would end with her aching, sweaty and covered in dirt that never got fully washed away —but at least her body would be her own.

The Rankless had touched something in her because they were still real and human, not some sculpted creations of the gods. They were not the only ones who had received hope.

But the face that surfaced again and again in her mind was the Half-rank overseer. *I thought the Half-ranks had a better existence than the Rankless. But they don't, do they? He had his flesh ripped apart and reassembled as the gods saw fit. Then all the Rankless hate him for doing what the gods require. That's no life.*

The weight of her thoughts wasn't one she could lift. She would have to bear the burden. There was more suffering than she'd imagined, and she'd been a fool not to see the truth before. She knew the Half-ranks were used for experiments. Neriso's lab had even shown some of the ways they were used.

Hope existed in the Rankless, and it renewed her, but

there was no hope in the plight of the Half-ranks. They had none of the freedom of the Rankless and none of the privileges of the Chosen and Companions.

With a sigh, Jaisa spun around and headed to the portal. No point dwelling on the Half-ranks. Not when there were finally positive thoughts and feelings. Had Tavar been below? She didn't know, but her belly fluttered at the idea of going home and sending him a message.

"Take me up," she said to the portal, then she steadied herself waiting for the lift. Going up couldn't be as awful as going down.

# CHAPTER 27

N eriso found Jaisa in her room the night he heard she'd traveled below. Having learned of her excursion, it was important that he remind her of her purpose. Everything she did must be aimed at elevating him. How under the gods' sky did she see this as beneficial to their image? He stood in the doorway silently and allowed her eyes, feral as an alley cat's, to appraise him. Her breath went in and out evenly. She did not seem upset or apprehensive. He'd thought she might, but then, he admitted to himself, he did not understand much about this woman he owned.

She seemed almost... happy.

"You went below," he said.

Jaisa stretched out on her bed, long, pale limbs sliding over the covers. Dirt ran over her white dress like angry slashes. "I did. I asked your permission to wander. You gave it."

"I would've given you an escort." *She should have been escorted. What was she thinking? Sometimes she behaves like a toddler. I should scold her like one.* All that she did reflected on him. As much as he worried about how this would make him look, the most worrisome part was that she'd tried to deny him.

She's denied her name, and in doing so, denied him.

Her limbs curled in again, leaving only that blood-red hair fanning over the bed. Her white dress bunched between her thighs and the soles of her feet were oily. "I didn't need an escort."

"Your dress is dirty." It wasn't what he wanted to say—wasn't what he'd come to say. But her beauty and the dark streaks on her dress made her more powerful. More dangerous. The admonishments he'd intended wouldn't come.

Her eyes moved away from him to the white gown tangled around her white limbs. "I suppose it is. Shall I change for you, husband?"

"Why did you refuse your name?" He tried not to sound annoyed, but even to his ears, his voice sounded harsh. She did not so much as bat an eyelash. If anything, her expression grew sweeter, more innocent. How easily her face lied. How often did she lie? The rules were quite clear on such behavior. He should report her. He wouldn't, but the least she should do was act her part.

*I saved her life when I chose her. And still, she denies me my dominion. I own her, and she denies me.*

That she was a rebel in spirit, he was aware. It just didn't matter. No rebellion would ever stick. The gods were there to stay, and neither she nor any like-minded people she found would change that. It seemed to make her happy to keep the old world and old feelings alive inside her. It was scientifically proven that happy people made more productive team members. If this kept Jaisa from some sort of temperamental breakdown, what did it matter?

But it must be kept under wraps.

Soon she'd forget the old world, anyway. They all would, except for a few of the truly powerful like Neriso. If she behaved properly, her intentions didn't matter much. That was why she needed to *actually* behave properly.

"I'm amazed that you're aware of what I said." Jaisa stood. Her bare feet were red and the hand she motioned with was blistered on her palm. "How did you know?"

"I asked for a transcript from the computer."

She laughed, as if nothing pleased her more than him spying on her. The sweetness of her laugh alerted him to how off-balanced the comment had made her.

"Do they play it for you in my voice?"

"They could, but I didn't request that. Don't get mouthy." He grabbed her arm and tugged her roughly toward him.

She flinched as his fingers dug into her flesh. *I'm hurting her.* He forced himself to let go. She fell back onto the bed, rubbing her arm, her eyes going wide.

"I wanted to know why you went down there," he said, letting her retreat from him, "and now I want to know why you stopped that man from naming you."

Jaisa slunk up to him and took his hand in hers. Her body still angled away from him. "They didn't have names to give me in return. It wasn't a place for names."

"That's not a real answer." He gulped down more angry words. She already looked afraid. *I own her, but I can't take advantage... Some words, like some actions, I will regret later.*

"That's my real answer. I wanted to be myself, just myself. Up here, I'm your wife, your property. I'm yours. If I said who I was, that would be all I'd ever be down there. Neriso's wife is all Jaisa can be. I wanted to be me. And none of them have names. I can be at home there without one."

"And when you go back, what name shall you take then, Jaisa?"

"When I go back?"

"This is what you desire. I will allow it, as long as you proceed in a fashion that reflects well on us. Whatever you do, you must do beautifully. You can't be nameless there any more than here." He touched her face and leaned to kiss her soft mouth. Had she thought he would deny her? No, he had to keep her content. Perhaps he even wanted her to be happy. "And you must do it in a way that improves our image. That is your primary duty."

"Neriso?"

"Jaisa."

"Why not just tell me what's truly bothering you?" The green eyes that stared up at him were feral.

"Why? Why did you go down there?"

"I want to know what my city does, above and below."

"It's not *your* city."

"Of course, husband. It's yours." Jaisa smiled, a smile that made him forget everything else. She was a woman who could do anything, be anything, and she was his.

All the Companions in Third City were talking about what Jaisa had done. Tavar listened to their ongoing discourse without interrupting, but the whole time, his amazement grew. For the gossip of her going to the undercity was a larger effect than he could have hoped for. The most amazing part was—none of them seemed to know who she was.

"I don't think it really happened," one woman said haughtily as she walked with her friend toward the exit of the Companion training center.

"I've never even thought of going down there, have you?" said another to his friend.

Tavar lingered near the door, watching them exit.

"She must have had her Chosen's permission. It can't be what everyone is making it out to be."

"But what Chosen would give permission for such a thing?"

"I'm pondering asking mine. It sounds thrilling, doesn't it?"

They might not know who the Companion in question was, but Tavar had no doubt. He knew Jaisa, not well, but well enough. He knew he'd given her a map of the city. He'd advised her on how to descend into the undercity. She'd even communicated her impressions back to him.

Tavar listened a while longer to see if anyone even speculated her name. But no one else seemed to know the name of the Companion who'd dared walk among the Rankless—who had dared to entertain them.

The situation was safer for her if she remained nameless. And she wouldn't for long, especially if she kept going. And he knew that she would continue.

He wasn't a fool—this was her victory. But his information had played a part in it. That was what Riuti had been saying the whole time. Everything was about contacts.

She'd used him, and he would use her, and somehow, it would lead to a better world.

Knowing this and believing it were two very different feelings. For the first time, Tavar believed. She'd done it. She'd taken the first step and managed to stay within her rights as a Companion.

On his way home from the Companion training classes, Tavar stopped to stare over the edge of his city. The world around him was like a desert, but when he looked over the balcony, all he saw was undulating mist.

He held on to the vision of the white mist until he arrived back at Ruiti's house and wandered into the back of his own rock garden. It was the only place in the house that felt like it was legitimately his, and Ruiti gave it a wide berth, as if he understood what that meant.

Tavar knelt in the middle of his sea of unmarked gravestones and began to whisper about the world below. He carefully touched the stone that was for Wendy. This time around, he was going to make her proud.

# CHAPTER 28

Dirt crunched under Naeemah's nails, leaving dark lines etched over her knuckles. She dug deep before lifting a seedling from her cart into the hole and smoothing the soil around the edges. Behind her, the camp stirred—new sounds and voices mingling. When she'd finished her planting, she turned, without lifting herself from the ground, and watched the new arrivals.

Her heart fluttered—they were just as she had been, fresh from the gods' world and unsure how to adjust. They were her seedlings, too. It would be her care that saw them flourish or wilt.

Connor and Jayden would turn them into an army. Those suited to war or espionage would be trained. Those suited to hunting or scientific pursuit would be trained. But many would not be suited to warring against the gods in any fashion, and those Naeemah would teach. They must learn to survive.

"So many things could go wrong," Jayden remarked.

Naeemah jumped, her hand flying to her heart and leaving a smear of earth. "I didn't hear you approach."

"I know." Jayden chuckled. "You've got your talents—perception ain't one of them."

"Optimism isn't one of yours."

"I'm plenty optimistic, just not blind."

Naeemah shrugged. "We fly or we fall. There is no purpose to contemplating the ground. If we soar, it doesn't matter, and if we do not... Well, thinking of it will not soften our descent."

Across the camp, Connor stepped out of the woods with one of the new recruits. Her eyes stuck on him. He moved with the directness and confidence of someone who had never considered how far they had to fall. Personal experience told her that wasn't true, but she was still certain that failure was far from his mind in the moment.

Their success was tied to his shoulders, and that was all she needed to know. He wouldn't let them fail. *She* wouldn't let them fail.

Jayden gave a braying laugh. "You've been good for him."

Connor and several recruits glanced in their direction.

Naeemah dropped her eyes to her freshly planted seedlings. If the green shoots lived long enough, they would help produce new food that wouldn't need to be foraged from destroyed cities. This was the future, and that was the only direction Naeemah wanted to look. She said nothing more until Jayden sauntered away.

Inside her, something fluttered, her wingspan extended. They were all good for each other. This place, Connor, Jayden, and time were healing her. This was not another cage, though she'd thought it one at first. In time, if she fought hard enough, she'd fly free.

Looking up, she caught Connor's eyes, which remained on her. He paused in whatever he was saying to the new recruit and smiled. His teeth were crooked and yet the smile was perfect, reaching inside her and making promises.

*He's a warrior... and that is exactly what this world needs.*

A warrior with an army.

Jayden was correct. A myriad of factors would play into their success in the days to come. Failure would be easy. But Connor wasn't one to take the easy path, and she'd learn to do the same if that was what it took to guide them through peril.

Naeemah returned Connor's smile, lifting one earth-covered hand to wave. The bells on her wrist chimed—a careless birdsong. Then she tilted her face up.

Up, up, up, to the blue sky hidden between the black web of the gods' ships.

Not too long before, she'd never thought she'd see the sky again. Under that bright blue, nothing was impossible.

Each morning for a ten-day after her descent, Jaisa's blood sang with power when she woke. She'd done it—she'd reached out and found a way to help those who were suffering. And Neriso hadn't denied her return! On the tenth day, before she could fully enjoy this new concept, the door to her room opened.

As pale as a moonbeam at midnight, Lyra stood in the doorway, enveloped in a floor-length green gown with a short, hooded black cloak. Her mouth, which peeped from under the oversized hood, was painted a deep maroon. How striking the girl-child was—though she looked less like a child every day. Her eyes were downcast, and her hands clasped in front of her.

Jaisa's smile came naturally. "Speak, Lyra." She slid her legs to the floor.

"The priestess of the fifth temple has come to see you." Lyra's voice lifted high, as pure as a bell.

"Message received." Jaisa stood from her bed and went over to her wardrobe. She swiped through her options, eventually choosing a draped red dress that matched her hair. The machine expertly applied her choice to her body, and she turned toward the door. Lyra still waited, her eyes downcast.

Jaisa would have liked to shield her from this encounter, but Lyra's presence seemed to imply she wanted a further command. And hadn't she discovered in the undercity that sometimes a little entertainment was all it took to make a life livable again?

Jaisa shook out the folds of her red dress. "You and Melody shall come down to join us."

"Yes, lady." The single window in Jaisa's sleeping chamber flooded Lyra with light, making her skin appear to glow.

"You look lovely, Lyra." Jaisa lowered her voice as she spoke, but her hands set to tingling anyhow. *How do they understand my words? Maybe there's a time limit to how long I may converse with the servants, or maybe even the walls here spy for the gods.*

Neriso had said he could know every word she spoke if he chose.

Lyra bowed her head, strands of soft, white hair falling from beneath her hood. Her face was flushed red a shade more than a little akin to her eyes. She fled the room. Jaisa followed her, but instead of heading up to the rooftop terrace and the instruments there, she went down the stairs. Melody must have already been downstairs. Jaisa descended.

In the lobby, lit only by the tinted lights of the hall, sat the priestess, skin crawling with metal and stare as vacant as any beast's. She was not alone.

At the priestess's metal-clad feet lounged a golden lioness, adorned with a collar of red light. Jaisa blinked hard against the suspected mirage. Yet the lioness remained. Her golden eyes moved over to Jaisa, and her jaws parted in a wide yawn—teeth sharp and powerful.

Jaisa took a step back. "Priestess..." A lion could deal a bloody death, long and painful. Perhaps a drone's touch was preferable.

"Lady Jaisa," the priestess offered a tight smile but extended both hands palm up.

The lion's mouth closed, and its eyes locked on Jaisa. Muscles rippled down the beast's legs and chest as it rose.

"The gods heard your prayer and offer you a gift." The priestess kept her hands held out.

"A lion?" Jaisa took another step back.

"Now you have a pet, just as you desired." Finally, the priestess lowered her arms. "I reported to the gods what you said. Your plea must have truly touched them for such a generous gift. They do what they can for us."

"A lion is not a pet." Jaisa stared into the lion's eyes. How powerful it looked. Those jaws could undo her in an instant, and yet... There *was* something beautiful about the creature. Despite Jaisa's prayer at the chapel, she had never been one for cats. They'd always seemed so distant and superior. But this cat had every reason to feel that way. It didn't offend her.

The larger wonder was that her words in the temple had been heard and acted on.

What she said and did could change the world—albeit not much. But put together with giving some hope to the undercity, it lifted her soul. It was enough for the moment.

"The collar tames it, lady. You do not need to fear. The lion will never harm you or yours."

Jaisa dragged her eyes away from the beast. *It's only natural that even their gifts are capable of death and destruction.*

"This is a thoughtful gesture," she said. More than that, the lion was a sign, a physical manifestation of the change Jaisa held in her hands. As long as she followed the rules.

She'd walk the line.

"Isn't it?" the priestess crowed. "And now pets are offered for purchase. Yours was free, but anyone else who wants a pet need only give credits."

A low gasp burst from behind Jaisa. The girls must have arrived. They probably wouldn't see immediately what the lion really meant... what it stood for. Power.

She wanted some of that power in their hands. "My girls must be taught to care for it," Jaisa said.

"Instructions are in the system." The priestess shrugged. This was beneath her notice. She probably believed all Half-ranks were beneath her notice.

Jaisa strode up to cat and knelt at its side. Lyra and Melody were splotches in her peripheral vision. She stroked its head, though her hand trembled. They were only children, and they needed to see strength.

"She's my pet now." All this because of one comment about wishing the gods allowed pets. *And my comment changed the system. It... No, a lioness. She... will be a constant reminder that I may not have power in the old way, but I can change this world.*

"Yes, lady," the girls said in chorus. Their eyes were wide and their hands held tightly clenched in front of them.

"I'll call her 'Grace.'" Jaisa moved one hand over Grace's powerful muscles and the beast trembled. *With a desire to attack? To run? I'll never know.*

"A fine name," the priestess said.

"Sing to us," Jaisa commanded her girls and then turned to the priestess. "We'll take a walk in the garden. I had several lovely viewpoints built in to overlook the city."

Lyra's and Melody's voices came out soft. One of them trembled, but without looking over, she could not tell whose it was.

Grace trailed behind Jaisa. *But this silent predator answers to me.*

# BOOKS BY THIS AUTHOR

## Spider's Kiss

They exterminated her species...
...that was their first mistake.
The second was keeping the Spider Queen alive.
Book one of the Drambish Contaminate Trilogy

## Spider's Gambit

As one of the last survivors of a race of shape-shifting spiders, her will to survive and her lust for revenge both point to the same strategy—exterminate her enemies before they find her.

Book two of the Drambish Contaminate Trilogy

## Spider's Choice

Book three of the Drambish Contaminate Trilody COMING SOON January, 12, 2020

## Visit Jesse Sprague's Webpage For More Information Or To Join Her Mailing List At: Www.jessesprague.com

Sign up for Jesse Sprague's mailing list (or reader's group as she likes to call it) for updates on her latest projects and extra perks like character interviews, early release information, insights into my process, and best yet FREE exclusive short stories!

Did you miss reading The Drambish Contaminate trilogy? Start with book one!

Printed in Great Britain
by Amazon

63124046R00138